Red Sulphur

THE GREATEST MYSTERY IN ALCHEMY

A Saga by Robert Bosnak

BOOK III

THE PHANTOM SORCERER

ISBN: 978-1-957176-02-4

Cover design by Cover design by: Baki Boquecosa
www.jbaki.com

EMPRESS
PUBLICATIONS
WWW.EMPRESSPUBLICATIONS.COM

For

Jonathan Lipsky
Playwright, Dreamer, Friend

James Hillman
Teacher, Alchemist, Friend

Eddie Michaels
Life Enthusiast, Friend

Book Three

The Phantom Sorcerer

Part Eleven

Clara

Chapter Twenty-Four

Vienna, December 1676

Count von Waldstein rushes up to Venier, rapier drawn and pushes it into Venier's throat until he draws blood.

"No!" I hear myself scream. "Don't kill him. That is not Wenzel Seyler!" I am startled and appalled with myself that my first concern is not for my daughter or son. Actually, Maximo feels like a stranger to me: a mere carrier of Red Sulphur, and not my heroic son who saved his sister. Count von Waldstein looks up at me in total surprise while at the same time carefully forcing his rapier deeper into Venier's throat to wake him with pain.

Aunt Marianne sits on the floor holding the unconscious Maximo, rocking him softly in her arms and whispering sweet gratitude in his ear. Mundanus stands next to her holding Johanna tightly against his chest. She doesn't cry but just stares with puzzled curiosity at Venier. I am struck by the absence of fear in her eyes. She pushes against her father's shoulders insisting she be put down, and walks over to the harpsichord spinet. An explosively rousing music rises up, rumbling like the eruption of an angry volcano. Her fingers race wildly across the keys.

Venier and Maximo awaken simultaneously, each with the same look of incomprehension.

"You're under arrest, Wenzel Seyler. You'd wish you were dead once we're through with you!" the Count growls at him in utter disgust. A man threatening to kill a child is the lowest of all scum. I can feel how Count von Waldstein – his rapier slightly trembling – has to exercise self-control so as not to kill Venier on the spot.

Venier looks like an aged version of the vulnerable young man I had met in Venice nine years ago during those brief moments when Mantis had left him alone. I hate the sorcery we have been practicing, even if it gave me my twins – and I know that this situation is entirely my fault. I had been swept up by the beguiling magic of my own weavings. My pride had created Wenzel Seyler and fed Mantis with Red Sulphur. I realize that Seyler had not just been making gold for profit here at the court in Vienna: he had been feeding the Red Sulphur cravings of Mantis.

I turn to the count, at a loss for words, knowing only that I have to save Venier and cast a pleading glance towards Mundanus. But he looks at Venier with hatred in his usually gentle eyes. Aunt Marianne is equally revolted by the man who threatened to kill our daughter. I feel desperately alone.

"This man was possessed by a demon," I exclaim. "Maximo exorcized him. Couldn't you see? It was right in front of us in the glow-cloth train. You puncture the throat of an innocent man, Your Excellency. The attacker is gone, back to Hell. Wenzel Seyler is gone!"

"But Madam, how can you say such things? This man attacked your daughter, for heaven's sake!" He looks at me with complete incredulity.

"It wasn't him," I point at Venier. "It was the Devil." I sound insane, even to myself.

Venier looks up at me. "Signorina Clara, what is happening? Where am I?" he asks in a feeble voice.

"You were about to shoot my daughter. You cut your mother's throat, you stole my Red Sulphur, you stabbed Marianne and Clara half to death, you caused the death of my Grandfather…" Mundanus hisses like a cobra.

"Mundanus, stop it!" I scream and rush over to Venier to protect him from the sword. I feel excommunicated by the looks of everyone I love in this room, but am fiercely driven to protect Venier. "It was my fault. I caused this. You know it," I yell at my husband and my aunt, grab the naked blade of the rapier – sharp on both sides – and feel it cut deeply into my hand. The pain is strangely comforting as I yank it away from Venier's throat. The count looks apoplectic. Johanna shrieks as she sees the profuse bleeding of my hand, her previous calm shattered. "Mother!"

The only dispassionate one in the mayhem is Maximo. He has been rubbing his eyes since having been roused from his swoon by his sister's volcanic music, and now he stares intently at the attacker. He looks away and then stares again, trying to make sense of what he sees. "You are not the man who tried to kill my sister." He speaks thoughtfully, like an old man. "It is a trick. You were exchanged. Where did he go? How did you do that?" He looks curious, as if he is trying to solve a puzzle. Turning to his father he asks again: "Where did he go?"

"What do you mean?" asks the Count, finding his tongue.

"This man is not the same," Maximo explains. "His eyes are different, his whole face is different. He just looks like the man with the pistol. But that man escaped. Where did he go?"

The words of our son finally make Mundanus come to his senses.

"This man was possessed by a Devil, Maximo. You drove that Devil back to Hell. This is the man who stayed behind. You not only saved your sister, you saved him too."

Venier seems to understand all at once. "You drove Mantis away." His tone towards Maximo is one of complete devotion. The same voice I remember him using towards me back in Venice when I momentarily seemed to have rid him of his demonic jailor. I'm oddly envious of my son. Actually, he feels like Aunt Marianne's son now, and a rival for the affections of Venier. My instant self-loathing is boundless.

"Indeed you did," Mundanus concurs, suddenly immensely proud of his son. "Not even the Pope could do what you did; he tried but he couldn't." Aunt Marianne goes over to Maximo and hugs him.

But Maximo is not satisfied - not at all. He turns to me, realizing that I have the answer for him.

"Tell me, Mother," he commands.

Mundanus comes over to me and looks at the deep gash in the palm of my right hand. He leads me to a small basin and pours wine over the wound. Then he wraps my hand in a scrap of leftover material from the glow-silk train. I instinctively withdraw my hand, finding it blasphemy to use the precious material as a bandage. Maximo has followed us. "Tell me, Mother!"

I can feel Venier looking at me intently. Even the Count seems curious, though his rapier is pointing at Venier's throat again, although this time he holds it a few inches away.

"This man is called Venier Solario. He is the stepson of your great grandfather," I explain to Maximo. My hand is hotly hurting, making me highly alert. "When he was a little older than you there was this horrible creature from Hell, a demon called Mantis," I begin, restraining myself from describing Mantis; I don't want the children to end up with nightmares and thus continue Mantis' reign. Johanna is listening, spellbound. "This demon took over his body and drove Venier out. In Venice, where he is from, where your father is from, I tried to help him get rid of Mantis so Venier could return to his body. And for a while it worked. But then Mantis struck back and did horrible things. The demon took total possession of him and changed his name from Venier Solario to Wenzel Seyler. He stole your father's Red Sulphur, the material that can change sickness into health and metals into gold." I look intently at Maximo and realize that he completely understands what I'm telling him. He keeps nodding with great earnestness. "The demon loves the Red Sulphur and feeds on it. So Wenzel Seyler came to the court here in Vienna to feed Mantis and lead a mean life."

"Red Sulphur has two faces, Maximo," Mundanus finally comes to my aid. "It has a nasty face that loves the fires of Hell. That's partly where Red Sulphur was made, in the fires of Hell. But your great ancestor I told you about was able to refine it and gave it the power to do good."

"Salomon Trismosin," Maximo replies, full understanding dawning.

Mundanus nods, "When Red Sulphur recognized the demon from Hell it longed to get back to its origins, to be fed again by the Devil's fires. So Red Sulphur and Mantis both used Venier to get what they wanted: to feed on each other."

"And they used me to get what they wanted. I didn't know enough and was tricked by them," I add, more for my own sake than as an explanation.

"Is Red Sulphur alive then?" Johanna asks.

"Yes," Mother Marianne replies. "It is alive but in a different way than you and I are alive. We live and we die. But Red Sulphur lives forever."

"Like God?" Johanna asks.

"Like God," Mother Marianne concurs.

Count von Waldstein lowers his rapier. "So this man was truly possessed by the Devil?" he asks.

"He was indeed," Aunt Marianne replies, her initial rage at Venier disappearing. "Our Red Sulphur magic made his demon grow all-powerful."

"So how was the boy able to drive him out?" asks the Count.

The three adults look at one another, waiting for one of us to talk. An awkward silence ensues.

"My sister and I are children not just of our parents. We descend from Red Sulphur directly. There are moments when I feel I am not really here but there is someone else living my body." Johanna nods vehemently, indicating that Maximo is speaking for the both of them. "So I can understand that a demon can live in the body of a man." He sounds astonishingly mature, not at all like a seven-year-old boy. This dramatic fact gives enough weight to his words so the Count does not doubt him for a moment. "When I saw the man with the pistol threaten my sister, it happened. I was pushed out of my body and watched it all from the ceiling. Below me I heard my voice say things that didn't come from me. It was the other me. Or maybe not me," here he gets confused.

"It was the Son of Red Sulphur who spoke directly to the demon," Mundanus explains with deep love in his voice.

Maximo nods enthusiastically. "Yes," he exclaims, "it was the Son of Red Sulphur. He is me and I am he. And at the same time he is not me at all." His voice carries the clarity of subtle understanding. My love for him rushes back into my soul like water through a sluice that has been opened. I walk up to him and take him in my arms, loving my son with the warm heart of a mother. I see Mother Claudia rise up before me in Dolfin Chapel, dressed in the blue of the Virgin, and I express my profound gratitude to her, feeling intimately related to the Mother of God.

"If he stays at court he will be hanged," Count von Waldstein tells us calmly, now fully understanding what has happened.

"No one needs to know what happened here," I plead.

"I will have to tell the Emperor. It is my duty."

"Then we must flee," I conclude, with clear lucidity. "I will take him with me to The Hague tonight. The wedding dress is finished. There is no reason for me to stay a moment longer."

"With all respect Madam Dolfin," Count von Waldstein responds gently, "that would be an insufferable affront to His Majesty." He sees my defiance.

"It would reflect badly on the Prince of Orange," Aunt Marianne adds. "We are here at his pleasure." I refuse to listen.

"Count, could he stay in my room? Red Sulphur would guard him, I'm sure." The simplicity of Maximo's words, in his high-pitched child's voice, make Count von Waldstein waver. I can see how he is torn between the obligation to his Emperor and a new respect for the alchemical miracles he has just witnessed.

"The Holy Roman Emperor has other things on his mind with all the grand guests pouring in for the wedding. You could tell him afterwards that Wenzel Seyler has fled. He seems to have been displeased with Seyler to begin with," I support my son.

"His Majesty is ambivalent about him. Seyler has performed miraculous transmutations before his very eyes."

"But he was specifically asked to stay away from the wedding," I insist.

"Seyler is a consummate performer," the Count replies, with a puzzled glance at the obviously timid Venier. "He especially charms the Ladies, and the courtiers can't stand him. His indiscretions have reached the ears of His Majesty. His reputation would have appalled our future Holy Roman Empress."

"I will be responsible for him," Mundanus says quietly, stepping forward. I feel a flush of love for my husband and his generosity. I know he is doing this for me; he still feels little charity for Venier. Theodore Mundanus stands before the Count with the full authority of the most searched after alchemist of his generation. Count von Waldstein relents.

ꟹ

When I enter Maximo's room in our family suite, he is having an intense conversation with Venier. They don't notice me. I stay very still, hardly breathing. Johanna has moved to Aunt Marianne's quarters and Venier is sitting on the bed that had been hers, while Maximo sits across from him on his.

"I remember it all like a dream. Much is lost," Venier muses.

"That happens to me when Red Sulphur takes over. My memory doesn't work as clearly after it leaves. It feels like waking up and dreams fading away," Maximo replies in a pensive manner.

Venier nods. Even though there is a 30-year age difference between them, they converse as equals, sharing the same quality of experience. Venier is deathly pale and I notice the deep lines in his face. In the brief moment I had seen Wenzel Seyler, his skin had been taut and youthful like that of a man in his late twenties. Venier, with his ravaged countenance, looks over 45. The transformation is startling, underlining the truth that this is *not* Wenzel Seyler. Mantis has pillaged Venier's body, sucked him dry, leaving him behind like a rag. Deep down I notice my fear that Mantis will return. I waver between an unshakable faith in my son – and daughter for that matter – and my memories of the past, when I had seen the possession take place before my very eyes.

Maximo leans forward, and I can't suppress the thought that they are alien brothers.

"Do you remember when Mantis first entered?" Maximo asks with intense curiosity, his feet not reaching the floor as he sits on the fluffy white down comforter of his grand four-poster bed. The Hofburg palace provides us with generous quarters.

"I remember how he kept me down in the cellar at first. At that time there was a difference between me and him. He tortured me, and I was his victim. But then…I don't know how it happened; suddenly I *was* him. He had jumped into me, like someone jumps into water. After that my memories turn vague, and what I remember is like a story someone else told me long ago."

Maximo nods avidly. There is an expression of deep gratitude on Venier's face for being so completely understood.

"When did *you* first notice?" Venier asks him. I hold my breath, waiting for Maximo's answer.

"I was with Johanna in Mother's weaving studio. It was a long time ago. There was a problem with one of the looms. The weaver was very distressed and I wanted to help her. Suddenly someone else was looking through my eyes. This other someone saw instantly what the problem was, and his hands fixed it in a flash. I could clearly feel that they were not my eyes and hands."

"How did you know that it wasn't you?"

"The eyes of Red Sulphur see differently. Johanna has it with her ears. She tells me that her Red Sulphur ears hear music all the time. When it is just her, the world is silent. For me I think it starts in my hands. I can feel it tingle in my hands and they become restless; they want to make something. It's like being very hungry and you need to eat something or you'll faint."

I am filled with gratitude to get these profound insights into my twins. Maximo could only have told this to someone like Venier - never to me. My son continues,

"Red Sulphur eyes see the world alive. Everything breathes and colors become very bright. At the same time I'm floating somewhere outside my body knowing that all of this is happening. It was very frightening at first. But now I'm used to it. And when I'm suddenly back in my body I remember most of it vaguely, like a dream that rushes backwards away from me. I'm always very surprised that the problem is fixed, like with the loom; or more often, there is a completely new thing in my hands. Most of the time I have no idea what it is or how it got there, but it always turns out to be useful for something. Then people praise me and I know for sure that I had nothing to do with it. But I can't explain. I can only talk about it with Johanna. She understands exactly. She says that not only does her music come from somewhere else, but that the ears that hear it are not hers. By now she can listen in whenever she wants to. She says it's like walking around with a complete orchestra in your head. I can see it in her eyes when it happens to her. What I do now is walk around everywhere in the morning and find scraps that have a different feel to them. I can see them breathe. It's like I'm collecting stuff for Red Sulphur. And then I find these marvelous new things in my hands and it is evening and I have to go to sleep."

Listening, I'm happy that Maximo has Venier to talk to, and in my mind I'm devising ways so I can listen in on their conversations all the time. I feel I'm tricking my son. But I can't make myself announce my presence to them. Instead, I actually move behind a curtain to continue my eavesdropping.

"I have these horrible memories," Venier says softly, almost in a whisper. "I remember being told that your parents were getting married and then I remember nothing until I woke up one day in a monastery and they called me Brother Wenceslaus. I was under the protection of an Augustinian Abbot in Moravia, in a place called Bruna. That Abbott was an alchemist. He had a stone that could change things it touched."

"Red Sulphur," Maximo exclaims. "That must have been the Stone that Mantis stole from my father. Was it in an ivory box?"

Venier nods. "The same box in which your father kept his Stone."

Maximo explains, "My grandfather Maximo had two identical boxes made in the Holy Land and gave one to my grandmother Claudia. She kept a sacred relic in it and Grandfather Maximo kept the Red Sulphur in the other. Then when Mantis stole the box with the Stone, Father put the Red Sulphur in with the relic."

"At the time when I first became aware of being Brother Wenceslaus, I thought the sorcery stone belonged to the Abbott. There was a legend that it had been buried by the first Abbott of the monastery but was never discovered until my Abbott found it around the same time I, or Mantis or Brother Wenceslaus, arrived at the monastery."

"The Abbott was a liar," Maximo concludes simply. "Mantis brought the Red Sulphur he stole from Father in Venice to the monastery in Bruna. You don't remember, because you weren't there."

I'm glad the Count had told us the corroborating story about friar Wenceslaus Seilerus recorded by His Excellency Johann Joachim Becher, so I know Venier Solario is telling the truth.

"I really thought the Stone was his. He took me into his confidence and showed me how he transmuted pewter plates into gold. The next thing I know is that I have the ivory box, the Abbott has mysteriously died and I'm at the Court, now called Wenzel Seyler. There are so many periods that are black. No memory at all."

"Mantis must have killed the Abbott and taken the Stone to the Court so he could eat the Red Sulphur. Mantis loves Red Sulphur," Maximo concludes with fairy tale certainty.

"Do you think Mantis will come back for me?" Venier asks, in the small voice of a child talking to a trusted authority.

"Yes," Maximo replies without hesitation. "He will come back and then I have to drive him out again. He will always come back for more Red Sulphur. But he smells a bit like rotten eggs, so I know when he's here before he can catch you. I will guard you." I cannot believe this is my 7-year old son talking. And yet I know this is his voice, and he is not currently possessed by Red Sulphur. The Twins must be maturing much more rapidly than ordinary mortals. It's the only way I can explain it.

Venier looks at his young benefactor gratefully. I hide more fully behind the curtain as I hear my daughter enter. She sits down next to her brother on his bed.

"Are you feeling any better, Signor Solario?" Johanna asks him in a polite, concerned voice.

"He's like us, Johanna," Maximo explains as Venier nods. "But *his* other spirit is mean and green and called Mantis."

"I figured," Johanna responds without surprise. "That's why I came. Can I ask you something, Signor Solario?" Venier consents with a graceful bow. I remember one of those bows from moments he was fully himself without a trace of Mantis, and feel relieved. For the time being he is clean.

"Do you remember wanting to shoot me?"

"Oh no, Signorina, I have no memory of it. And I can't imagine how I could ever have done such an awful thing!" Venier responds emphatically. He looks bewildered.

"I thought so," Johanna answers, satisfied. "Because you don't look like him. The Mantis man was much younger than you, and he looked like my mother." I almost give myself away as I gasp with surprise.

"Yes," Maximo concurs, "that's true. Mantis *does* look like Mother. I hadn't thought of it until you just said it. But yes…"

"Why do you think that is?" Johanna asks Venier, as if it were a simple puzzle to which he had the missing piece. I am dumbstruck. All my thoughts vanish. And then they rush back in one gigantic wave: my attraction had not been mine at all. It had all been caused by the mercurial passion of my Red Sulphur textiles to Mantis! At first I had thought it was *my* attraction to Venier but finally I came to believe Mundanus who insisted that it had been Red Sulphur's longing for the fires of Hell. The divine longed back for the demonic, for the time of Origin before Heaven and Hell were separate. Red Sulphur and Mantis had fused and this produced a shimmer of my face over Venier's, using my magical youth as a veneer over his visage. It made Wenzel Seyler look young and now that the film of my youthfulness had been removed Venier's face looked old. It gave Mantis-suffused Wenzel Seyler traits of my face covering Venier's physiognomy like transparent clouds over his olive Roman tan.

"But your mother doesn't look at all like me. And I look like Mantis," Venier responds, incredulous.

"That's true," Johanna tells him. "You look not at all like Mother now. But Seyler did. It is the same face in a different key, like in music. I saw it right off and that's why I wasn't really scared of Wenzel Seyler. He felt familiar. But I don't understand it at all. Did you know Mother before?"

"I loved your mother. She was the first one to cure me of Mantis' tortures. She led me out of Hell." He sounds transported. "Mantis wanted her all to himself. He wanted to possess her. So I fought him for days, but of course he was stronger and expelled me to the place of no memories." Venier speaks in sobs, though he is not crying.

"Mantis played Mother's face as a melody over yours so he could be with her forever," Johanna concludes. To her musical mind this is as clear as it is abstruse for me. The Devil singing her mother's mask over the face of his captive is no problem to her mind, or to Maximo's, who instantly gets it. I am arrested by the icy awareness that next time it will not be Venier Solario who Mantis is after. It will be my children! I shiver uncontrollably and give myself away. Maximo jumps up and pulls back the curtain next to the French doors between Mundanus' and my bedroom and the twin's room. When he sees me he laughs with uncontrollable mirth, as if we are playing a game of hide and go seek.

"Mother!" Johanna exclaims, "What are you doing behind the curtain?"

"She's playing," says Maximo. "She was going to surprise us, but I spoiled it. I found you! I found you!" he chants as he dances around me. Suddenly he is a 7-year old again, and I take him in my arms, hugging him tight. He coos with delight. I see that Venier looks very embarrassed.

"See how much she looks like Wenzel Seyler!" Johanna turns to Venier in triumph, as if she were stating the obvious and he would instantly see the truth of her words. "Completely different, of course. But exactly like him," she clarifies in the way children can see what is obvious to them, not understanding that adults have trouble participating in their vision.

"I don't understand it either," I say to Venier.

"But it is so clear!" Maximo insists. "Johanna is completely right. There is no doubt, Mother: your face was floating on top of his," he adds, pointing at Venier. I am surprised by the complete lack of a sense of the unusual in his words. To his mind this must happen all the time, people carrying the faces of others as a mist over theirs. When you're seven, everything is new; why not this?

"You have remarkable children." Venier says to me finally, a blush spreading from the top of his curly head to the neckline of Mundanus' nightshirt he is wearing.

I notice that my face is hot. It is the first time I see Venier as a man, not a boy. And he appears to look at me as a woman. Yet I'm wearing no magic fabrics. First Christiaan Huygens, now Venier: my love is out on the loose! I don't know if I should feel happy or guilty about this. After all, my husband's heart belongs to my aunt. When I notice that I'm arguing for the rightness of my emotions, I realize I must be feeling guilty. Most of all I am truly surprised by these erotic affections. Something new is definitely waking up within me. Now I blush even more, realizing that I'm feeling all this in front of my children. Yet I desire to go back to my bedroom and dress in the radiant flesh-colored morning robe I use when I want to have Mundanus all to myself. I mentally shake my head to get rid of these musings, but they keep hanging around.

"Yes, they are quite extraordinary." I concur with Venier's compliment a bit less gracefully than I would have liked.

"You have not changed since last I saw you," he gallantly continues our stilted conversation.

"Nine years ago," I reply. He certainly looks like a changed man. Deep furrows in his face and a slight bend in his upper back give this man an air of maturity after suffering; and it makes him much more attractive to me than the mere boy he had been before.

I notice that The Twins are observing us with their uncannily perceptive eyes and I make a valiant effort to mask my feelings, using my lifetime of Regent training in stoicism.

"I came to say that later this afternoon we have an audience with the future Holy Roman Empress. Just us. She's arrived for the fittings of her wedding dress and wants to see you two. She tells me she has heard a great deal about you," I say to Johanna. "Maybe you could play something for her?"

Johanna nods absentmindedly. She's already listening in on a concert in her mind. I know my children's expressions.

"Will the Prince be there?" Maximo asks. "There is something I want to show him."

"No, but I could ask Mother Marianne to request he come see us. What do you want to show him?"

"A little something I made," Maximo replies, non-committal. When he speaks in that tone I've learned not to push. He will reveal his intentions at a moment of his own choosing.

"Well then," I say, pushing back my hair so it flows away from my face and noticing the brief glint in Venier's eyes, "I'll leave you three to it. I have to go back to prepare the fitting room for Her Majesty."

"Prince William had just returned from the hunt and gotten off his horse in the courtyard. Maximo comes up to him," Aunt Marianne tells me in a flush, "and says 'Prince, I want to show you something' in that way of his that knows no fear no matter who he's talking to." I can see the conversation between Maximo and Prince William happen before my eyes. Aunt Marianne and I feel intimate in the way we do when we talk about our children. It's almost like talking to myself.

"So he goes up to the Prince and hands him something. Clearly Prince William doesn't know what to make of it. So he asks, and Maximo says 'It is a bullet wrapped in Mother's cloth dipped in bees wax. It is much quicker and easier to load than bullets wrapped in paper.' I see the Prince smile like sunrise. He takes out his pistol, fills it with gunpowder and stashes the bullet in with his loading tool. I can see that surprise is building on his face. Then he turns around and fires at a tree and hits it in the center. 'Incredible!' he exclaims. 'This is indeed much more accurate than bullets wrapped in paper!' Then he explains to me that bullets are little lead balls wrapped in paper and pushed against gunpowder in the barrel. This is a very careful and slow process because if the bullet is not firmly packed against the gunpowder the bullet will fall out or the barrel will explode. He explains that Maximo's bullet is not only faster to load, but also much more accurate. He is now checking if it can be used for muskets as well. So the Prince told me to ask you for more cloth. He says it will change the fortunes of the Dutch Republic. He wants this to remain an absolute secret. Then Maximo told him that the bullets could be given to the soldiers already wrapped to save even more time. And no one will ever find out what the cloth is made of. He can't believe that Maximo came up with all this by himself. Most of all that Maximo made the wax thicker to one side so the bullet spins and finds its target more accurately than a straight bullet!"

"The son of Red Sulphur did, not Maximo," I reply, feeling sour that my cloth will be used to deliver death. I remember that Red Sulphur likes destruction as much as it enjoys creation and that's why it had craved for Mantis. I don't know from which side of Red Sulphur Maximo's invention stems, and I decide to consult my husband before going any step further.

"We must speak to Mundanus about this. We could be creating the next Red Sulphur monster." Aunt Marianne looks annoyed, stopped short in her maternal pride over the genius of her son. "The Prince of Orange needs a lot from me lately. I need to get his army their spinning bullets and his future wife her wedding dress."

"The Prince told me that this is much more important than the wedding dress."

"I can't go to England now anyway," I mutter, annoyed, realizing that I can't leave Venier without Maximo, or Mantis will return for sure. I need Maximo and Venier to stay with me in The Hague. I want to speak with Mundanus first and foremost. And my day is full of fittings. This afternoon we have tea with the future Empress. I want to talk with Mundanus before that.

༄

"I wonder what will happen if we wrap the activated Red Sulphur in that same material when we do a projection," Mundanus muses after I have told him about Maximo's invention, upon his return from his day-long search through Wenzel Seyler's laboratory in the heart of the city. We are in my atelier where I make the final changes to the dress before the Empress-to-be comes. His response annoys me: he has not heard my concern at all.

"You can wonder about that later. Now I need us to decide what I'm going to tell the Prince. I'm afraid that using Red Sulphur to deliver death will backfire. I feel that we put it in the service of Mantis and his cohort. I worry that it will start loving all the mayhem and it will affect our children. They're *made* of Red Sulphur. I'm afraid the lethal uses of Red Sulphur will injure The Twins. We've used it for harm once before, with Monsieur Delamarche, and look where that got us! Don't you worry about our children?"

"You can't undo Maximo's invention, darling. Prince William will impound every piece of cloth you make. You would have to stop weaving altogether. Would you be willing to never again weave glow cloth?"

"If it would protect my children, of course!" I respond with stronger emphasis than necessary. Would I sacrifice my craft for my children? Would I?

Mundanus sits very still, looking at me intently. Aunt Marianne enters with The Twins through the large glass paneled French doors at the far side of the studio in anticipation of the meeting with Her Imperial Majesty-to-be. She immediately notices the tension hanging in the room and looks at Mundanus who doesn't respond to her eyes. He is fully focused on mine. Then both children rush up to him, having not seen him for a day, since he had gone to Wenzel Seyler's laboratory to retrieve the ivory box and what was left of the Red Sulphur. Happy feet tap out their excitement on the parquet floor.

"Was there still any Red Sulphur left, Father?" Maximo asks him eagerly, after pressing his body ardently against his father's. Johanna is still holding on to Mundanus, enjoying the moment, eyes closed.

"More than I had initially feared, Maximo. Apparently, Seyler was a better alchemist than I had thought based on Waldstein's accounts. The Count must have been wrong about the amounts of Red Sulphur Seyler used per projection. But he did grind it to powder. It is no longer a stone. I'd say he used about half; a hundred and fifty years' worth of projections." Mundanus is pensive for a moment. "Maximo, where did you get the idea for the bullet?"

"The lead ball fell out of Wenzel Seyler's pistol. I thought 'That's not supposed to happen. It should stay in there. Something is wrong with the mechanism.'"

The adults burst out laughing and Maximo looks surprised. "But weren't you scared?" I ask, unable to hold back my laughter.

It seems too comical that he would think about the mechanism when his life was in danger.

"Why would I be?" Maximo asks, truly uncomprehending. "There was no danger. Red Sulphur is much more powerful than Wenzel Seyler. Red Sulphur could make him shrivel without lifting a finger!"

"Then why did you faint?" Johanna asks, in her practical voice.

"Because there was a flash of lightning and then everything went black," Maximo responds, equally matter-of-fact. Johanna nods, indicating that his answer fully satisfies her curiosity. She moves over to the clavichord spinet and begins to improvise.

"That's the battle between Mantis and Red Sulphur," Maximo explains, recognizing her music.

Then there is a staccato succession of single notes, each softer than the previous. Distractedly I'm reminded of old Constantijn Huygens' amazement when he told me, "It is impossible to have soft sounds and loud sounds on a harpsichord. They all twang the same. But she has found a way. I don't know how she does it, playing sounds of varying volumes, but somehow she does it!" He had been shaking his head.

"That's the bullet dropping," Maximo elucidates.

Venier was right: these are remarkable children, I think drily.

By the time Johanna plays the flash of lightning, we all recognize it.

Before we can continue our conversation a herald announces the arrival of the Empress-to-be.

Countess Eleonore Magdalene of Neuburg has changed from last time I saw her in Dusseldorf. Then, she had been a timid child-woman, leaning away from her daunting future. The woman who enters, followed by Count von Waldstein and a small retinue, is almost stately. Her neck is stretched upward, her blond hair done up in elaborate vertical curls which show off her slightly elongated fair face to advantage. Her lips, which seemed pouting before, now appear full and determined. Her dark eyes look out at the world with distant calm. This woman is no longer cowering before her future: she has stepped into it. The slight blush on her face looks real and not a powdered artifact.

"What heavenly music!" she enthuses.

"Did you recognize it, Count?" Maximo asks, completely ignoring the future Empress. Maximo is very fond of Count von Waldstein and happy to see him.

"May I introduce Your Highness to an exceptional young man? This is Maximo Dolfin," the Count smiles broadly, obviously proud to make this introduction. I instantly know that the Prince of Orange has talked to him about the bullets. The Dutch Republic and the Habsburg Empire are the closest of allies against the French Sun King Louis XIV. I sense with dismay that the matter is out of my hands. The great powers will rule me; I feel much more sympathy now for the young Countess who is reluctantly following the path of her destiny, and absentmindedly notice an attractive dimple in her chin. The freedom I thought I had, compared to her gilded captivity, turns out to have been an illusion.

She looks at Maximo like one who meets a younger brother, and her posture relaxes from the erect formality that must have kept her in a tight corset since she arrived here at court.

"And you must be his sister, creating that divine music," she says to Johanna in a warm conversational tone. Johanna gets up from her spinet chair and curtsies perfectly. They are so different from each other, our twins. Johanna is all grace, aware of rank and social custom, while Maximo is like a noble peasant, blind to all decorum.

Then she sees the magnificent wedding-train and is overcome with awe. It still hangs down horizontally across the entire length of the atelier radiating moonshine. I see that the countess is crying involuntarily over the sheer beauty of the garment, at which moment she steals my weaver's heart.

"Look, it sparkles," Maximo points out. It seems to me that the cloth recognizes its purpose in the emotions of the Countess.

Johanna instantly begins to play, and now I can hear that she is expressing the emotions of the young bride. All her fears and hopes ripple through Johanna's music, while the cloth seems to be experiencing a pure joy of being. I remember all those years ago in Venice when I had been trying to weave patterns of water into my fabrics. Now I recognize them in the glow-cloth train. But these aquatic patterns are more subtle and intricate than anything I could have woven. The subtle imagination of the glow cloth is so much more scintillating than anything I can come up with through my merely human vision. I feel a pang of envy of Red Sulphur and its divine playfulness. Johanna is now playing in a minor key and I realize she must be intoning the Countess' mourning over having been taken away from her calling as a nun and her desire to devote herself exclusively to our Lord. She must also be suffering homesickness, as the music turns into a dirge. The sparkle in the glow cloth ceases.

"Let me show you the dress," I say out loud, looking at Johanna. She seems to wake from her Red Sulphur trance, and stops playing. There is a stirring in the retinue, especially among the ladies in waiting. All men will have to leave.

"Let me spend a few more moments with your children," she requests. Disappointment ripples through her female attendants. "Of course," I concur, proud of my twins.

"Your music is more beautiful than any I have heard," she compliments Johanna, who takes it in stride. I know she doesn't consider the music hers; she's just hearing it. Johanna is innately modest.

"There's much more of it," she replies. The concert in her mind must still be going.

"Would you like to hear some more, Your Highness?" I ask.

The Countess looks as pleased as if the music were balm to her soul, which I'm sure it is. The court here must be like a desert to her, since all she craves for is our Lord. "Yes, could you play a bit more, Johanna?" she asks my daughter.

This time the music is bright with eager anticipation. I notice Mundanus has taken Count von Waldstein out of earshot, to the glass-paneled French doors. I see the Count nod with delight as he looks in Maximo's direction. I have never seen this much paternal pride on my husband's face. I realize we have entered a new era as Johanna's spinet reaches a crescendo.

ꟿ

"We need your help, Madam Dolfin," the Prince of Orange tells me in his study at the Hofburg, where he is spending a week between battles against proxies of his archenemy Louis XIV. The wedding has been a moment of respite for this man, now 26, who is carrying the weight of a sovereign Europe as the chief marshal of resistance against French imperial designs. Even his enemies respect him. I realize that he will have no trouble getting his bride and the ruse of the dress was just a rare moment of insecurity with Aunt Marianne, his closest confidante in matters of the heart. The air of self-confidence makes him almost look handsome, the hunchback close to invisible. Uncle Johann has told me that battles are good for his health and that he was in excellent condition right now. That's why it hadn't been necessary for Helvetius to come with us to Vienna as the Prince's personal physician. Rather, he stayed in The Hague to catch up with the plethora of requests for the Medicine. He could work without sleeping and still would lack the time to see all the prospective patients flooding in from all over Europe. Even courtiers from Paris came over in secret. It was just a matter of time until the Sun King himself should request his services. I know the Prince of Orange would be delighted.

"Madam, did you hear what I just said?" the Prince asks, a slight pique in his voice.

"Yes, Your Highness, I did. I'm just considering my response."

"There can only be one response, Madam," he says sternly. "The Fatherland needs you. Without these bullets we will soon be overrun by King Louis. The Emperor was very pleased to hear about this new ammunition and wants it for his troops as well of course. We need to go into production as soon as this wedding is behind us." He speaks about the occasion as a mere nuisance that needs to be suffered. Then his tone changes, "Your son is quite remarkable, Madam. This bullet is one of the greatest improvements in warfare since the invention of gunpowder! It works with all weaponry and because of its spin the accuracy is so much increased that it will save bullets. It makes our troops much swifter and we could overcome greater armies than ours. We need these bullets, Madam. It appears that only you can weave the cloth… We have plenty of bee's wax," he ends with a grin.

"Have you tried with other textiles?" I ask hopefully.

"The imperial engineers tell me that the weave of the cloth is exceptionally fine. They have not seen it before. I remember my grandmother raving about your remarkable textiles. Of course as a boy I didn't pay any attention. But maybe I should have. I won't ask you to tell me your secret. I know it must be related to this alchemist Theodore Mundanus everyone is looking for. I'm well aware that Helvetius is using this Mundanus' formula to keep me healthy. Johan de Witt told me he knew the true identity of this man, but never revealed it to me."

"He didn't owe you much now, did he?" I remark drily, still angry at the Prince for not having intervened in the gruesome mob assassination of the brothers De Witt four years ago. He had even rewarded the leaders of the rabble. The Prince looks at me uncomprehendingly, not noticing my insolence, and I decide to leave it at that.

After a brief silence he continues his request - which I know to be an order. Since I am a Van Os and Aunt Marianne's niece, he won't have me tortured into submission as he might have anyone else, but he could exert a great deal of pressure nonetheless. "I will supply you with a small army of weavers if you need them. The engineers tell me that the cloth is made of some kind of wool that is thinner than silk, impossible to make, yet existing in front of their eyes. They are baffled. The Emperor has ordered them to examine the material of the wedding gown to see if it is made of the same cloth. He is willing to have it taken apart bit by bit and be used for bullets."

At this moment I hate men.

"Don't bother," I remark with a profound lassitude and a bitter taste in my mouth. "The dress is made of silk. Maximo took a piece of my woolen cloth. It is slightly thicker and absorbs the wax better. I don't know how he could have known. But he did take the right material."

"I have never heard of such a child," the Prince marvels.

"My children are different from ordinary mortals," I reply without pride, sad for this to be the truth. I crave an ordinary life now more than ever, but I know that it is not to be. "My daughter plays music Monteverdi could only have dreamed of. My son has a technical prowess that would stun Leonardo. And I am their mother…"

"That must be hard," the Prince responds in an unusual moment of true compassion.

"Not as hard as losing them!" I speak fiercely, suddenly deeply concerned again about the effects of this new ammunition on my Red Sulphur twins.

"Why would you lose them?" the Prince asks surprised.

"I can't explain it," I say and wait, hoping a decision will present itself. Then I realize that the decision has already been made. The men have decided, and I am just a woman; the great powers of Europe have decided, and I am just an ant under their marching boots.

"I will weave for you," I say, tired as I haven't felt since Venier assaulted me nine years ago. This feels like the next assault. My womb is cold as ice. "Now I have to go back to get ready for tomorrow." It will be a joyless wedding.

"The Fatherland is grateful," the Prince concludes simply.

'The Fatherland can go to Hell!' I refrain from saying out loud.

ꕤ

As a special honor to our family we are seated near the front of St. Stephen's cathedral in a pew next to the Prince of Orange. I'm sure

Maximo's invention has raised our status immensely, and the rumors about this secret must have spread fast, since I see everyone look at him with great curiosity. He, of course, is utterly unaware of all this attention and only marvels at the enormous cavernous heights of the ceiling.

"Look at the roof, Mother," he points out to Aunt Marianne and me, as if we were one person, "It looks like it floats."

"It imitates the vaults of heaven," Mundanus explains.

"It's like giant birds. It's kites flying up there. Kites of stone," Maximo marvels, oblivious to the fact that he is surrounded by Europe's dignitaries in ornate regalia.

Johanna is equally unaware of the solemnity of the moment. She is completely entranced by the sounds of the gigantic organ, and I realize that she has found her calling. I know she is going to be one of the great organists, piping out music never heard before. Tears are running down her cheeks, but she is not really crying. She is just overfilled with heavenly breath. I want to take her in my arms and tell her that I know exactly what she is feeling. To me she is a weaver of sound and we share the jealous intensity of our calling. But I refrain from touching her, respecting her at this moment not as my daughter, but as a fellow slave to an art. Standing between my children, I look up at the Cross, and dread the fate of our Savior's mother.

The ceremony progresses. A gasp is heard as the bride enters in my dress, which clearly enjoys its environment, the train floating in like a lustrous cloud. The cloth becomes the vanishing point of everyone's perspective and instinctively I press myself close to Johanna, who leans into me, transported by the organ music. I feel an overwhelming pride in my family.

The giant pearls around the Empress' flushed throat, the bulbous golden imperial crown she wears on top of her hair woven in with her gold tresses – all these adornments disappear behind the intense adoration with which she stares at the gold cross she tenderly holds in her hands. On the cross a beautiful golden Christ reveals his heart of suffering to her. The moment between the

Empress and her Savior is of a fragile intimacy that almost makes me look away so as not to intrude upon her public privacy. There is no doubt whom she is marrying, and her canonic vows are those of a nun. The man standing behind her with his sharply protruding Habsburg jaw is only incidental, completely excluded from her devotion. His eyes are sad. The forest of ornate golden bishop's miters and staffs belie the utter simplicity of the bride's true Christian piety. Maximo touches me with his elbow while looking up at the vaulted ceiling. "She is a bird," he whispers, "I saw her fly up."

Part Twelve

Marianne

Chapter Twenty-Five

The Hague, October 1677

Clara insisted on taking Venier back with us to The Hague. He now shares a room in our home with Monsieur Delamarche, and the two of them are getting along really well.

Old Constantijn Huygens introduced Johanna to the organist of the Great Church where Mundanus and Clara were supposed to have been married. Now Johanna is there daily, breathing her miraculous music through the grand pipes.

We're all surrounded by the bodyguards supplied by the Prince of Orange, now that Clara is weaving ammunition in a large warehouse transformed by the military into a giant armory. Our whole life has suddenly become a single-minded war effort. Maximo is diving ever deeper into the spirit of invention and is directing a team of craftsmen. Everyone has had to get used to being guided by a boy not yet eight years old, but his clever machinery makes people forget he is a mere child. He has designed a cast iron mold covered with waxed glow cloth. The cloth is divided into small perforated squares over semi-spherical holes that each fill with a drop of lead on top of the cloth. The individual squares of fabric automatically curl up asymmetrically around the metal, and seamlessly fuse into an off-center ball when the upper mold is lowered like the waffle iron Cook uses on Sundays. Maximo loves waffles.

In this way mass production of glow cloth spin bullets has been made possible, and it was just a matter of time before all the spies in Europe would descend upon us. And they did, one by one, usually badly disguised as diplomats stationed in the Residence. Gerda received exorbitant offers on her wool. We told her to sell everything she produces near The Hague and on our farm in Altensteig. Since the production of glow cloth is a well-kept secret anyway, Gerda may as well move up in life. It keeps the foreign powers guessing as large amounts of useless counterfeit bullets flood the market.

Rumors have it that the mysterious Theodore Mundanus is the originator of the magic cloth, and the hunt for him takes on feverish proportions. King Louis is beside himself with fury – a fact we all enjoy – especially because in the King's mind, Mundanus is purported to be French.

In all of this turmoil, the Prince has asked Helvetius and me to accompany him to London to ask officially for the hand of his first cousin, fifteen year old Lady Mary of York. It is a matter of haste, since the young Princess, second in line to the English throne, is being wooed by King Louis' son, the Dauphin of France.

The ostensible reason for our company is that my Prince's health has deteriorated during this brief interlude between battles with King Louis. Battles are tonics he needs as much as the Medicine Helvetius provides. But the real reason we travel with him is that he needs me close, because like any grand philanderer to whom women are mere quarry, he is terrible in matters of the heart. With me accompanying them as Helvetius' wife, Prince William will be able to kill two birds with one stone. He will have a physician at hand in case his withdrawal from battle makes him truly ill, and he will have me around to guide him through the mysterious labyrinth of Woman.

ꙮ

When Helvetius and I first arrive at Whitehall Palace, Prince William is still with his uncles King Charles and the Duke of York at Newmarket Heath, at the famous horseraces that are always held the first week of October. The Prince had hurried there from Harwich to confront his uncles in the matter of his proposed marriage to Cousin Mary. Rumors have it that William had refused to accept the terms they had offered him: to receive her hand in exchange for favorable terms in a peace agreement in the current war between England and William's Allies. He would not sign off on peace before the marriage and was reported to have said that he refused to sell his Allies for a wife. The marriage was hanging dubiously in the balance.

My Prince's hand is actually quite strong. As a fiercely Protestant Prince of Stuart blood, he is the unofficial head of the English opposition. He is loved by the people of England, who are disgusted with Stuart brothers James of York, a Catholic, and by pseudo-Protestant King Charles. They are passionately against any kind of papist French rule. On a personal note, they admire my Prince for his superb horsemanship, honed by years of battle.

Now he has arrived at Whitehall and it is the first time I will meet him since we came to London. The King is still absent, traveling back from one of his other castles to entertain a mistress. It appears to be his primary pursuit, entertaining mistresses. It sounds to me like a vacuous life, but then again, maybe he truly loves them; who am I to say? I know nothing about love, really. I know Mundanus, and that's about as far as I know romance. It is ironic that Prince William trusts me so completely on this score.

Since I first met him that day in front of the Grand Pensionary's office at the Inner Court, he has treated me with the respect due to a mother, though this respect is pervaded with a twinkle of romantic attraction which has always struck me as comical. His own mother had never shown him any affection. She felt trapped in Holland, always professing her close allegiance to her brother Charles whom she frequently hosted during his continental wanderings as a hapless King without a crown, lavishly spending her son's money. After the Restoration when Cromwell was ousted and Charles II regained the throne, she made it known publicly that she was rather in London at her brother's court than in The Hague with her son. I had instantly recognized Prince William for the orphan he was, and he had found in me a mother-in-waiting, hiding from herself how much she truly wanted to have a child. I hadn't really known this myself until the birth of The Twins. A world I'd never known gave me a new heart, and with the overpowering love I felt for Maximo – and if I'm truly honest with myself, to a lesser degree for Johanna – my maternal affections towards the forlorn young Prince deepened.

By distinguishing himself in acts of subtle statesmanship and battlefield wizardry, he rapidly rose in power and reputation, but it made him ever lonelier. He was innately shy, because of his hunchback, and had been taught to be suspicious of everyone's motives. I was the only one with whom he felt entirely free to speak honestly in matters of the heart, and rightly so. I knew with absolute certainty that I would never betray his trust.

Whitehall is the largest palace in England, and with its 1500 rooms larger even than the Versailles King Louis is building. It's an entire village on the Thames actually, a place of a certain hard and material gorgeousness where one gets lost. It reminds me of the North End Palace for its lack of true taste and patronage of the creative arts, full of drab paintings that would make a Dutch Master cringe. There are sumptuous velvet hangings, gilded chandeliers and elaborate marbles. Everything is copied from Versailles. It has actually been brought over here by Louis – possibly left over rejects from his massive Versailles project – and paid for from his coffers as an open seduction to his cousin Charles to become Catholic and aid the French King in his imperial Charlemagne dream. The liaison to Paris, as everybody knows, is Charles' French mistress, the clever Louise de Kérouaille, Duchess of Portsmouth, with whom he is currently cavorting somewhere.

"I'm used to this. Uncle Charles is always between castles; he likes to make you wait. Last time I was here he made me wait here at Whitehall for days. The shorter the wait, the higher the esteem. He'll be here soon; he needs me," Prince William assesses the situation. We are in his elegant suite with cedar wood paneling and a large arched window overlooking an unimaginative yard. "I miss our walks in the gardens at North End," he tells me wistfully.

It feels incongruous that this hero of the battlefield would have such a love of plants. It's been there ever since I've known him. Sometimes I feel he'd be so much happier as a gardener. But we don't get to choose our destiny. We're part of a plan when we enter the world as pawns on a chessboard in the middle of a game in which our side may be winning or losing. A Prince destined for battle will have to forego the horticulture of his heart.

"Do you like battles, my dear Prince?" I ask. "My husband tells me they make you vigorous."

He ponders for some time. I like it how deeply he always considers my questions.

"I will tell you as a soldier, not as a Captain General." He pauses again, his forehead in a concentrated frown, seeing before his eyes what he is about to tell me. "There is a breathtaking thrill when the great moment comes and the horses ride out. We move in step irresistibly towards enemy lines. A boiling mad rage takes hold of me and the others. The overwhelming wish to kill gives us wings. The monstrous desire for annihilation hovers over the battlefield. It thickens our brains to a red fog. We call to each other in sobs and stammer disconnected sentences. A neutral observer might believe we are seized by an excess of happiness…" He sounds lyrical. Then his voice turns somber, "But all the death is horrible; the wounded disfigured. I always vomit when I inspect a battlefield afterwards, even if we win: it makes no difference. So yes, I love going into battle and I hate the outcome."

"Would you avoid them if you could," I ask him, not knowing which response I'd prefer.

"We all dream of the one great battle that will be decisive and will end all war. But that's just a momentary dream to make us fiercer. We get restless and crave the next red fog. If I'm honest I have to say that I couldn't stay away from it. Thank God I have a just cause!"

"You must be grateful to Louis," I respond drily, pointing up at the opulently gilded Versailles chandelier.

He smiles at me with the pleasure of being known.

"A nauseating field of dead bodies and screaming wounded must be a lot more comfortable than asking a 15 year old girl to marry you," I jest.

"Endlessly so," he concurs. "I'd rather lose an arm."

"You may lose your heart."

"Oh Madam, you're such a tender-hearted soul. Hearts don't get lost. At best they stray."

I reflect upon his philandering life, so much in line with most royals, and compare it with my own heart that got lost once and for all.

"Madam Marianne," he asks me, obviously weighing a question he has been pondering for a long time. "May I ask you a question of a very personal nature in return?"

I feel myself blush and nod quickly.

"I know it must be related to your alchemy, but could you tell me how it is that you now look younger and more beautiful than when I first met you when I was 16 years old?"

His question embarrasses me. I have discussed this only with Mundanus and Clara. We have been set apart from ordinary mortals, aging considerably slower than anyone else - a disparity that is becoming increasingly obvious. Currently it just incurs the envy of others, but soon voices of witchcraft will sound and our youthful appearance may become dangerous. I fear for my Red Sulphur twins, whose aging will be entirely unpredictable. For now, they are merely growing intellectually far more rapidly than ordinary children, but in the company of the Huygens family that is not yet such a glaring fact. Christiaan spoke five languages by the age of six, after all. I dread the future. As I look up I see the Prince awaiting my answer.

"You are indeed correct, my dear Prince," I decide. "It is the alchemy. I have received large doses of the same formula my husband gives you for your health. It has saved my life several times. And as one takes large quantities of the medicine, the aging process becomes unpredictable."

"The outcome seems far from unpredictable to me. Madam Clara and Signor Dolfin also age much slower than the rest of us. With such odds I would ride into battle any time. Do you think it would have the same effect on me if I ask your husband to dispense the medicine to me in higher doses?"

"I am not a physician, so I can't answer your question. But I doubt you would want it. People who age in the ordinary way always wish to live longer and avoid the ravages of time. But when you are the only one to do so you become a freak of nature and finally an outcast."

"I don't think I would mind aging a little slower. I would enjoy my mistresses more," he concludes with a grin. "And I'd be on par with a 15 year old Lady who appears to dance like a dazzling wood sprite."

"She's dancing in a performance, I hear," I respond, glad to change the subject. Lady Mary's upcoming pageant, a ballet based upon Ovid's 'Callisto', is the gossip all over Whitehall. Allowing Lady Mary of York, a Princess second in line to the throne, to make an appearance on stage, is considered a scandalous flaunting of public opinion by her uncle the King. Women are only just appearing on the public stage, and those who do so are mostly considered creatures of the lowest character.

"I could arrange for you to be at this ballet. That might actually be a good idea. She would not want me in attendance. But you could get an impression of who she is. It might help us in devising a strategy," the Captain General concludes.

ꝏ

Before Helvetius and I go to the pageant with the young Princesses Mary and her sister Anne, I read up on Ovid's myth of Callisto in one of the many unused libraries at Whitehall Palace. My father used to fulminate against this habit of aristocrats to hog valuable books they never read, just for the purpose of owning them and smoking their pipes by the fire looking well bred. The room is cozy, lined with books ordered by size and color. Over the fireplace hangs a picture of the Lady Mary of York dressed as the goddess Diana, painted last year. At 14 she looks remarkably womanly. She has the beginnings of her mother Ann Hyde's voluptuous outlines, a rose petal, sensuous mouth, and self-contained eyes looking at the world with a wary distance suited for a young Princess of England, whose every move is the gossip of the court. She gives off an air of elegant grace and pale melancholy, accentuated by the beautiful white complexion of the Stuarts. Her abundant hair, worn in long curls reaching almost to her waist and framing her brow in short ringlets, is dark brown with the Stuart auburn in the glints of the tresses. What strikes me is the crescent moon resting atop her forehead with a blonde curl rivulet flowing over the concave hollow. Together with the bow in her left hand, arrow in her right and behind her a placid English hound, she carries all emblems of Moon Goddess Diana the divine Huntress.

Turning to Ovid, I am reminded that Callisto is an ancient princess devoted to Goddess Diana. The Goddess' devotees were virgins, sworn to never be with a man. Shape-shifting Zeus was entranced by the young girl and approached Callisto in the guise of the Goddess, her beloved Mistress. In this way she was tricked into letting down her guard, and was ravished by him. No one could understand why such a ribald myth was chosen for the staged presentation at court of an innocent young Princess and possible future Queen.

But sitting here, looking at the painted Lady Mary in her guise of Diana, I am struck by the fact that the young princess would appear as a devotee of the Huntress twice. Maybe underneath all of her ostensible guilelessness, she is sending a message to all suitors saying that she is a woman's woman, not a man's, ready to defend her virginity against any of them; and that the man who took her would be a rapist ruining her life, even if he were the King of the Gods himself.

Deep within me an admiration begins to take hold for this defiant young slave of fate, defending her body against the inevitable invaders. I must tell my young friend to be most gentle with her, or he will be forever cast in the role of the Grand Ravisher and his life will be Hell.

Helvetius and I are delivered to the court in a black lacquer carriage with the Austrian imperial emblems prominently displayed. Prince William, showed excellent maneuvering skills by having us be the invitees of the Habsburg emperor. It makes our attendance both a matter of state that can't be refused and an event of minor importance. I'm uncomfortable being a person of interest here at Whitehall.

When a lackey opens the door, I am very pleased to see Austrian ambassador Count von Waldstein descend to greet us. It is a relief to have a friend at court.

"Madam Schweitzer, Doctor Helvetius, what a pleasure!" he intones gregariously, his voice genuine and warm. He kisses my hand; a restrained, courtly gesture, yet one that conveys fully how he has been looking forward to this meeting. Helvetius, who up until this moment had been his usual fussy self, worrying how he would look at a function of this magnitude, clears up instantly, and for a moment I fear his relief will make him behave in too familiar a way. But his Germanic upbringing puts some restraint on his momentary ebullience.

"Your Excellency," he exclaims in his German voice, too loud for the occasion, "My wife tells me you have been a most gracious host when my family was your guest in Vienna."

I fleetingly ponder the fact that Helvetius becomes a more gregarious man when he speaks his mother tongue and nod, underlining his gratitude, remembering that fateful night when the count's rapier had pressed into Wenzel Seyler's throat. Helvetius was never told the details and had been introduced to Venier as Mundanus' step-uncle. By now most of the salient details of my life are unknown to my husband. Count von Waldstein knows considerably more about what matters to me than does Helvetius. "Thank you for taking us to the pageant. We don't know anyone at court and Prince William isn't favored by the Lady Mary," I say in warm understated German.

"Then it shall be up to you and Madam Clara to change her mind," he concludes simply, thereby closing this delicate matter. "How are the remarkable young Maximo and Johanna? I was sorry to hear they didn't accompany you. I had hoped they would be here with their parents…" he lets his voice trail off, making me realize he is particularly disappointed about the absence of Theodore Mundanus, whom he reveres. It weighs on Count von Waldstein that he is the only one who knows Signor Dolfin's true identity, apart from Clara and myself. The Count had asked us while still in Vienna if he could take any of the English alchemists like Isaac Newton or Robert Boyle into his confidence, an idea Mundanus had adamantly rejected. We trust the honor of the Golden Fleece, upon which Count von Waldstein had made his oath to not divulge his knowledge. But Mundanus wouldn't trust another soul.

"Signor Dolfin sends his special regards," I tell him as we ride the short distance to the ballroom where the pageant will take place.

Count von Waldstein shines with delight. "There is someone I want you to meet," he replies with obvious pleasure, "An adept I have known for as long as I can remember who has come to the court recently, a close friend of the great Robert Boyle himself."

The carriage comes to a halt in front of the grand ballroom and I have no chance to ask for any further details. I descend, holding up the long gown I'm wearing for the occasion: sky blue with a mixture of glow cloth and azure made from the sky-blue precursor to the Stone. I had asked Clara to make me powerful dresses to impress their gorgeous nature upon young Lady Mary of York, who has an outspoken liking of rich materials.

To my relief, we are announced by the stately lackey by the door as Imperial Ambassador von Waldstein and guests. The stares are brief and mercifully unimpressed, although some of the Ladies at the court notice the remarkable quality of my dress. I know the difference between someone looking at my person or at one of Clara's creations, and am grateful to my niece that at this moment I disappear behind the gown.

The grand ballroom is in colors of pearl, made festive for the occasion with pink garlands and a forest of trees indicating Diana's sacred grove. I now understand why this event is not just referred to as a ballet, but as a pageant. A sea of voices waves gently in early night restraint before wine and ballet may lead to exuberance. In the center of the room I note a gigantic chair, much like a throne, and I realize that the King shall be present. The King's presence indicates that this ballet is an orchestrated matter of state, a formal presentation of the Lady Mary, second in line to the throne after her father the Duke of York. I am interrupted in my musings by Count von Waldstein.

"And may I introduce Madam Schweitzer, a noted adept; and the illustrious Doctor Helvetius you must have heard about." I see a man of indeterminate age and disturbingly familiar eyes looking right through me. His face seems to exude forward as if it were bursting towards me.

"Signor Ricaldo Rossini," the Count introduces him proudly.

"I am very pleased to make your acquaintance," a mellifluous baritone of an accomplished Magus chants in a rolling Italianate cadence. I have rarely been as curious about a man as I am right now.

"Of course I have heard of the remarkable Helvetius transmutation and have read your report of the December '66 projection. It is said that you have met the great Mundanus. And you Madam, Robert Boyle assures me that you have achieved the heavenly blue caelum together with Signor Dolfin."

"How does he know?" I ask, taken aback.

"Anthonie van Leeuwenhoek has reported about it to the Royal Society. He says your niece uses it for one of her remarkable dyes. All of Europe seems to be talking about her accomplishments."

Count von Waldstein beams with pride about the obvious reference to the marvelous wedding gown of his Empress. Ricaldo Rossini's voice carries, even though it is soft and melodious, and some of the courtiers around us grow silent. I'm embarrassed.

"Your splendid gown must be of her making," Signor Rossini concludes. Now all of our neighbors stare at me for seconds longer than is proper. I am saved by the entrance of the King and his mistress, the stunning Louise de Kérouaille, Duchess of Portsmouth, who looks strikingly like the statue of Mundanus' mother Claudia in Dolfin Chapel. They are followed by the King's brother, the melancholy James of York, Lady Mary's father. I am particularly intrigued by the Duke of York, Mundanus' principal adversary - a man who has been chasing my beloved for 15 years. The Duke's long visage appears wasted by dissipation, different from the thick gregarious face of his brother the King, who has the air of a man successfully devoted to carnal pleasure. His favorite illegitimate son and two of the latter's mistresses are to dance in the prologue to the ballet. The King has left a trail of bastards, but his marriage to the queen has remained barren. My Calvinist self has a hard time with all this abundant lust. I feel prim.

As soon as the King is seated, holding on tightly to his Louise, the orchestra intones the prelude to the prologue. Now I too am filled with anticipation. A new life is about to dance onto the world stage.

Servants dressed in horned Pan-costumes walk in with rich candelabras, replete with dazzling candles. From outside, the sound of fireworks is heard, and the reflections of their colorful lights enter the ballroom like specters. The jaded audience cheers like a crowd of enchanted children. The ballet has our undivided attention. But the prologue is dull, with cavorting courtiers in daring dress rushing through unimaginative choreographies reminiscent of a bawdy nursery. The supposedly seductive movements of the English fauns and nymphs display their profoundly un-Mediterranean nature. Ovid would not have been pleased. I sense Mundanus smile behind me in Italianate superiority. Not liking this side of him, I turn around to dismiss my invisible beloved – and am met with Signor Ricaldo Rossini's disconcerting eyes, crow's feet rising in arrogant amusement. I'm reminded of a moment in Venice when Mundanus was holding forth about the Nordic lack of playfulness compared to the Latin cornucopia of sensuality. Clara had waved her magic sleeve and his self-importance had almost ended him up in the Grand Canal. I raise my arm, slightly ruffling Clara's textiles, and am aware that Signor Rossini notices the sky-spirit blue exuding from the cloth. His breath skips a breath. I miss my niece.

The scene on the stage before us changes. The prologue has ended, and the dull music prepares us for a next act.

Suddenly we are transfixed by a figure moving like a twirl of fog, almost immaterial in appearance; a floating child-woman embodying a forlorn sprite in search of her Mistress Diana. She moves with the spellbinding grace of moon rays. I feel myself becoming lyrical while at the same time my heart sinks as I compare her to the clumsy physical presence of my deformed Prince. As I cast a quick glance behind me I notice Signor Rossini's intense gaze as he absorbs this apparition of grace. I find him disconcertingly intriguing.

On the stage, Callisto moves to pick a narcissus in a clear reference to the myth of the virgin girl Kore, who was picking narcissus flowers just before being ravished by Underworld god Hades. As she bends forward I have the urge to yell out "Don't!" as if I were a child at a puppetry show. I can feel a woman's solidarity with the girl about to be raped by forces beyond her control. When the young Princess looks up at us, I see a tear rolling down her face. She knows what is about to unfold and looks the King straight in the eye. Charles acknowledges her with a gallant gesture of his head, completely unaware of the message he has just received. Louise is all loveliness, shamelessly courting the young Princess as the representative of the Dauphin of France. World politics is being enacted before our eyes in the guise of a young woman dancing her destiny. I can feel an instant rivalry between Mistress Louise and myself since I represent Prince William, King Louis' archenemy. Battle lines are drawn and I notice Count von Waldstein leaning towards me, underlining our Habsburg alliance. Behind us Signor Rossini smiles almost audibly. I don't have to turn around to notice his pleasure about the unfolding intrigue. I wonder who else notices, but it seems everyone is simply riveted by the elegant innocence of the young Princess picking her flower of doom. With clumsy movements a courtier matron dances upon the stage carrying divine Diana's attributes. A splendid hound follows her obediently. We all know she is Zeus in disguise. A great actor might have been able to portray an Olympian in lust employing a woman's body for his sordid scheming. But this courtly Lady fails miserably, and her stilted movements might have given a comical aspect to the unfolding tragedy were it not for the gossamer movements of a Princess whose childhood grace is about to be ravished. Her loveliness stands before us with the piercing accusation of a pawn about to be captured on a grand chessboard looking at her king. The King in the flesh is utterly oblivious as he shamelessly paws his French mistress.

"What a beautiful dress," the Lady Mary tells me when she's introduced to me by Count von Waldstein after the ballet. The sounds around us are abundantly festive, as the court has reached the early foothills of full-fledged Bacchanalia. The King has led in the ample libations to Bacchus and is all but copulating with the incomparable Louise, both conspicuously enveloped in a luscious haze of wine. James, Duke of York, left right after the ballet, with no more than a curt nod to Lady Mary of York, who curtsied in distant regard. Now that the Duke has become a pious Catholic, his relations to his very Protestant daughter are chilly.

"It is made by Madam Schweitzer's incomparable niece Madam Clara Dolfin, who made my Empress' wedding gown," Count von Waldstein gushes. Now that she is no longer dancing on stage the young Princess is but a shy girl wishing she could be elsewhere with her young Lady friends. My gown gives her a moment's respite from her obvious desire to be gone.

"May I touch the material?" she asks me, with diffidence that belies her arresting stage presence.

"Of course, Your Highness," I respond with an involuntary blush as I hold up the sleeve Clara cut like modest butterfly wings. It flutters beneath my slight tremble. As she touches the material I hear her gasp, enchanted by the force of Clara's mastery. She looks up at me and I am moved by the innocence in her almond eyes, reminding me of Prince William's when I first encountered him at her age; and suddenly the affair of state has become a personal mission. This Princess has a lot in common with my Prince, and it could actually turn out to be an intimate marriage if the chips were to fall the right way. I notice Ricaldo Rossini observing the scene with the perspicacity of a Magus who can see behind veils. I will need all my Regent education to keep my mind in occultation, shielded from his view. I realize this instant that Signor Rossini is about to play an essential role in my life, the manner of which is as yet obscure.

"I have never touched material as rich as this," the young Princess exclaims in unabashed admiration. Her face is now flushed as after a large gulp of wine. I can see in Count von Waldstein's eyes that the dress is doing its intended diplomacy.

"I brought some gowns with me I could show you," I encourage her. "My niece made them especially for you, hoping you'd do her the honor of accepting them."

A momentary suspicion lights up her eyes, trained as she is in the knowledge that gifts to royalty usually contain requests. But the power of Clara's alchemy overrides her caution and she invites me to her quarters the day after tomorrow. Before she turns to other guests, I gift her with a small glow cloth kerchief, which she accepts with delight. I have not yet visited grand St. James's Palace here in London, where the young Princesses Mary and Anne of York are being brought up far away from their Catholic father. To my surprise I'm looking forward to the visit.

After the Princess has drifted to another part of the ballroom, Signor Rossini approaches me. "That is the Red Sulphur cloth your Prince's bullets are wrapped in," he concludes, with a clarity of knowledge it would be insulting to contradict. So I remain silent, awaiting his next move. Noting how the blood draws away from Count von Waldstein's cheeks, I conclude that he has been equally taken by surprise, indicating that this knowledge didn't come from him. An uncomfortable silence ensues between us, offsetting the resounding intimations of impending debauchery throughout the pearl ballroom. I can't wait to leave.

"I recognize the Stone when I see it," Signor Rossini remarks. "Theodore Mundanus has left you with ample riches." Helvetius, whose attention had been occupied by a court physician, has returned to us, and looks at me quizzically.

"Your niece's textiles have been made with the same Red Sulphur you use as the Panacea," Signor Rossini explains slowly, in the way one teaches a rather dull student. His insights are altogether too discomfiting and I look pleadingly at the Count, hoping he will suggest our departure.

"Robert Boyle has requested a meeting with the both of you," Signor Rossini adds to my already significant consternation. Helvetius is instantly delighted and forgets the remarks about the textiles. Any literate man in Europe would wish to meet with the great scientist who, next to Isaac Newton, is the prime luminary of the Royal Society. "Maybe you would wish to be present?" Signor Rossini bows in Count von Waldstein's direction. The momentary alarm about Signor Rossini's disconcertingly exact knowledge of Maximo's ammunition seems to evaporate as we set out on an animated conversation about Robert Boyle's remarkable vacuum pump, surrounded by outbursts of outlandish festivities and increasing demands of the flesh.

ꕤ

Princess Mary has gathered her closest playmates in her room at St. James's Palace for the showing of the dresses. First of all, of course, there is 24-year old Frances Apsley, with whom young Mary is ecstatically enamored. Their childish play has become so romantically heated that everyone in Whitehall wonders if there is more going on than just the infatuation of young girls. Rumor has it that Frances' father has asked his daughter to see less of the Lady Mary, who calls Frances 'my husband.' Their love is the glowing center of Princess Mary's life.

Mary's timid younger sister, Lady Anne of York, has taken up the same kind of romantic play with the brilliant and imperious Sarah Jennings, who at barely 17 is already a power at court to be reckoned with. Her sharp wit is indiscriminate and she has been known to challenge even the King, who takes the matter good-heartedly because he enjoys the young woman's acerbic tongue.

When I enter, followed by two of my Prince's women servants carrying Clara's creations, Sarah Jennings stops us before we can place the trunk and unpack the gowns.

"You are an emissary of William of Orange," she says bluntly. "These magical textiles are to bribe our friend in the matter of his courtship." Her voice is haughty and her maturity well beyond her years. She is a full figured blonde and looks positively stern and self-righteous. Even Lady Mary's "husband" Frances Apsley, who is seven years her senior, looks bashful by comparison. I see the Lady Mary take a step back as if this fact were new to her. Young Lady Anne stares blissfully at Sarah, the heated romantic feelings towards her idol unmistakable. "I've heard about them and seen a painting of the wedding dress of the Habsburg Empress which the Emperor has had so kindly sent over." Her voice is dripping with sarcasm. "He is William's ally, as we all know."

"And whose side are you on?" I hear myself asking her in the same tone. I'm surprised by my combative response and wish I had kept my composure.

"On the side of my friends the Ladies Mary and Anne of York," she growls shooting sharp icicles.

I've heard about this girl and her bossy nature. The Princesses are completely under her power. If I am to have any chance with my mission, I will have to get by this belligerent young shrew. I decide to treat her sour attack in the way of sulphuric acid and isolate it, refusing any interaction. If you allow the acid to interact with any material it will corrode it because of an unquenchable thirst for water – and if it does interact you douse the material with water, plenty of water. Putting this encounter in the context of my laboratory calms me. Utterly ignoring Sarah Jennings, I instruct the women of my Prince's retinue to place the waterproof trunk, able to resist the rigors of a sea voyage, on a round table in the corner of the room close to one of the windows, so the light will stream directly onto Clara's creations.

"Is it true that you are of Prince William's court?" Princess Mary asks timidly, backing away into the protection of her beloved Frances.

"No Your Highness, I am not," I reply honestly. "I am the spouse of his physician, Doctor Helvetius."

"Is he so sick that he has to travel with a physician?" Sarah asks sardonically. "Is he so ill that his physician alone does not suffice but that he has to take his wife as well?" Lady Anne giggles.

"I have been asked to accompany my husband to present the gowns my niece has fashioned for your Highness," I address the Lady Mary directly, making it a point to neutralize Miss Jennings vitriol with emphatic inattention. I pointedly never look in Sarah Jennings direction again.

"A wedding dress maybe?" Sarah scorns.

"Will you permit me to show you the gowns, Your Highness?" I ask in a neutral manner.

"I think we should send her away, Your Highness," Sarah insists. "She's come with bribes you shouldn't accept."

Lady Mary looks desperately at her Frances for guidance. The atmosphere in the room, balancing uneasily between nursery and boudoir, is notably colder than the fall temperature outside.

I wear a stole made of glow cloth and take it off in a billowing wave of magic fabric. Princess Mary instantly recognizes her desire to see more of our sorcery and silently nods. Sarah folds her arms and looks huffy, but in her eyes curiosity has been lit. Frances puts her arm protectively around her young spouse. They indeed look like the couple they fancy themselves to be, and I understand the King's orders to separate them as much as possible. If my Prince has any interests beyond a formal marriage-alliance he will have to win her away from this 'husband.'

As I lift the lid off the trunk I am reminded of that moment in Helvetius' study when Mundanus first opened his ivory box with the Red Sulphur to me. A thrill of reflected light off the magic glow-cloth fabrics mirrors the outside autumn sunshine like the blossom of a full moon. I can hear even Sarah Jennings gasp.

"That is so beautiful!" Princess Mary exclaims clapping her hands like a young girl.

"It's a trick!" Sarah warns her adamantly. "Your cousin William is trying to seduce you through sorcery. This woman is a witch!"

I realize instantly that she is going to spread this calumny at court and remember Clara telling me of witchcraft rumors having gone around the Hofburg in Vienna when she was working on the Empress' wedding gown. The King's mistress Louise de Kérouaille, a consummate master of court intrigue, will use it immediately to further the Dauphin's cause. I must discuss this with Count von Waldstein immediately. Mundanus had warned me of the English when he told me how he was chased out of London, thought to be a sorcerer who had caused the Great London Firestorm of September 1666.

I sense all eyes in the room resting upon me, even those of the servants, and feel I must do something.

"They say that her husband Helvetius is keeping Prince William alive through sorcery," Sarah Jennings bursts out.

I respond by taking out the first item from the chest, a simple glow-silk night gown enchanting to any woman or man. Clara had packed it on top to set a moonlit mood and I see instantly that she has succeeded. Lady Mary looks at her Frances adoringly and I can read in her eyes how the glow cloth has made her love visible. It shows us the world through the fantastic eyes of imagination.

"I hear the Prince is a hunchback," Sarah Jennings exclaims mean-spiritedly. "He must be used to hiding his ugliness behind finery!" I cringe involuntarily.

"Sarah!" Lady Mary scolds her unexpectedly. "He's still my first cousin! I'll never marry him but his mother *was* my father's sister."

"He's just Zeus dressed up as a member of your family," Sarah disparagingly refers to the *Callisto* ballet. Now I realize that it may have been Sarah Jennings' idea to portray any suitor to Princess Mary as a wily old rapist. Men are not welcome in this virginal grove of the Goddess.

I hand Lady Mary the nightgown and she parades it seductively in front of Frances who is embarrassed by her young 'wife's' inviting sensuality. I can see that their romance is mutual as Frances' eyes all but burst out of her flushed face.

"You were sent here to drive us all mad!" Sarah Jennings accuses me. She is right, of course, so I don't dignify her with even a glance in her direction. Truth can be the most biting vitriol of all.

She rushes over to the trunk and franticly begins to pull out the gowns. "Where is the wedding dress? There must be a wedding dress! You were not sent here for nightgowns." Before I can stop her she has found the stunning wedding gown at the bottom of the trunk. She pulls it out, ripping the gossamer pearl cloth, and holds it up triumphantly. "See! This is what the witch was after!" I have never in my life been treated as atrociously as this and need all my Regent restraint to not slap this insolent girl. But Sarah's sulphuric attempt to show me up as an evil pawn in Prince William's chess game backfires.

The Lady Mary exclaims excitedly to Frances: "Let's be wed right here and now so no one will ever separate us again! I'll wear the gown to make it official." I realize that that the reflecting glow of the magic cloth has seduced the impressionable young Princess into firmly believing in the actuality of her romantic child's play.

"Madam, you had better leave," Sarah Jennings utters curtly. "You've done enough damage here."

I don't look at her.

"Yes, Madam Schweitzer." Young Princess Anne politely speaks her first words of the afternoon. "You had better go."

Princess Mary is too wrapped up in the reality of her make-believe to be aware of my presence. Her face is flushed as she perfunctorily drops her dress to the floor and pours herself into the wedding gown, which fits like a glove. She looks enchanted.

I bow to the Lady Anne and make my way to the door, Prince William's maidservants in tow. I realize I am as disgusted with our sorcery as is Sarah Jennings.

"We could preempt it by spreading the rumor that Louise de Kérouaille is enchanting the King by way of witchcraft. Everyone would wish to believe it. That way an accusation of you by Miss Sarah Jennings would lose its sting. You are much less interesting to courtiers than is the Duchess of Portsmouth. She is one of the most powerful forces at court," Count von Waldstein is musing out loud as we are riding in his carriage to the London quarters of Signor Rossini on our way to Robert Boyle's residence. Helvetius nods. He has been agitated since I told him about Sarah Jennings' potential accusation of witchcraft.

"I could add periwinkle, leeks and earthworms to the Panacea. Albertus Magnus has given us that recipe." I suggest. "It would instantly go around the court and make everyone lovesick. Then we could have a Lady at the court find the bewitching potion in Louise's boudoir."

"I could add green powder of Spanish flies. They will inflame the senses. Whitehall will become one big orgy!" Helvetius adds. "The accusation of witchcraft would stick instantly."

"It will lead to a frenzied search for more potion. They wouldn't leave a stone unturned. Love magic meets a craving need at this court," the Count says with a grin.

"Why do you carry green powder of Spanish flies?" I wonder out loud, before realizing that it is for my amorous Prince's dalliances. Helvetius keeps a studied medical silence.

"Let's wait a bit before we unleash these epic bacchanalia," I suggest as we stop in front of Signor Rossini's Covent Garden quarters at the Cock and Magpie Inn on Drury Lane. The Inn is a many-windowed three-story building next to a barber shop, under various attic roofs pointing in all directions on a lively street full of carts and donkeys. Over the entrance awning a colorfully painted rooster looks up at a magpie against a blue sky under a rainbow. When the liveried coachman opens the door of the carriage I absentmindedly notice a man urinating just around the corner and become aware of an intrusive smell of excrement and vomit. This is a street of many drinkers. Birds overhead give the impression that death is a frequent visitor here. Rats are foraging everywhere. Since it is common knowledge that cats are the cause of the plague, they have been slaughtered and outlawed, leaving the rats with no natural predators. This is an unusual place for an esteemed foreigner to make his quarters.

"Good afternoon," Signor Ricaldo Rossini jovially greets us, as he enters the luxurious black lacquered Berlin carriage, one of the first of its kind in England brought over by Count von Waldstein to impress the continent-gazing English. "I am so pleased I will be able to introduce you to the illustrious Boyle." Our momentary visions of court intrigue vanish at the prospect.

I try not to stare at Signor Rossini as we ride towards the house of Robert Boyle's elder sister Katherine Jones, Lady Ranelagh, in Pall Mall where Boyle has lived for the past decade. Signor Rossini explains to Count von Waldstein that the house on the Mall was beautifully refurbished last year when she gifted her brother with a large state of the art laboratory.

In a way Ricaldo Rossini reminds me of Mundanus' grandfather. The fluidity of his face is like a thin film of fog over a mutable surface, as if he is both present and absent at the same time. The result is a fascinating mixture of charisma and emptiness. But I am most attracted to his eyes. They remind me of Mundanus before he went through his transformation. Maybe it is the expression of Magi who have labored extensively with Red Sulphur. I wonder if Signor Rossini is an initiate to the Great Arcana. I'm convinced he is an advanced adept. Suddenly he turns to me: "Do you carry the blue caelum with you, the precursor to the White Sulphur you have achieved with Signor Dolfin? I had hoped you would bring it to Boyle to have him test it. It is all Boyle has been talking about since he heard about it from Leeuwenhoek earlier this year. He has been very excited to meet with you and of course with you, Doctor Helvetius. You know your pamphlet was published in English four years ago?"

Helvetius and I nod at the same time. There is something downright eerie about Signor Rossini. It is as if he can see through my purse and is actually looking at the small pouch of blue powder Mundanus and I had decided I would present to Robert Boyle, were I to meet him. I shudder at all that is revealed to his gaze and feel naked – which is strangely exciting at the same time. There is a momentary whiff of musk in the air. My heart beats faster and I hope I'm not blushing. I can't fully concentrate as he tells us that the home of Robert Boyle's sister had been for almost thirty years the meeting place of what had become the Royal Society of London fifteen years ago. He is praising her intelligence as an exciting woman scholar who can use her mind on par with any man – as he looks at me directly with disconcerting frankness. It seems as though he is talking about me and I feel increasingly uncomfortable under his hidden praise.

"I know Signor Rossini to have a very sweet tongue," Count von Waldstein jokes wryly, to deflect attention away from me. It indicates that he is close enough to Signor Rossini to joke about his manner.

Signor Rossini smiles back in a conspiratorial way. "You must admit, dear Waldstein, that being in the company of a woman of high degree is thrilling to the soul."

"You're embarrassing yourself and the splendid Lady in our midst," Count von Waldstein retorts with stern amusement. It is obvious that we all enjoy one another's company. Even Helvetius grins conspiratorially.

"He's not talking about me," I remark with a calm skillfully belying the actual spinning in my head.

"But I am, Madam, I am! It is a delight to an aspiring adept to meet a woman Magus who can produce the blue caelum." I decide not to remark on the obvious fact that I'm not a Magus, and let his warm Latin wind pass over me like an inconsequential summer breeze. But to my dismay I notice that some of his honey sticks to my heart. I remind myself of the disaster that occurred when I let myself become enamored of Monsieur Delamarche, and focus on the horrible moments when the chevalier had gone through his atrocious agony caused by our poison.

Count von Waldstein stares at me intently with the fascination of an aspiring adept, not with the eyes of the consummate diplomat. "Can you explain the blue caelum to me? All I know is that it is the precursor to the penultimate White Sulphur that can transmute metals into silver; itself the last step before the ultimate Red Sulphur."

I look at Helvetius, hoping he will come to my aid and deflect all the unwelcome attention I'm receiving. But my husband looks at me with pride on his face and I realize that he wants to bask in my glory.

"You know of course that all matter organizes around sparks from the cloud of Creation when space itself came into being," I begin. Count Waldstein nods; this is common knowledge among alchemists. Signor Rossini refuses to hide his alarming interest in my person and I want him to shade his gaze. "Those scintillating sparks are called the Heaven, the caelum of matter and animate it constantly," I continue. "But of course you know all that."

The Count nods impatiently for me to continue.

Signor Rossini takes over and I'm grateful for it. "Caelum is found at the root of the indivisible corpuscles of matter Democritus called 'atoms', and feeds them. Without it, matter could not exist and would evaporate like a dream," he holds forth, and I feel we are at the outset of a dangerous duet.

The Count nods. "But how do you fashion it?" he asks.

"You extract it from copper. Ask Boyle. He has experimented with it and wants to compare his blue powder with the color of the dye of the dress you were wearing. When I saw your heavenly dress I knew instantly Boyle had to see you. But now it's even better since you brought the caelum itself," Signor Rossini gushes.

"We didn't derive it from copper only," I say with hesitation.

"And herein lies the secret," Signor Rossini exclaims with excitement. "But let's wait till we meet the great Boyle before you explain your experiments any further."

I hold my breath, realizing that I can never tell any of them that the secret ingredients were grown from the placentas of our Red Sulphur twins. I'm losing my balance as my body succumbs to the seductive presence of Ricaldo Rossini.

࿇

It is a shock to see Robert Boyle. He is of a tall and slender stature, pale and much emaciated. Actually he looks thin and miserable as a skeleton. I had been told that Boyle's body had worn away from constant studies through sleepless nights, and rumor has it that he is wearing leaden soles to prevent being overturned by the wind. But I'm taken aback by his ghostly pallor. He embodies the great genius of our age, far outranking Isaac Newton, who is said to be envious of him. Here is the founder of the Royal Society, the leader of the chymists, the spirit of the age, looking almost blue, as if rigor mortis is about to set in. At fifty he has the air of an old man, looking twenty years older than Signor Rossini who must be of the same age. His sister Lady Ranelagh, his elder by twelve years, looks downright spritely by comparison. In stature she reminds me of Princess Amalia van Solms: voluminous and of portly elegance, hosting to perfection.

"Welcome to our home!" she exclaims jovially, with genuine hospitality, after having greeted Signor Rossini as an old friend. "What an honor. Your Excellency Count von Waldstein, Doctor Helvetius himself, and the producer of true caelum I am told," she says, turning to me with the solidarity common among women of intellect in an instant acknowledgment of our anomalous position in a world of scholarly men. I feel honored, since I hold her in high esteem. She is said to be a close collaborator with her brother, and has for decades been the hub of scientific London, including a circle of prominent alchemists.

"Did you extract it from copper?" Robert Boyle asks me directly in a high-pitched voice that has no time for small talk.

"Let's go to the drawing room," Lady Ranelagh proposes in a calming voice, dousing her brother's excitement. We are standing in the marble hallway of the gorgeously appointed home, modestly indicating great wealth. Our voices echo slightly and I agree with our hostess that this is hardly a place conducive to serious conversation.

Boyle looks at his sister with the slight irritation of a child who has to wait before he can go and play. The intimacy of their relationship is obvious and it is clear that she makes his life possible well beyond providing him with a home that is entirely arranged around him now that she has been a widow for eight years.

When seated in the comfortable room to the right of the marble entry hall, I take a moment to familiarize myself with my environment. I'm with my back to two imposing marble Doric pillars that reign over the room with classical dignity. A fire lights up the white marble fireplace. The room is warmed up from its stern spare frame by sumptuous Persian carpets and leather ottomans. A variety of exotic boxes and statuettes remind us of the many foreign dignitaries and scholars that have come to visit the great Boyle in order to receive his advice. The chair I sit on, with its sumptuous blue velvet upholstery, seems French-made. Lady Ranelagh serves tea. Until she is finished, custom has it that even Robert Boyle must restrain himself.

When the last of us has been served his patience is used up.

"It *must* be extracted from copper!" he says. "I have done so myself. It leaves behind a colorless white metal and the extract is blue. It can be transplanted back into the white metal and it becomes common copper again, but that's all it does. It has no further use so it can't be the caelum. Van Leeuwenhoek reports that he has studied your blue dye under one of his microscopes and he says it's alive, in the way the gold you produced, Doctor Helvetius, was alive."

I am struck by the complete acceptance Boyle displays of the fact that Red Sulphur is a living being. Christiaan Huygens had been considerably more circumspect. It confirms the common opinion that Robert Boyle is indeed an Adept.

"Is there any relationship between this caelum and the person of Theodore Mundanus?" he asks in his slightly nasal high-pitched voice. I look at Count von Waldstein who stares at his nails, a non-committal look on his face.

I have prepared myself for both questions, but now that they are being asked, I don't know how to respond.

Helvetius speaks up, to my relief. "Well, as I have written, 11 years ago I performed the transmutation with Red Sulphur given to me by Theodore Mundanus himself. And when I later received the panacea you must know I'm using, it was fashioned by a person who left it in my care signed with the letter 'M'. I suppose Mundanus wanted me to have it. But I have no idea where he is."

"I hear Signor Dolfin is from an ancient alchemist family from Venice," Signor Rossini remarks in an uncharacteristically delicate manner.

"Might he know something about Mundanus?" Boyle asks with increasing interest.

"I was wondering the same," Signor Rossini responds, his voice trailing off.

Now everyone in the room is looking at me intently.

"Signor Dolfin looks entirely different from Theodore Mundanus, though," Helvetius interjects quickly in order to ward off any suspicions about our nephew-in-law.

"Advanced alchemists in possession of the Red Sulphur have intricate ways to change their appearance unrecognizably," Signor Rossini posits politely. This is the first time anyone has ever made a remark of this kind. It frightens me. "May I tell you all something completely confidential, something that will not leave these four walls?" Signor Rossini asks in conspiratorial fashion.

We all nod.

"The Venetian Ambassador to the Dutch Republic is a close friend of mine. He was given the adoption papers of Giovanni Dolfin VII, born Giovanni Theodore. It gives his birth year as 1624. My friend called it a clerical error. It should of course have been 1644 since Signor Dolfin can't be a day over 33 at present. Everyone will attest to that." I must have turned a deathly pale, a bit like Robert Boyle I imagine, and notice that I have stopped breathing.

Signor Rossini turns to me directly. "I would so love to talk to your nephew directly. He sounds like a remarkable man!"

"It is a clerical error for sure. I first met Signor Dolfin in 1667 and then he looked in his twenties. I remember first thinking that he was an albino actually, because his skin was pale and soft like that of a newborn baby," Helvetius remembers out loud.

"That could have been the result of an alchemical blanching agent, which is part of the rejuvenating process inherent in the Red Sulphur," Signor Rossini counters very politely.

"Do you mean to say that Signor Dolfin actually is Theodore Mundanus?" Boyle asks Rossini, the pitch of his voice almost falsetto.

"He most definitely is not!" Helvetius exclaims indignantly. "Not even Red Sulphur could change a man so completely."

"What is your opinion, Madam Schweitzer?" Lady Ranelagh asks me, mainly to put me at ease because I must be displaying a pitiful expression. I feel dizzy as if I'm about to faint.

"How serious is everyone in this room about their oath that nothing spoken here shall ever leave these quarters under any circumstance?" Count von Waldstein speaks up. I understand his intention and think feverishly about what I shall do next. I know Magus Ricaldo Rossini has guessed the truth and whatever I say really no longer matters. It is better to keep him sworn to secrecy than to pretend to an untenable position in the face of a Magus.

"Absolutely!" Robert Boyle exclaims. "I shall take it as a grave personal affront if anyone betrays the confidence of this moment!"

"Hear, hear!" the others concur.

"No one will speak, Madam Schweitzer. I vouch for them as a Knight of the Fleece."

"No one will intentionally cross Count von Waldstein, I assure you!" Signor Rossini ejects with a grin. "I've seen the consequences." Count von Waldstein does not return his expression or his compliment. His gaze is completely focused upon me.

With rising consternation, Helvetius looks back and forth between Von Waldstein and me as if at a court of tennis. I feel for my husband. He will be publicly betrayed by what I'm about to say. I have kept this secret from him for ten years. But the die is cast and there is no way back.

"You are right in your conjecture, Signor Rossini. I will not try to mislead a Magus. Giovanni Dolfin is indeed Theodore Mundanus after an accidental overdose of a blanching formula made from the Red Sulphur he holds in his possession. It all but killed him. It was made to hide his identity when Johan de Witt and the Duke of York were chasing him after the Helvetius transmutation. He had fallen in love with my niece and wanted to stay in The Hague to start a family."

"The blanching formula," Signor Rossini mutters. "It is said to have extreme rejuvenation as a by-product. In the days when alchemy was still strong the Magi used it to escape from authorities. I thought as much when I heard Signor Dolfin's date of birth from my friend the Venetian Ambassador."

Helvetius looks thunderstruck.

"I am so terribly sorry Johann Friedrich. I don't know how I can ever apologize enough to you," I say with deep concern. It is very uncouth to make such an intimate marital statement in public and everyone looks down at the floor.

"So that's how I came into the possession of the universal medicine!" he muses after some time. The silence in the room had been very loud and oppressive.

"Your wife's secret was a small price to pay, Doctor Helvetius," Count von Waldstein reassures him with warm kindness. Helvetius' face clears up as he realizes that he is now related to the most sought-after Magus in the world.

"You knew about this!" Signor Rossini looks at Waldstein.

"I was sworn to secrecy," he replies.

"When may I meet Signor Dolfin?" Robert Boyle asks with overwhelming eagerness.

"I would gladly travel to Holland to bring him your personal invitation," Signor Rossini offers.

"Your oath prohibits it." Count von Waldstein speaks calmly, making it clear that he is serious about his task to carefully administer the closed circle of secrecy. "Only Madam Schweitzer is at liberty to ask him."

Again all eyes are on me.

"I will ask him," I relent. I know that Mundanus won't like anything better than meeting with Robert Boyle. "But you shall meet him as Giovanni Dolfin. Nothing may leak or James of York will have him locked up in the Tower in no time. He has been after Mundanus since his first visit to England in 1662."

"Yes, Dickinson has told me about that encounter, as has Newton about Mundanus' visit in '65 when he performed a transmutation before him. It changed both their lives profoundly. It made lifelong alchemists of them. I have always been most envious." Robert Boyle's face is no longer bluish, as a flush has managed to make its way to his cheeks.

"I have brought you a present from him," I say as I take the pouch with the caelum powder from my purse and hand it to Boyle. Lady Ranelagh is radiant. It must be the answer to a deeply held wish of her brother's. I am moved by her quiet devotion.

"I will most eagerly study it and will report back to you and His Excellency Signor Dolfin very soon," Boyle says, with a deep bow. It takes me aback to hear Mundanus addressed in so exalted a manner. Count von Waldstein had done the same when he first was made aware of Giovanni's true identity. I smile, remembering the ill-reeking beggar I almost sent from my doorstep at our first meeting.

ꝏ

When I arrive back in my Whitehall quarters, a letter from Mundanus is waiting for me. I always marvel at the course of destiny that is so frequently punctuated by coincidences. Helvetius goes for a brief evening visit with Prince William to check on his health, which does seem to be a bit in decline, so I have time to savor a simple supper sent to me by the Prince's kitchen. Now that he is an eminent soldier with powerful enemies, he trusts no cooks but his own, since poisoners are ubiquitous. He always travels with a kitchen staff. I find pleasure in the ache of postponing a perusal of the writing of my beloved.

I hold the letter in my hand. Mundanus always uses parchment. I note how his hand is a mixture of individualized letters and sometimes flowing shapes with momentary gregarious extensions. It is the precise hand of the laboratory doctor, easy to read and well considered. I especially enjoy his 'd's: they dance like backwards-arching ballerinas. I feel how my palm is caressing the parchment texture.

His epistle opens with warm greetings, less intimate than usual since he wants to avoid talk in case the letter were to fall into wrong hands, as had happened in Baden when Monsieur Delamarche got hold of one of his ardent letters to me – with ghastly consequences.

He gives good tidings about Clara and the children. Clara seems to be spending much time with Christiaan Huygens, whose health is declining. Johanna is playing the organ at every free moment, and Clara is considering building a small organ in the ammunitions factory across the street. This news excites me. I shall be able to listen to Johanna because the organ will likely be heard in the laboratory.

But then follow some alarming sentences:

"Gerda has spotted the Phantom Sorcerer again. She saw him in close proximity to Maximo as he was walking over to the factory without his guard. We will now have Maximo accompanied at all times by two soldier-guards. Maximo laughed when I told him. He seems to be incapable of fear. He just said that he hoped to encounter the sorcerer and whip him good. I had to laugh, but Gerda looked terribly sad. Maximo is around the age her brother Peter was …"

My mother-heart convulses and I want to go home right away. I hate being away from my children.

☙

I get an urgent message from Prince William in the morning. I am to join him in his suite of rooms at my earliest convenience – immediately, that is.

When I enter I am instantly aware of the similarities between my Prince and the Lady Mary. They both have the long oval Stuart face and almond-shaped eyes with heavy brows and lashes, the full Stuart mouth and masses of dark red-brown hair. Like hers, his nose is aquiline and his chin slightly cleft. I know how much he dislikes amusements and frivolities, and am glad for him that he didn't have to attend the *Callisto* Pageant.

"The King has consented," he exclaims unceremoniously when I enter. "We are to marry in a few days. He has accepted all my demands and I will not have to sell my honor for a wife," he adds haughtily.

"I hope you're not going to say this to the Lady Mary!" I reply, certain of my right to say anything I feel, almost like a court jester.

"The Lady Mary's feelings no longer matter," he retorts mercilessly.

"She can make your life Hell. You can't ride out to battle all the time and you will have to spend some time at home; and some moments in her bed even. You'd better consider her!" I exclaim, offended. I know his Stuart obstinacy, his pride and temper; they are the worst parts of his character and can make him a monster.

"She will be my wife on my terms or not at all!" he mutters stubbornly.

"You can say that to your uncles, but not to a woman," I insist. "Does she know the King has decided?"

"I suppose so," he mumbles. I now realize he is scared. Matters of the heart terrify him. "I'm told the King has said that I am an honest man – in fact the 'honestest man in the world' were his exact words," he says with a grin, "and that he trusts me. He has told his minions to go to Uncle James and tell him that it is a thing he is resolved upon. I'm sure Uncle James is delighted," Prince William adds with irony.

"But we don't know if the Duke has told the Lady Mary," I insist.

"I assume so," he replies, annoyed. "I told you, it doesn't matter."

"In that case, why did you ask me to accompany you if you're going to act in total disregard of a woman's feelings?"

"Women's feelings are going to be disregarded entirely in this matter," he replies. "Louise de Kérouaille has been sent back to her home. The King wants me to marry immediately before King Louis finds out. Uncle Charles is deeply in his debt."

"Soon you'll be in bed with a fifteen year old girl who hates you," I say quietly.

"I will bring wax to plug my ears," he responds in a failed attempt at levity.

"Please admit that you are scared, my dear Prince. You don't have to tell anyone else. It would do you good."

"Damn right I'm scared!" he responds in battlefield language, which I excuse on this occasion.

"Good, thank you. Now what are we going to do?" I wait.

He remains silent.

"Might you go to St. James's Palace and check how she is doing?" he finally asks in a small voice.

"What good would that do? She has already been set up against me by her friends. It just might make matters worse. She'd probably refuse to see me."

"To the contrary. She seems to have been enchanted by Madam Dolfin's dresses, or so I'm told. She was wearing the wedding gown inappropriately for days and used it for her child's play with Lady Apsley. My informants tell me that she has asked Sarah Jennings, who behaved so rudely towards you, to leave St. James's because she had caused a tear in the veil. I hear it has made the Lady Anne very upset."

This detail shows that his information must be correct. I remember Sarah tearing out the gown from the bottom of the trunk with great force.

"But that doesn't mean she wishes to see me," I counter, not wanting to ever see the inside of St. James's Palace again.

"Again you are wrong, my dearest Madam Schweitzer," the Prince says amiably, his fears abating, "she wants to know all about the materials and wishes to use them for her next pageant."

"So that is information from before she knew about the wedding then," I conclude, "After the wedding there will be no more St. James's or Whitehall pageants, as she'll be living in Holland."

Prince William nods. "I would be most obliged if you would go to see her, Madam Marianne," he says gently. He never uses my first name unless he wants to appeal to our intimacy.

For a third time I'm on my way to Pall Mall. St. James's Palace is close to the home of Lady Ranelagh. I'm traveling in an ornate old-fashioned carriage that used to belong to King Charles I, father to the current King. Compared to Count von Waldstein's extremely modern Berlin carriage by which we had traveled to Robert Boyle's, this feels like a quaint relic of a period gone by. I realize that England is behind the times, even with great minds like Boyle and other advanced thinkers of the Royal Society. The English depend on handouts from Cousin Louis and are no match for my Prince and his Habsburg allies. William is right: in the matter of the marriage, he is in charge, not his uncle Charles II.

We arrive in Pall Mall at the large square in front of the palace. Soldiers in bright red stand guard beside the dark entrance between two rigid 7-story towers with octagonal mock battlements. When they see the carriage they salute stiffly, indicating that I am under the protection of the highest powers. The large black wooden gates creak open slowly, as if responding to a heavy mechanism in need of lubricant.

Henry VIII built his Tudor Palace in red brick and designed it around four courtyards. After close to a hundred and fifty years it still looks as defiant as King Henry himself. It faces the Mall broad-chested and determined, arrogant almost. Deposed King Charles I slept here the night before he was beheaded in 1649. It feels like a piquant detail that I'm riding in a carriage that belonged to him. It reminds me of how the young Lady Mary must feel this very moment. I gather that she has been crying ever since her father told her on October 21st, now two days ago. I had checked to see if the invitation still stood, and was assured that the Lady Mary eagerly wanted me to come. I was told that she had isolated herself in her bedchambers, dressed in Clara's wedding gown, weeping in heart-piercing sobs. I'm not looking forward to my mission. Only my deep fondness for my Prince could have gotten me here.

Princess Mary's bedchambers are appointed in a lovely moss green. On a dark shining oak parquet floor, a pine needle tinted carpet with pale pink flowers spreads out like a forest clearing. The bed with its high canopy in green damask with golden fringe is mirrored by a moss bed spread on which the Lady Mary cuts a tragic figure in her gorgeous pearl glow-cloth wedding gown with its opalescent sheen. From the opposite end of the room, a ceiling-high four-panel lead glass window shines brightly with afternoon sun over a boudoir table with an ornate gold-framed looking glass. The reclining Princess looks delicate as a glass figurine.

She does not move when I'm shown in. Hesitantly I walk over to the fireplace, and after a time I sit down on a rust-colored velvet chaise lounge, under a sumptuous needlepoint tapestry of frolicking women. I look around at the delicately carved wooden mantelpiece reaching all the way up to the high ceiling and wonder about King Charles I's last night on earth, before Cromwell took his head. A melancholy atmosphere pervades the chamber.

"I am told that you are my cousin's only true friend and that's the real reason why you have accompanied him to London," she whispers in a tiny voice.

"He is very dear to me indeed, Your Highness."

"I must apologize for the way you were treated, Madam. It was inexcusable. I hope you accept my apologies. When I heard who you truly were I sent Sarah Jennings away from St. James's. I was told that you are the only one who truly knows his heart."

I remain silent and wait for her to find her words and move through the morass of emotions.

"I know that my marriage to him is unavoidable," she continues after some time. Then she utters some heart-rending sobs but restrains herself with some effort.

"It must be painful to be promised like a slave to a man you don't love," I say softly. "I understand." She begins to weep softly, with tears that seem to give her solace instead of the piercing angry sobs. I wait several minutes for her emotions to subside.

"I asked you to come here and tell me about him," she says, her voice sounding much more mature than her 15 years. This is the young woman hiding behind all the child's play, maybe only truly known by Frances Apsley. The court does not know her like this and she must hide this aspect jealously from her chroniclers. I am surprised. It is not what I had expected, even though I have no idea what I *did* expect. I wait again, this time to gather my thoughts.

"It will not change my feelings about him or the marriage, I assure you. But I want to know what I am facing," she clarifies. She has pushed herself up on her elbows and we look at one another.

I nod. "I understand, Your Highness. I'll try to be as honest as possible. My Prince would wish for no less than that. You are much like him, in fact. In your position, he would gather intelligence as well. He always does before going on a campaign." Princess Mary smiles faintly.

"You have known him for a long time, haven't you?" she asks.

"Since he was just about your age, Your Highness."

"So what is he like?" she asks, not eager to know him, but resigned to the necessity.

"He is a shy man who loves botany. He is a consummate soldier who loves riding out to battle. He is self-conscious about his deformity and sees women as conquests only." I decide to be painfully honest in order to gain her trust. It is most important that she form an alliance to me.

"I appreciate your frankness, Madam. Truly."

"He is afraid to encounter you, and if I might be so bold, your wedding night fills him with dread." She wails for a brief moment and I'm afraid I have gone too far. But I decide to forge ahead. "To him you are different from other women; not just because of your high rank. He told me that when he first met you 7 years ago, you felt like a child sister to him. He told me that he did not have these affections for the Lady Anne, but just for you. He has never spoken about it to anyone but me, because he is a scrupulous statesman and does not want emotions to interfere with political matters. Under all his bluster, he likes you, and he knows you hate him. I know that he would much rather have displayed brotherly affections. But he wears a deadpan mask of studied indifference in the way we are taught in our Calvinist Dutch Republic. Everyone believes that he is not a man of feelings, that he is a cold and calculating Captain General. Only I know that the opposite is true, and that's why I'm so very fond of him. He was taught very well by his brilliant teacher Johan de Witt, his primary mentor and adversary. You must have heard of him."

She nods, indicating that the rumors portraying her head as silly and vacant are erroneous. She seems an astute observer with knowledge of history. I wonder what other common gossip about this young woman will turn out to be false.

"May I ask you a question, Your Highness?" I ask. She assents with a 'go ahead' gesture of her right hand. It seems that we have moved past the merely formal.

"Was the choice of *Callisto* yours?" I hide my eagerness to know the answer. It will reveal a great deal about her. I am sure my Prince will ask me a hundred questions.

"Yes, it was." She gives me a melancholy. "It was indeed. I feel much like Callisto these days."

"I thought as much," I respond, grateful for her candor. "It was a courageous thing to do."

"Uncle Charles didn't understand the reference, nor did Father," she says ruefully. "Father doesn't understand anything. He only rages about the egregious insult done to his person and doesn't pause to think that I have to allow myself to be raped!" she exclaims with furious indignation. Enraged sobs pierce the moss green room.

We are both silent for a long time. I wish I could shield her from the impending ravages of her unprotected existence. I'm reminded of the prostitutes I saw that night in Venice who must make a life from unspeakable submission.

"Will you be there for my wedding, Madam Schweitzer?" she asks unexpectedly.

The smallpox epidemic began that day I visited St. James's Palace.

ꟈ

First Princess Mary's beloved governess fell ill, then her sister Lady Anne. The Primate who was to perform the wedding ceremony got sick, which seemed a bad augury. The wedding most certainly was being conceived under ill omens. Helvetius became very busy and the abilities of his universal medicine soon made him in overwhelming demand. He treated the royal family to prevent disaster, but couldn't keep up with all the requests from the court, or from the people of London. I was grateful for Clara's foresight to demand that Mundanus give Helvetius ample amounts of the Panacea in return for her hand in marriage.

We have to get out of London as soon as possible. The last thing I want is to bring home smallpox to my children. The wedding date is set for Sunday, November 4, my Prince's birthday, and that of his mother's. It's also the anniversary of his father's death – of smallpox. Fear is rising.

Smallpox or not, the people of London are ecstatic over the wedding and my Prince is the toast of the town. The Protestant city magnates have always found him a better friend than the much-despised Charles II or his brother James of York. Louis XIV is enraged, having received the news of the wedding as he would have done the loss of an army, and has started intrigues by way of Louise de Kérouaille, who has not been seen at court recently. Charles's ample pension from Cousin Louis has been cut.

The City is to present the couple with a stunning banquet where King and Queen, the Duke of York and his very pregnant Catholic young Duchess will be present. It is the first meeting between William and Mary since the announcement of their wedding. Mary has kept herself away from him, refusing all encounters. My Prince has tried but has been petulantly rebuffed. Tonight they are to sit next to one another. Both he and the Lady

Mary have asked me to stay close to them. I am now an official member of his retinue, acknowledged by all sides. Ample inane gossip about my relationship with the Prince of Orange bounces about. I am usually portrayed as his official mistress.

The court is to travel by water from Whitehall with the Lord Mayor, sheriffs and alderman in barges carrying the banners of the various guilds. Helvetius and I are assigned to the guild barge of the Worshipful Society of Apothecaries. The moment we set foot on board, Helvetius is surrounded by physicians and apothecaries wanting to know all about the by now legendary universal medicine.

"Madam Schweitzer," a familiar voice behind me intones, "what a pleasure to see you again."

Ricaldo Rossini, wearing a white sash with the Apothecary emblem of golden Apollo riding a silver dragon with bow and arrow, bows elegantly.

"Signor Rossini," I exclaim. "I was not aware that you were a member of the London Society of Apothecaries! I'm a bit confused to see you here. I thought you were a foreigner."

"I'm an honorary member," he responds modestly.

Even as an honorary member I don't understand how he got himself invited to this very exclusive banquet.

As if he reads my mind he says, "Like you, I am a friend of the Prince of Orange. I was a physician traveling with his troops. That's how I met Count von Waldstein as well."

Helvetius has momentarily been released from the barrage of questions by his colleagues and joins us, greeting Signor Rossini effusively. The secret from Lady Ranelagh's drawing room unites us.

"Did you know that Signor Rossini was a physician to the Dutch Republic troops of our Captain General?"

"No, I didn't!" Helvetius sounds surprised.

"Oh, but you must," Signor Rossini insists in his sonorous baritone. "We've in fact met on several occasions…"

Helvetius is silent for a moment and stares up at the night sky.

"A beautiful night," he says. Then he looks back at us. "But of course I remember, Signor Rossini, we've met on several occasions."

"Why didn't you tell me?" I exclaim. "It seemed that your acquaintance with Signor Rossini was entirely new when we met at the Lady Mary's *Callisto* pageant! You didn't tell me you knew him!"

"He probably just forgot," Signor Rossini says amiably.

"Yes, that must be it. I probably just forgot," Helvetius repeats.

I experience a bolt of suspicion while at the same time feeling an irresistible attraction. In some way it seems as if I have known this man all of my life. Before I can ponder it, we have arrived at the opposite side of the Thames, where the festivities are to take place. My last sense impression before we get off the barge is an imaginary whiff of malodorous Drury Lane where Signor Rossini is staying, an odd location for one of his esteemed standing.

I'm surprised to see that the royal guests of honor have already arrived. I had expected them to enter as usual: in a formal procession through a boisterous throng of applauding courtiers and dignitaries. It appears to be an informal feast, with these spacious army barracks transformed festively into a din of celebration. The royalty is seated on a dais behind a long wooden table laden with a profusion of venison pies, huge pieces of roast beef and mountains of jellies, cakes, custards and side dishes. A sea of silver goblets promises ample supplies of wine. An army of servants flits about like honeybees inspired by the momentous atmosphere of the occasion. The mood among the principals appears artificially aloft – except for the Lady Mary, who looks openly uncomfortable, like a stiff cut-out figure against a full motion background. With pleasure I notice that she is wearing one of Clara's subtle green organdy dresses, the crisp cotton fabric shining, both earthy and angelic.

"Rossini!" a voice next to her calls out in our direction. James Duke of York invites him over from his seat next to the Lady Mary. I'm surprised how well known Signor Rossini is and that he is the first of the entrants to be acknowledged. We have entered with a gaggle of dignitaries.

"Your Highness!" Rossini replies jovially and walks over to the main table. The Prince of Orange motions Helvetius and me to come up to the dais as well so he can make formal introductions. I sense everyone's eyes on me as I follow Rossini and Helvetius to the King's table. Thanks to my father's decidedly republican attitude, rank doesn't faze me, which gives me occasion to observe sharply. I notice Helvetius walk in front of me with heavy steps, burdened by the weight of being publicly singled out. Signor Rossini all but bounces up to the dais and moves over to the Duke of York.

"Your Majesty," the Duke turns to his brother the King, who is already acquainting himself with the ample supplies of food and wine, some fat dripping unceremoniously off his sensuous lips. Despite my Calvinist disapproval of his lascivious person, I can't help but like him. He is the only one in the crowd who is unpretentiously comfortable with himself. "This is the famous alchemist I have told you about."

"The one who helps you finance your ill-advised African adventures?" The King barely looks up from his serious engagement with a leg of lamb, his elegant long fingers glistening with animal drippings. "So you can make gold," the King says to Signor Rossini, without glancing up. "That's very useful. Keep it up," the King concludes, losing all interest.

"Your Majesty is too kind," Signor Rossini voices in a low silver timbre I know so well from moments when Mundanus has used this beguiling Magus resonance in the past.

Charles looks up as if waking from a dream. "Ah but of course," he beams at Signor Rossini. "Of course I know you. We have met before. I remember it well."

I am suddenly acutely aware that Signor Rossini knows the advanced Art of the Magus to insert himself into the minds of others. I am greatly alarmed. I know he has done so with me and that I am powerless in the face of his well-honed charm. I am falling for a man whose motives I cannot fathom. Since I can't resist it I promise myself to remain sharply alert. From the rear of my mind a nasty doubt arises that I may not have acted of my own free will and that I betrayed Mundanus' identity under the influence of his magisterial persuasion. But before I can think any further about it the Duke of York turns to Helvetius.

"And you are the man who knows the whereabouts of Theodore Mundanus and won't tell anyone," he says haughtily. I am taken aback that even while his mind must be painfully occupied, the Duke of York is still thinking of his pursuit of my beloved. I realize that there is more going on in the mind of York than just a lust for gold, and suspect a profound fascination with Magi. Or maybe Rossini is implanting this question in the Duke's mind. Helvetius doesn't know how to reply.

"This is my physician, Uncle James," the Prince of Orange comes to our aid. "You had better stay in his good graces, with a pregnant Duchess and smallpox going around. You might need him. He is the only one I know who stands a chance in the face of the scourge." His voice is artfully lighthearted.

James of York looks at his nephew with hatred in his eyes. "How like you to defend mere physicians!" he responds disgustedly, implying that to him physicians are just lackeys who would not enter his palace by the front door.

"Madam Schweitzer," the Lady Mary says gracefully, in a gentle voice, "the dress is of some solace to me. Thank you for it." She looks at the Prince of Orange, and tears begin to flow.

The Duke of York looks at his daughter with disdain. A display of emotion in public is shameful.

I wave a glow-cloth kerchief in front of her and hand it over. It instantly calms her; she looks grateful.

Unable to help myself, I begin staring again at Signor Rossini, who is now talking animatedly with King Charles in a familiar way as if they have known each other forever. I suddenly wonder if he actually knows any of the people whom he charms so expertly. I drift away from the main table after casting a supportive glance at my Prince; exasperation darkens his eyes. Indeed he'd rather lose an arm than court his cousin. He leans away from his future wife and she sits very still.

I notice Count von Waldstein entering at the other end of the room and push myself through the throngs, needing to urgently talk to him. He is happy to see me, instantly breaking off all conversation with the surrounding dignitaries to welcome and introduce me. It takes some time before I can take him aside. In a quiet place outside overlooking the Thames I ask him: "Do you remember when you first met Signor Rossini?" He looks puzzled. "Exactly where was it?" He seems to draw a blank.

"Why does it matter?" he asks, after a time of fruitlessly searching his memory.

"Did you meet him while visiting the troops of Captain General the Prince of Orange?" I ask point blank.

"I've never visited troops under the command of the Prince of Orange," he replies with certainty.

"I think that you might have met Signor Rossini only a short while back. He is a Magus who can insert memories in your mind that have no historical basis. He can make you feel that you've known him for most of your life."

"But that's impossible!" he exclaims.

"Then try to remember when you first met him. Did you meet him before you came to England?"

"Oh, long before, years ago," the Count dismisses any other possibilities with a wave of his hand. Around us the noise is beginning to increase and a voice of the master of ceremonies announces a welcome speech by the Lord Mayor.

"Then see if you can remember him in any context other than English," I say as we walk back inside to hear the official celebratory address of the engaged couple by the City of London.

In his parting words a flushed Lord Mayor reads a faded poem by some tepid courtly muse which ends in these lines:

"Thrice happy pair! So near allied
In royal blood and virtue too!

Now love has you together tied!
May none this triple knot undo!"

My stomach turns at this pious tripe. Everyone knows there is no love between the couple. But this is the play being performed. No one can escape the gilding of hatred glossed over with sweet lies. I look at the table on the dais and see the Princess with the haunted look of a caged deer about to be slaughtered, my Prince like a trapped wolf trying to chew off his paw to be set free, the Duke bitter as bile, his unhappy pregnant Duchess the age of his young daughter, a barren Queen looking forlorn, and the King eating away without listening to the Lord Mayor. I can't help but smile at the graceless poem set against the truth of this intimate Stuart family tableau. But it seems no one notices. They want the lies and the wine to flow richly.

"You're right," the count mutters when the Mayor has finished the final stanza. "I can't find any memory that does not involve England."

"And how long have you been here?" I ask rhetorically, knowing full well the count arrived last February, a little over half a year ago. He nods, thoughtfully. "We must find a way to investigate him," I ponder. "It is going to be different than usual because he has the kind of awareness that can see behind curtains and around corners. He will have no trouble with any spies we send his way. Within no time he will know who they are and they will have known him for decades and swear that he is the godfather of their children."

"The Duke of York said that he could make gold, might we investigate the transmutations he has created?" the Count suggests.

"We don't know if these were actual transmutations or implanted memories. The Duke is an easy target because he is so much in need of gold for his ill-considered African adventures," I say, repeating King Charles' description. "It is easy to implant a memory that is the materialization of such wishes."

The Count bows to me, acknowledging without words his admiration for my reasoning.

"The only person who could find out is Mundanus," I say hesitantly, not wishing to involve him; but I instinctively know that the true identity of Signor Rossini needs to be known for the sake of us all. "We have to entice Rossini to come to The Hague with us when we return with the Lady Mary," I conclude.

The Count looks thoughtful and doesn't object.

I'm filled with a great sense of foreboding: we may be face to face with the phantom sorcerer himself.

Chapter Twenty-Six

The Journey Home; November 1677

It is Saturday November 3rd, the eve of the wedding, and the Prince of Orange craves distraction. I have suggested we invite his old friend Signor Rossini to join us for supper. My Prince remembers him well from their many years of acquaintance when Rossini was a superb physician to the troops. It will be enjoyable to exchange memories with an old comrade in arms. Helvetius, who has fond recollections of Signor Rossini as well, will join us at what my Prince calls his pre-gallows meal. The Captain General's best friend William Bentinck will also be in attendance as will be two other friends. Bentinck had been puzzled at the mention of Signor Rossini, whom he couldn't recall for some reason, though Bentinck had been close to Prince William during all of his military campaigns. He was assured that he would remember Rossini once they met.

The cedar wood-paneled suite of my Prince smells cozy, like wood fire mixed in with fragrances of the exquisite foods prepared in abundance by the Orange-court cooks to honor their master. They have created a memorable private meal that handily competes with the massive culinary feast put on by the City of London. The English chefs have nothing over their Dutch counterparts! The table for seven is set festively with the precious golden goblets the Prince has brought among his rich gifts to his wife-to-be. They had been part of his mother Mary Stuart's dowry, and they were a fitting adornment for a last meal before they would pass into the possession of Mary Stuart the Younger.

My Prince likes intimate dinners, as did his grandmother Amalia. They put him at ease and make him talkative, unlike his usual taciturn behavior – a famous trait running in the Orange family ever since the liberator of our country, my Prince's great grandfather William the Silent.

Signor Rossini is holding forth about the many intimate details of their collective past. Count Bentinck now remembers Rossini as well, as do the other two friends of the Prince who enjoy the wine like true soldiers.

I wonder how Signor Rossini gets his information, but decide not to reflect on that and focus mainly on keeping my mind in occultation so he will not be able to read it. I focus on particular alchemical experiments, particularly those related to the extraction of the blue tincture from copper. I go over and over the details of this arduous procedure, putting a hedge of noise between the world outside and my inner self. Sometimes I sense an incursion by Rossini. I can feel it by a heated excitement starting from my pelvis reaching up to my heart. His eyes look at me with slight puzzlement, which makes me feel my plan is working, though I'm unable to resist the effects of his charm. Yet I do stay aware of his seduction while I fall for it, which is all I can do. It is a strange experience to become increasingly infatuated with a man who may turn out to be my worst enemy: I long to be possessed by him, while at the same time steeling myself against his masterful advances. During the day before this dinner I walked around with a gold coin under my tongue, an ancient prescription for the protection against evil spirits. Whenever I feel I am unable to resist his charms I acutely remember the sensation of the gold coin and I feel protected while succumbing. Halfway the meal, at a moment I feel strong, I open myself to an instant of envisioning the Red Sulphur in Mundanus' possession. Signor Rossini immediately notices and unmistakable craving claws forth from his eyes.

"Signor Rossini," I ask sweetly. "I know that you want to meet my nephew Signor Giovanni Dolfin. Maybe you should join us on our journey back to Holland. There would be place on board, don't you think, Your Highness?"

"It would indeed be a great pleasure to continue our long acquaintance at my court. I remember how much you enjoyed my country in the past," my Prince concurs enthusiastically.

By now Signor Rossini has seduced everyone around the table, and each guest, aided by the free flowing wine, passionately supports the Prince's invitation.

I think intensely of my laboratory, walking around it in careful mental observation. Then I allow a few moments of envisioning Mundanus and Clara. I know Rossini is exploring my mind. I almost faint with desire.

There is a moment of labyrinthine pondering visible on Signor Rossini's countenance. I can feel that he is weighing the situation very carefully, at a speed considerably greater than that of ordinary human thought. If this were a game of chess he'd be thinking 20 moves ahead. I admire his perspicacity and feel everything within me turn moist, flowing unstoppably towards him.

"We are leaving as soon as possible after the wedding," Helvetius explains. "The Lady Anne has fallen ill and it is difficult to keep Princess Mary away from her sister. Also, her beloved governess, the one she calls 'my mam' is on her deathbed of the smallpox. We should leave immediately." As the physician in charge, my husband sounds authoritative.

"The governess will die, but Lady Anne will not," Rossini ponders out loud, as if adding this detail to his inner calculations. It is as though he is looking straight into the future.

"I think so too," Helvetius prognosticates. I can hear the difference in tone between a physician who assesses the future based on current facts and one who can see a future already accomplished. Trismosin tells us that the true Magus can envision past and future in one single swoop, the way one sees a long stretch of river flowing through a valley below from a mountain top. I'm overawed when I realize that Signor Rossini calculates back from future events. I know that Rossini notices my thoughts, but I am incapable of hiding them.

He smiles, knowing my game. He is fully aware that I'm intentionally luring him to The Hague to uncover his identity and his ponderings end. "I will surely accompany you. It is exciting to have the chance to meet with the creator of the true caelum." He throws down the gauntlet in my direction. Checkmate: I surrender. If he so pleases, he can have me right now.

ꕤ

It is now the Monday after the wedding and it turned out that only close relatives were to attend the wedding. So the invitation from Princess Mary was moot. But I was told details:

At nine at night, on Sunday in a gloomy chamber of St. James's, by the haunting light of flickering candles, the wedding was performed like an execution. The only one in good humor was the King, who made constant inappropriate bawdy jokes about the impending wedding night, increasing the level of discomfort dramatically. The young Duchess of York was very pregnant and the King told the priest to hurry or the wedding might no longer be one of an heiress of the throne of England, if the Duchess were to give birth to a son right there and then. And at the moment when the groom had to endow the bride with all his worldly possessions and as a symbol put gold coins on the altar, the King exclaimed: "Put those in your pocket, niece. It's all clear gain."

When this marriage made in Hell was sealed, King Charles drew the curtains on their bedstead and shouted in coarse jest: "Hey for St. George!"

The Devil himself couldn't have performed it better. All the women were crying and the men filled with mutual hatred.

My Prince remained silent about the whole affair, but for one statement to me.

"I brought pig's blood and soiled the sheets. Then we slept in opposite sides of the bed."

I admired his tact in giving proof of her virginity without raping her. He had learned his *Callisto* lesson well.

"Did you have a chance to study it?" I ask Robert Boyle when visiting him this Monday afternoon, eager to know his opinion about the blue caelum. I'm now particularly interested in it because of the response Signor Rossini had displayed when I waved the butterfly sleeve of the blue dress I wore for the *Callisto* pageant. It caused him to stop breathing for a moment. I can use anything I get my hands on to change our unequal game and add an element of surprise because he handily outmaneuvers me on all counts. And worst of all, I *want* him to! My heated longing for him is most distressing. It makes me feel distant from Mundanus, and I'm convinced that this is the true purpose of Rossini's seduction.

We are in Boyle's laboratory on the third floor of his sister's large mansion in Pall Mall. It is an oblong room with ample light coming in through two large dormer windows on the sloping roof. Along the wall are shelves with vessels of all shapes and a variety of glass distillers. Various metal instruments hang above the open fire pit, ready to be used. There are two blasting furnaces of different sizes, several smaller ovens for heat at lower temperatures, a fixing oven, an athanor, and some instruments I don't recognize. In the center of the laboratory is Boyle's vacuum pump with its giant glass globe on a flask with handles and levers to pump out the air. I'd seen illustrations of what he calls his 'pneumatic engine' – however, to be standing face to face with the real instrument is another matter altogether. It makes me almost forget what I'm here for. But then I'm called back to the present and ask him my question about the caelum.

Boyle looks even more skeletal than last time we met. His eyes are set within deep black hollows.

"I've studied it constantly and experimented with it. It has a strange relationship with time. Some experiments I did I can only explain when I hold the notion that the effects happen to the caelum before I even know which experiment I'm going to carry out. I've hardly slept since I saw you. From the effects on the caelum beforehand I'm now able to deduce the experiment I'm about to conduct. And then when I try to thwart it by doing another experiment, the effects I had found before have disappeared as though they never existed, and now the caelum shows the effects of the other experiment before it is carried out."

I'm very excited. This may be the answer to my prayers. The great alchemist Geber tells us that the heavenly caelum lives like moisture at the root of every atom and makes its life possible. It creates the individual space in which atoms exist. Caelum is the heavenly essence of space itself. Master Descartes might say that it makes a thing from a *res cogitans*, a thing of the mind like a dream, into a *res extensa*, a thing existing in extended physical space. Caelum allows imagination to take on physical form. From the sky-blue moisture at the roots of atoms, Red Sulphur is made. I remember back to a night in my laboratory while working on the last phase of caelum when Mundanus told me how his father described to him with great excitement when he was just a boy how without caelum space would not exist. He spoke of Venice and being with his father in a small boat on the lagoon near the Lido. I'm grateful this memory allows for an intimate moment with him, however fleeting. I need it to counteract Rossini's magic. Now I know for a fact that Red Sulphur has complete freedom in both space and time. If Rossini is indeed the phantom sorcerer, he has not only mastery over space, since we know he can cast his phantom anywhere he pleases - he must also have mastery over time.

"I'll show you," Boyle says and walks over to a table where I see a peculiar instrument, one of those I didn't recognize. It takes me a moment to get back to the present. The device has a thick barrel like a pistol leading into a narrow snout on the bottom end and an eyepiece on the top. It is clamped to a proportional vertical carrying pole. Next to it on an elevated copper platform an oil lamp sheds light through a glass sphere filled with water through a lens in front of it.

"What is it?" I ask.

"It's a microscope," Boyle explains. "My assistant Robert Hooke has designed it."

"But it looks completely different from Leeuwenhoek's!" I exclaim.

Boyle nods. "We can't make lenses of the magnification level Leeuwenhoek creates. No one can. So instead Hooke has fashioned two lenses on opposite ends of the barrel. That way we can come close to Leeuwenhoek's magnification. But the improvement is in the light source. Look, the oil lamplight is magnified and bent through the spherical water flask and then led through another lens that focuses all the light on the specimen platform," Boyle points at a screw that holds a platform, similar to the one Leeuwenhoek used when I had viewed our gold dust. "Because of the focus of the light we can see more than even Van Leeuwenhoek can with his superior lenses."

I'm impressed with all this ingenuity and look again at the magnificent pneumatic engine Boyle has designed. I try to cast my vision of it back in time to Salomon Trismosin so he may behold the future. It feels futile, but I can't help doing it.

"Now, first we study the caelum before we design an experiment," Boyle suggests with the excitement of a schoolboy receiving a magnificent present. He puts a quarter grain of the Caelum on the viewing platform, focuses the light of the oil lamp to a point of intense brightness, and turns the focusing screw on the barrel. The entire contraption moves incrementally closer to the viewing platform until Boyle is satisfied. I see him marvel at the vision he beholds. A glow radiates off his face as if his soul has become starlight. His blissful fascination makes me realize why Boyle is the greatest scientist of our age. The vision of his heart has the same intensity as the light gathered at the focal point of the oil light beside the microscope. "Look!" he invites me.

I have looked at the caelum before with one of Anthonie's microscopes. But this time the boulders of blue stones shine brightly like under a giant sun, their impact almost piercing my eyeball. I withdraw briefly. Then I focus again and notice the breath of the caelum, immovable as if between inhale and exhale.

"Now let's design an experiment. Let's say we are going to add it to silver. We need to do an experiment that makes us not lose the caelum. With silver we can easily extract it again. This time we'll go through with the whole experiment so you can see the effects."

We spend several hours setting up the silver experiment, losing all track of time. Boyle is wonderful to work with. His precision is flawless, leaving nothing to chance.

Once the experiment is fully prepared he invites me to look at the caelum again before it is added to the molten silver in a small glass vessel.

When I look into the microscope again I gasp. The entire rock formation of the blue stone has changed. The boulders are completely rearranged and now shine with a glow of silver moonlight instead of bright sunshine. I pull away my head to see if the light source has changed, but it is identical. The shift in the light stems from within the caelum itself. Suddenly and without transition the caelum rocks have turned back to their original formation and the inner light has reverted to bright sunshine. I look up and see that Boyle has taken the molten silver and cast it in an ingot, destroying the experiment.

"So it responds to potential futures!" I exclaim.

Boyle nods. "That's the same conclusion I've come to. It appears that the caelum is mutable and so is the future. Better not tell your friend the Prince of Orange. He has bet his soul on Predestination. Wars are fought over this. And look at this elegant experiment. Science is a microscope pointed at religion. It has deepened my faith enormously while changing my mind completely."

Boyle and I stare at one another in awe, having just witnessed one of the great mysteries of the universe. My heart goes out to my father, who has always maintained that the future is free to become what it will through the influences we exert on it. It was a brave thought that could have had him hanged in a land where the future was believed to be rigidly predestined by an all-knowing Lord.

When I come back to our quarters at Whitehall Palace I go to the closet where Helvetius hides the bottle of the Medicine he has brought. He never carries it with him when he goes on his visits to his patients; he always takes only minute quantities. I grab the bottle and pour a few drops into the tiny flask Boyle has given me, filled with several spoons of the highly distilled alcohol he had poured from one of his alembics. As an initiated fellow adept he had asked no questions. Then I add the quarter grain of the caelum I carried with me in a pouch from home for good luck. I have been wearing it under my garments whenever I feel I need protection. I now have to wait four days for a full moon on Friday November 9th at 22.45 hours.

Prince William gave his Princess Mary of Orange forty thousand pounds in jewels. William Bentinck brought them over the day after the wedding in a large casket. King Charles had never repaid my Prince for the vast amounts of money the King had borrowed from William's father when he was a crownless Prince living on Orange largesse. Nor had the dowry for my Prince's mother Mary Stuart ever been paid. His fastidious and immediate exact payment of the dowry owed was a haughty act, stinging both his Uncles Charles and James, who resented him for it.

To Princess Mary herself he gave a small ruby and diamond ring.

In her despair Princess Mary refuses to leave St. James's Palace and join him at Whitehall. A dispute arises when my Prince commands her to leave her sister's bedside. Both William's parents had died of smallpox in the bloom of their maturity and he is terrified of the disease. So for the first time he exercises his undisputed spousal authority, asking me to make sure his command is carried out. In a serious affront, Princess Mary of Orange has refused to obey her new lord and master.

I'm not keen on going to St. James's, where the scourge has been taking a grave toll. But Helvetius assures me that if I take a drop of the Medicine under my tongue it will protect me. Prince William is terrified for the fate of his new wife if she is to stay by the Lady Anne. I notice true affection well beyond his injured pride as a husband being defied by his wife and am moved to honor his request.

Meanwhile, the young Duchess of York has given birth to a healthy boy and thus Mary is no longer Heiress to the throne of England – news received with a rude display of acidic glee by William's uncles. But my Prince seems at this moment not to care about her titles and is exclusively concerned about her wellbeing, probably as the only man in all of England who doesn't care about her loss of rank.

ஐ

I arrive at St. James's Palace, a place I had hoped to never see again from inside, on the morning of Friday November 9. Count von Waldstein had offered us his grand Berlin carriage, as an honor to the Prince of Orange – since it was intended to carry the Princess of Orange to Whitehall – and a friendly convenience to me. The delicious drop of rich Red Sulphur has left an aftertaste of my favorite dessert, strawberries and cream. It has filtered down to my throat where it spreads a cooling haze over my vocal chords, giving a veiled sound to my voice. I enter through the dark gate onto the right hand courtyard, heading for the rooms of the seriously ill Lady Anne. I've been asked to remove Princess Mary from these quarters.

The atmosphere in St. James's is even gloomier than it had been last time I was here, a little over two weeks ago. The disease has hit with sudden fury and the mood around is one of terror. The younger people, especially, have been falling ill, and everyone fears for the Lady Anne, who is just 12 years old.

I'm led through a long cold corridor with bright red curtains drawn over open windows. It is said that the color red has curative effects by rooting out the evil spirits. Servants dressed in red cast furtive glances at me. I'm wearing a warm woolen cape with a high caelum thread count mixed with glow-cloth and red silk, giving off a peacock shine of variegated hues between purple and pink with moments of blue-green. Amongst all the bright red, my textiles flow like moonlight at the break of dawn. The young lady in waiting who is leading me to Lady Anne whispers to me in front of the door to her Lady's bedchambers. "You are the wife of Doctor Helvetius aren't you? Do you carry any of his medicine with you?" She looks desperate. I see some small sickly white pustules forming on her forehead. My heart cries for her and I tell her to open her mouth and quickly drop some panacea under her tongue from the small bottle I carry with me for the Lady Anne. Helvetius has given me strict instructions not to give it to anyone else or there would be a stampede. But I can't help myself. The young girl looks so frightened and I have visions of my own daughter Johanna and of Clara when she was the age of this child. "Don't tell anyone!" I say with a mysterious voice of powerful authority that takes me by surprise. "If you tell anyone it will not work. It must remain a secret!" She falls to the ground, kisses my feet and scurries off. My heart pounds as I look around to see if this sad scene had been noticed by anyone. Thankfully it hasn't.

With profound hesitation, I knock on the red-draped door.

The doorway opens to a freezing cold room where every inch is covered with bright red cloth. The carpets are red and so are the sheets; and on the bed, the Lady Anne is dressed in a thin red nightgown and wearing a red veil. They have been very thorough, I think to myself, while doubting it will do any good. Red had been the smallpox treatment of choice a century ago. I remember having been told that Queen Elisabeth was wrapped in a red blanket when she caught the illness. Helvetius doesn't believe the red treatment works, but Mundanus is more open-minded. He will try anything that doesn't do harm. He says that if everyone believes in the red treatment it gives strength to the spirit and that can only be good – if you combine it with other treatments you know will actually have some direct effect.

The windows are wide open, the room as cold as winter. Outside cold is understood to be curative. Helvetius had told me that the Lady Anne was prescribed twelve bottles of beer mixed with spirit of vitriol every twenty-four hours and was given medicine to induce vomiting. Copious bloodletting was done from her tongue. Helvetius had mentioned that he might have ordered the same treatment before he had the use of the panacea, and that he never knew if his patients died of the disease or of the treatment.

The freshly minted Princess Mary of Orange is sitting by her sister's bedside dressed in a warm royal ermine coat with broad wing-like lapels checkered with the black ends of ermine tails. It is said that the ermine would rather die than be defiled, so the coat sends a defiant royal message. She looks up when I enter. I see that under the red veil Lady Anne's child-face is covered with ugly white pustules like popped maize from the New World. I'm surprised by the sudden detachment of my gaze.

"You can tell him I'd rather die than leave my sister's bedside!" ermine Princess Mary welcomes me stubbornly, in a tone my Prince might have used. They are truly alike. I know that going counter to her set mind will only make her haughtier.

"Will you hear my proposal, Your Highness?" I ask her directly in a veiled voice that is alien to me.

"No," she replies.

"Well, here it is anyway. I will give your sister some of the magical medicine my husband Doctor Helvetius has prepared. It has healed people who would otherwise have died. If it is not yet your sister's time as measured by the clock we all carry in our heart, she will be cured by this medicine, I can assure you. But I will only give it to her – and to you for prevention – if you leave her bedside and join your husband at Whitehall." I know that she heard my Prince tell her father at the Lord Mayor's celebration that Helvetius' medicine is the only hope against smallpox, so she needs no further explanation.

"That is Scottish blackmail! That is evil!" the Princess exclaims.

"It is," I concur. "I'm not proud of it. But my husband assures me that you will get smallpox if you stay here and will likely die."

"So my cousin is protecting his property, is he?" she bites with sarcasm. Now she sounds like a copy of the Duke of York, her father. She makes a point of not calling Prince William her husband.

"You might see it that way, Your Highness," I say calmly, my voice exuding conviction. "I'd say he truly cares for you." When I look down I notice for the first time that she is wearing the beautifully simple ruby and diamond ring Prince William gave her as her personal wedding gift on her right hand ring finger. I stare at it emphatically. Ill at ease, she covers her right hand with ermine. I know she is torn and that I will have to wait her out.

"May I sit down, Your Highness?" I request.

She makes a gracious move with her bare left hand to a chair nearby.

We sit in silence for a long while. I notice her casting loving glances at her sister as her right hand under the ermine plays nervously with her wedding ring. Tears roll quietly down her cheeks.

"I may never see her again," she mutters, with despair in her voice.

"You will see her again, Your Highness. My husband's medicine is remarkable. It has saved my life many times," I reply with focused certainty.

"So then why can't I just take the medicine with my sister and stay here?" she exclaims exasperated.

"That's tempting fate, Your Highness. The medicine is miraculous but one should never count on miracles alone."

Her jaw is set with Stuart intransigence. She'll make a great Orange matriarch on day, the Oranges being famous for their unrelenting tenacity.

"Your ring is very lovely," I say, non-sequitur. From the shoulder down her right arm pulls back deeper under cover. She glares at me as though I've just been impertinent. I can't help but smile. She knows just as well as do I that if she doesn't go with me voluntarily she will be carried out by soldiers, kicking and screaming; hardly a dignified prospect. No one will defend a woman against her husband. I know that this is the last thing my Prince wants to have happen, so I strengthen my resolve to persuade her. I wish I could match Signor Rossini's voice.

In the long silence that ensues I notice my Red Sulphur throat with its silver haze. I wonder if I could mimic Signor Rossini's Magus voice. I concentrate on the silver mist covering my vocal chords and attempt an interior form of the distillation I do in my laboratory. I gather together the tiny droplets of silver fog and heat the flask of my throat with the fire in my heart. I know that I have to convince Princess Mary for her own sake and focus that certainty in the pulse of my blood. I breathe into this pulse like I would use my laboratory bellows until I can feel my blood pumping loudly in my ears. I gather the steam and suddenly loosen the stopper on the vessel, transferring all of this intention at once by way of my voice to the mind of Princess Mary.

"You will come with me!" flows from my tongue like a concentrated distillate. My intent passes into her like breath.

"I will come with you," she repeats my will.

I am astounded. For the first time in my life I have used the voice of the Magus and I am exhilarated. I look intently at the horrible view of Lady Anne's puss-popped skin in order to stay grounded. I lift the red veil and open her mouth, her tongue swollen from all the bloodletting. She feels like a rag doll and reeks putridly. As I drip ten drops of the panacea under her tongue, my mouth tastes strawberry while my nose inhales death. I concentrate the Red Sulphur fog in my throat into a fluid shield against the spirits of malady that attempt to breathe into me from the mouth of the young girl.

Then I turn to Princess Mary. "Open your mouth," I command her. I am now the voice of her will and she opens her mouth instantly. Her breath is sweet and I feel loving compassion for this young girl about to be orphaned by her destiny.

ꕥ

I deliver the Princess to her husband who is greatly surprised by her sudden docility. I realize that I must release Mary from my voice now that it has fulfilled its service. I breathe out the fog and inhale the fresh winter air around me until the voice of the Magus has evaporated.

"At your service, Your Highnesses," I curtsy formally to dispel any sense of intimacy between my Prince and me, and return her will to the young Princess who looks momentarily bewildered and then wails, grief stricken. My Prince has to deal with at least some of her emotional distress and I feel a strong refusal to tame Princess Mary's wild spirit like one breaks a horse. I admire her courage and take my leave, to let these royal cousins who are so alike deal with one another directly.

I return to my quarters to wait for hour 22.45.

ꕥ

I have scouted out a small courtyard in the outskirts of Whitehall Palace frequented by no one, especially at night. I miss Hendrik as I walk there, dressed warmly and wearing my winter riding boots. Our old coachman has somehow always been there during these moonlight alchemical experiments, first with Father and then alone. I'm reminded of my preparation of the blanching tincture for Mundanus, when Hendrik picked me up from the ground after I had fainted and said, "You must have some strong stuff in that little bottle!" There will be no one lifting me to my feet this time, unless my efforts at occultation have been unsuccessful and Signor Rossini turns up. I can't help wishing he would be present, but hope I am able to make this particular desire invisible by folding it into my general erotic longing he has come to expect of me.

It has begun to snow and I am worried I will not be able to see the full moon and that therefore the caelum medicine I'm about to prepare may be lacking in potency. Looking up, I see the silver translucent clouds displaying diffuse moonlight, and realize that I have no idea what the light should be like for this kind of experiment. I don't even know what the experiment is for! Maybe the snow-filled atmosphere is just what's needed. All I know is that we have to be protected from a possible phantom-caster who eats the heart and liver of a child in order to remain powerful. I fear for my Red Sulphur twins, whose flesh he must be lusting after. I cringe at the thought that his phantom has already spied on Maximo in The Hague. I want Rossini to come home with us because I believe that his being around in one continuously visible body will be safer than having him materialize unexpectedly as shape-shifting imagination. In order to hide these thoughts from him I allow the lustful craving in my body to fully overtake me and feel like I'm walking through a hot shower of snowflakes. I will use the heat he provides to fuel my experiment and count on it that my desire for him will flatter his pride and thus keep him off my track.

The courtyard is already covered with an inch of glittering snow reflecting the diffuse overhead moonlight with scintillating refraction into the colors of a silver-toned rainbow, as if the earth were strewn with myriads of diamonds. As I walk to the center of the courtyard my boots on the snow send crackling music throughout the silent atmosphere. I glance about me, half expecting Signor Rossini to appear. But either he is not present or hidden. Around me is only night and I sense that I am entirely alone. My skin glows in the aftermath of the glorious bath I took when returning from Prince William's quarters after having delivered the Princess. I have scented myself in auspicious perfumes to be attractive to the caelum and to mix my ecstatic memories of the great transmutation at Mundanus' smithy with the heat of Rossini's blood seething magic.

I take Boyle's vial from my pocket and wait for the moon to reach the exact location I have calculated for her to appear at 22.45 hours in her momentary manifestation as Diana, the Full-Moon Huntress and the Sun's twin sister.

When the instant arises I hold up the vial to Diana bathing behind the clouds of snow, and incant my prayers to her. If anyone sees me at this moment I will burn at the stake for witchcraft. The familiar shaking from the earth below enters up through my feet, and my body wants to quake. But this time I carry in my bones the remnants of my brief authority as the voice of the Magus this afternoon. It steadies my spine, and makes the quaking an internal event while my body manages to hold still. My torso feels like a hermetically sealed vessel and the pressure rises to a degree beyond anything I have ever endured. I notice in my blood how the contents of the shaking vial achieve increasing subtlety until all physical matter appears to have vanished in favor of subtle body. I am left with a highly volatile substance that will evaporate the moment I remove the stopper.

Instinctively I put the whole vial in my mouth and enclose it firmly with my lips so nothing can escape, using my tongue and teeth to remove the stopper. Suddenly a giant gale explodes into my lungs. I sense my eyes pop forward in their sockets and feel a piercing pain, as sharply pointed pressure trepans my skull from the inside above the bridge of my nose. Invisible vision streams in through the breach. I hear colors and shapes reflect off metal surfaces, giving a view to an echoing world without light. I don't hear with my ears, but with the hole in my forehead, and I know I am experiencing what the Magi call the opening of the third eye. It gives voice to a world that flows directly into my flesh with immediate visceral certainty. A greater world than I have hitherto known now has access to me, and I'm acutely aware that I don't know myself. I notice a plethora of futures opening up simultaneously and realize I'm in Caelum. Life will prune these futures into a single one lived on the physical plane, while the others vanish like the instant reversion of the caelum boulders under the microscope preceding experiments that fail to happen. I wonder if, like Boyle, I will be able to deduce coming experiments from the current constellations of the future-telling caelum.

The future I note most clearly is one of powerful storms that rock a ship crossing the sea. I can't fathom whether the vessel goes down but I feel great fear around me. I will have to warn my Prince that our crossing may be fraught. I sense queasy intimations of seasickness. It is as though my body is on the ship, in the way of a dream. But unlike a dream it feels that the whole world is my body, as though I am the essence of space. Caelum gives access to innermost space and I cease to exist separately. I am the storm and the ship, they are my flesh; and my body is not mine, but is weather. Marianne van Os is no longer and I am terrified. Yet somehow that calms me, for I know that in order to feel terror there must be an 'I'. This terror is my *cogito.* I dread, therefore I am.

When I arrive back to our quarters I'm not surprised to find blood dripping from a wound just below the hairline on my forehead. I tell Helvetius I slipped on the snow while on an ill-advised night-time walk on the slippery grounds. He is greatly concerned and wants to put drops of the medicine on my wound, which I forcefully resist. I need the caelum to settle before adding more change agents. As he cleans and palpates the wound he notes with worry that it seems as if the skull underneath has been crushed. I reassure him many times that I don't feel any pain, which indeed I don't, before his alarm subsides. But he regards me with concerned suspicion and fear for my health.

ꙮ

Prince William is dead-set on leaving Monday November 19. He can't be persuaded by anyone, including me, to postpone our departure, even though storm winds have been gathering steadily. He wants to be away from Whitehall, away from the smallpox, and away from the pernicious influence of his uncles upon his impressionable wife.

I know that the stormy future I was shown when my third eye opened is true. Unlike the caelum boulders under the microscope when Boyle destroyed the silver experiment, my caelum visions have not reverted and remain in a storm formation that must be caused by actual subsequent events. It is confusing to have to think backwards from a future that has already occurred in Caelum time. I now live in two temporal zones simultaneously, and wish I could talk about it with Signor Rossini who appears to be very adept at this eerie doubling.

Mundanus has never spoken about anything like this and I doubt that he has access to the future in the same way I now do. I want him to go through this time experiment too so we may remain close and he will have the necessary abilities to outwit Signor Rossini. I feel close to Mundanus again, long for him – so it seems Rossini's power over me has diminished. He seems to no longer drive a wedge between my beloved and me.

I try to look deeper into the future, but I can't see past the storm and the seasick world. I wonder if over time the echoes of the future will reach me from further away. In my experience faculties often expand with use and become better honed.

Signor Rossini had left word that he can't join us until Wednesday November 28, by which time we all expect to long be back in The Hague. I am pleased to not have to deal with him yet

– until I catch a faint echo of his presence on our ship and realize that we will probably be prevented from leaving until November 28. Now that I've had my first inklings of caelum's ability to be patterned by events that are yet to occur, my dread and admiration around Rossini have grown exponentially. I decide to visit Robert Boyle the Friday before our Monday departure, and take him into my confidence. Count von Waldstein will join us and I feel supported by the anticipation of our meeting.

Now that the Lady Anne is visibly healing, patients are crowding in from far and wide so Helvetius will be too busy to join us, which I'm glad about. I don't want him to know what is happening. His fearful attitudes might do great harm. I need to be surrounded by persons of courage.

A strange consequence of my new Caelum life is an altered sense of equilibrium. It seems as though I am always falling without actually losing my balance. I have stepped off a cliff into a bottomless abyss of echo without origin. When a lackey opens the door to the Berlin carriage, I almost miss the step, and find myself falling upwards as if I were weightless – while knowing full well that nothing supernatural is happening to me. My physical body has its usual weight and responds to the unhinging circumstances much better than my troubled mind. I am prevented from tripping by agile muscles I've never used before.

"What happened to you, Madam Schweitzer?" Count von Waldstein asks me with alarm, pointing at the fresh crescent scar on my forehead.

"Let's say that I fell," I tell him. The consummate diplomat immediately realizes that I will speak about it later, and changes the subject.

"I'm so grateful to you for inviting me to your meeting with Robert Boyle. It is such a privilege!" Then he is silent for some time. "Do you have any idea when His Excellency might come to these parts?" he inquires, referring to Mundanus.

I tell him I have no idea and we talk about interesting gossip as we pass St. James's Palace.

"Your services to His Highness have been remarkable," the Count says, pointing at the palace. "Signor Rossini was right to call you a woman of high degree." Hearing the Magus' name makes me blush down to my throat. Count von Waldstein takes it that he has embarrassed me with his compliment and apologizes profusely. I wave his apologies away with a wan gesture of my hand. I feel drained. We are silent until we reach Lady Ranelagh's home in a matter of minutes.

We are told to go directly up to Boyle's third floor laboratory where we he is awaiting us eagerly. Lady Ranelagh tells us that he has been experimenting day and night with the caelum and can't wait to discuss his findings with me. I can't help but be flattered that the great Boyle is so eager to talk to me. Kings and Princes don't mean anything to me; scholars do. Count von Waldstein beams with vicarious pride, honored to be in my company. Lady Ranelagh looks at me with sincere approval – a regard, I'm sure, usually reserved for exceptional guests. Now I'm almost flustered. Combined with my general sense of disequilibrium, I feel I can barely make it up the two flights of wide stairs, though from the outside it must look as though I'm bounding up with exceptional zest. The Count can barely keep up with me. Lady Ranelagh has apologized for not joining us. Matters of household keep her tied up.

The moment we enter the laboratory Boyle begins to talk without any formal welcome, waving us over to Hooke's microscope. He starts in mid-conversation.

"The predictive abilities of the caelum diminish over time. I have been observing the caelum constantly, and since yesterday nothing changes, no matter which experiment follows. It seems that after some time the caelum becomes inert. I imagine that its ferment gets reduced. I wonder if its exposure to air diminishes the vigor in the way it does with usual fermentation. You brought me the caelum in a sealed vial, right?" I nod. "So I tried to no avail to remove all the air with the pneumatic engine to see if its abilities would return, but it remained inert," Boyle adds with a note of disappointment.

I quickly explain the previous experiments to Count von Waldstein, who looks astounded. Boyle by now takes it all as a matter of course and is no longer surprised by it as if the caelum had lost its prophetic marvel in him too. His gaze is intently focused on me.

I suddenly have a flash of insight. I understand that Rossini's Caelum abilities diminish over time so he constantly needs them to be tinctured with Red Sulphur. A strong echo from the future tells me that my abilities will only increase, probably because I took the caelum mixed with Mundanus' Red Sulphur tincture. Rossini must have ready access to caelum, but not to Red Sulphur.

As a first step, I explain Signor Rossini's magisterial abilities to insert himself into one's memory, and ask Boyle to remember the first time he met Rossini, which he instantly claims was years ago. But upon careful questioning no actual memories present themselves that are over a month old. Count von Waldstein reports his own surprise that he hasn't been able to remember any encounter with Signor Rossini outside of England. I tell them of my fears that Signor Rossini might be the phantom sorcerer who has been haunting us, and they look aghast when I tell them about Gerda's little brother Peter's cannibalistic murder. Von Waldstein tells us in hushed tones that in his native Bohemia there are tales of revenants, people who have died and return from the dead in need of the blood of the living. They are called vampires, he says, and wonders out loud if Rossini is one of those revenants. I remember Clara telling me of the Count's fascination with the Bohemian stories he was told by his local governess and note a tenor of childlike credulity in his voice, much unlike his adult perspicacity.

"I believe that Signor Rossini is alive, not dead," I counter with certainty. Count von Waldstein looks unconvinced.

Then I explain everything that has happened to me since I ingested the caelum tincture and point to the scar over my third eye. Boyle is fascinated and I notice him bowing to me in respect. Then he speculates, "It seems that caelum lives most concentrated at the root of sulphur; and Red Sulphur, being the most refined sulphur, may revive its memory after the caelum loses its abilities over time. Maybe its life-giving sulphuric fermentation stops when brought up to surface air and Red Sulphur may leaven it again." I am amazed by Boyle's quick acceptance of improbable facts. It makes sense to me that caelum might lose its memory of the future, like an old person becoming demented, like yeast losing its ferment. But we need an experiment to see if this is all just fanciful speculation. Both Boyle and I are experimentalists at heart.

"I carry some of the Red Sulphur panacea with me, the same we used to heal the Lady Anne. May we put a few drops on the demented caelum and see if it regains its access to the future?" I suggest.

Count von Waldstein looks blissful, as if he is experiencing a great moment in his life. I smile at the little Bohemian boy who used to believe in magic carpets, a faith that had made him travel the world as a diplomat.

"Might we do the experiment in the pneumatic engine?" I add. "In a vacuum the experiment may have more potent results, since no air interferes with the ferment."

Boyle looks very pleased, obviously having come to the same conclusion.

As a first step, we look at the caelum through the microscope. The boulders look dull and lifeless, no longer breathing. Strangely enough all boulders point in the same direction. I mention it to Boyle. "North," he says. "When the caelum dies it no longer has a will of its own and gets taken over by mineral magnetism. If the caelum comes back to life the formation will look much more unstable in the way it did when we first looked at it. So we know what we are looking for," Boyle concludes, satisfied with his hypothesis.

"But how will we look at it through the microscope inside the pneumatic engine?" Count Waldstein asks. I look at Boyle, having no idea how to answer the question.

"Indeed we can't," Boyle admits. "But we can let the interaction between the dead caelum and the Red Sulphur take place inside the pneumatic engine for an hour and then look at it under the microscope. That's as close as we can get. And then we can come up with an experiment we will perform to see if its future changes the state of the caelum."

We all agree it will be the best we can do.

I take out the vial Helvetius had given me for the Lady Anne. It is still mostly full. I had only used 20 drops for the royal sisters and 5 for the servant girl. Robert Boyle has removed the caelum from the microscope's viewing platform and put it on the small assay plate. I remember Plotinus' words that the incantation is as important as the medicine, and I suggest we need an appropriate chant. Boyle seems uncomfortable. He is enough of a follower of Galileo and his science to no longer believe in the relationship between experiment and ritual.

Suddenly I hear a very young German voice arise from Count von Waldstein:

"Revive the future
Sing brightly again.
Open your heart
To the breath of life!"

It seems very appropriate and I drip 5 droplets of the Medicine onto the listless caelum. Boyle instantly places the caelum and Red Sulphur mixture in the bulbous head of the pneumatic engine and pumps out all the air. I somehow expect to see a change take place when the vacuum is established, but nothing looks any different inside the glass bulb.

For the next hour we deliberate upon the test that is to follow and decide on a copper essay and the silver experiment we had prepared last time in this laboratory. But we carefully avoid making a decision between the two, in order to leave the future undetermined.

After an hour Boyle lets air flow back into the vacuum with a loud hiss, and takes out the assay plate transferring its content back to the microscope's viewing platform.

I get the honor of looking first. The blue boulders are fully alive, their breath held between inhale and exhale in a raw state of action potential. They look randomly scattered in many different directions of the compass. I keep my face stoic, in order not to influence the other viewers. Both agree completely with my observation. Then we toss a coin to determine the trial. It lands on heads, which we had decided to be the silver experiment. We look into the microscope again and this time the boulders have been redirected and glow with moonlight. In order to satisfy the experiment, we mix half the amount of the blue caelum with silver and obtain a metal with a deep red-copper tone. We look at the caelum again and find that it has reverted to its original formation before its admixture to silver. The count looks disappointed, but Robert Boyle glows like the caelum itself.

"That is supposed to happen," he says. "I had intended to do a second assay in which I will extract the caelum from the red silver so I can use it again for further experiments!"

For the next hours we help Boyle extract the caelum and I am reminded of the time at Brechtelt's goldsmith shop when Brechtelt was doing his careful assaying of Helvetius' gold. There is a similar excitement in the laboratory. Once the blue caelum is extracted from the red metal and the silver has returned to its full-moon shine, Boyle mixes the caelum back with its other half, places it carefully in the vacuum pump, and removes the air.

I now know Signor Rossini's game is based on alchemical experiment. It gives me a sense of safety, even though I acutely understand how truly dangerous he is, because he is in desperate need of Red Sulphur. I speculate that he may be running out of caelum as well. He is like Mundanus: he has access to the magical material, but he can't create it. And since we had the placentas of our Red Sulphur twins from which to grow it, our caelum is the result of an experiment that can't be repeated by someone who doesn't have access to this primal matter.

Fear for my twins closes my throat. Rossini will stop at nothing.

That dismal and stormy Monday, together with the Prince and Princess of Orange and a retinue of crying young Ladies, we set off in a barge from Whitehall and leave London. We are joined by a jovial King who keeps making inappropriate passes at the miserable young girls, and by a sour Duke of York. My Prince looks sullen and his bride red-eyed. Mary's beloved governess, Lady Frances Villiers, whom she called 'my mam,' has died, and her daughters Anne and Elisabeth Villiers are part of the Princess' desolate retinue. My soldier Prince gets very nervous from all the weeping, and not knowing how to deal with the distressed damsels leaves their care to me while he talks exclusively to the King and the Duke. The fact that he prefers his vile uncles over the crying girls is telling. He'd rather lose his right arm indeed!

The wind increases to a gale and to add to their misery all girls but for Princess Mary are prostrated with seasickness. I overhear one of the mates on board tell another that all the young beggarly bitches are suing for places at the railing.

In sight of Gravesend the King and Duke say their farewells taking several of the young Ladies back to Whitehall, and when they think they are out of earshot I hear the Duke remark with glee that his daughter's marriage is doomed to humiliating failure. My hearing has become more acute than it has been.

We go on board the yacht "Mary" that will take us on the crossing. But the captain of the ship refuses to take us any further than Sheerness, because he will not cross the North Sea in this slender vessel in the teeth of such a gale. We land in Sheerness on November 22.

My Prince has not counted on a delay and in his efforts to pay the dowry in full has used up all the coin with which he traveled. So now we're oddly unprovided. The usually resourceful Bentinck is sent out to secure a loan from the Corporation of Canterbury, but is most strangely refused. Finally money comes in through the Dean of Canterbury who gets our royal party out of its grotesque financial difficulty.

As the storm rages, the princely pair holds court in the Cathedral City where soon many of the gentlemen of Kent pay their respects to the young couple. This creates rumors that the Prince is delaying his crossing on purpose to show the King the full extent of his popularity. Even though untrue, the gossip demonstrates the public perception of brutal rivalry between the Prince of Orange and the royal Stuart brothers.

The storm abates on Wednesday November 28. Our party is transferred to Margate on a larger brigandine vessel "Montacute," and in the morning Signor Rossini presents himself to the Prince, who is overjoyed to be reunited with his old comrade-in-arms. It gives him new cause to pay no heed to the miserable damsels, Princess Mary and the Villiers sisters, who have by now flocked around me as their mother hen. I dispense lozenges of myrrh, cinnamon and angelica root – the same Mundanus had prepared for me for my trip up the Rhine during my pregnancy – and speak to the young women in soothing tones, while allowing them to mourn their various profound losses. William Bentinck is the only man who seems comfortable among the young ladies, and talks freely with them, especially with gentle Anne Villiers. He is a gallant young man of no particular talent but with a fierce loyalty to the Prince, a friendship that makes him accomplish unexpected results when needed. He'd give his life for Prince William's without a moment's hesitation. Because of our special relationships to the Prince, Bentinck and I have quickly developed a complete trust in one another, even though we have hardly met before this trip to

London. I tell him to be cautious around Signor Rossini, and ask him to be my eyes and ears around Rossini, now that I'm convinced Signor Rossini will avoid my presence. Echoes tell me Rossini knows of my personal transmutation. Bentinck is rapidly falling in love with Anne Villiers and I sense how that passion fills his soul with a fragrant and impenetrable rose fog, making our conspiracy invisible to Rossini's clairvoyance.

Maybe Rossini has read my mind, for he immediately searches me out on deck. I realize that one can change individual futures by acting in a truly unexpected manner; like that time when Boyle destroyed the silver experiment and the caelum reverted back to its original formation.

"Madam Schweitzer," Signor Rossini calls out from aft, where he is talking with Prince William by the main mast as the gaff-rigged mainsail is being raised in feverish activity. The two square rigs above it are about to go up as well. We are on the open sea with the wind in our back so his voice carries easily. The smell of salt is exhilarating. Above me, by the foremast, the three square sails have already been raised, as have the two jibs. Sailors are everywhere around us doing their work with grim determination. They are not keen on having passengers on deck when the sails go up. I turn in his direction and don't feign to be pleased to see him.

He takes leave of the Prince, walks over to the foremast and points at my forehead. "A fall?" he asks, non-committal.

"Are we going to play games?" I ask him directly, unable to hide my irritation.

He smiles. "I guess not. It is a pleasure to be with another Magus," he adds. "I called you a Magus before because I saw this in your future." To my great relief I notice that he no longer has access to my passions. I feel sharp icicles where the heat had been. "When you waved your caelum dress at me," he responds directly to a question I would have asked several minutes down the line about when he realized my future. He now skips all formalities and inserts himself at will in any point of the future. I am dazzled. "You had wanted to ask me, because I know how to do it. Once you know caelum you can inhabit multiple futures and try them out. You are going to be a master of it. It will be your curse – as Red Sulphur is a curse." For the first time I hear something besides breeziness in his voice; it is bitterness. "You'd better learn fast," he warns me as he turns around and goes back to the main mast aft, where he had been talking to my Prince. William Bentinck and Helvetius have now joined the Prince of Orange. All sails are up.

Shaken, I realize the full implications of the fact that my individual future is truly open, undecided until it is lived. I feel what it is like to be genuinely free in choosing a future: it is terrifying. I know I will not subject Mundanus to this curse, and am aware Rossini is counting on just this.

"Could you come below deck to see Her Highness, please, Madam Schweitzer," Anne Villiers voice behind me asks sweetly. The seasickness among the young Ladies has subsided, as has the storm, and young Anne looks as though she has found her sea legs. I like her because she is instinctively kind and because I like William Bentinck. I find her sister Elisabeth's open flirtatiousness harder to take. Around her I hear dark echoes approaching.

The Prince and Princess occupy the captain's cabin. When I enter the cozy quarters with light flowing in through five windows, three aft and one on each side, I see Princess Mary unceremoniously sitting on the bedstead, her legs dangling down, staring at her bare feet.

"Our people will love you," I tell her, anticipating her melancholy question. I know this future for a fact. Large-scale futures appear to be more stable than individual ones.

"My father lived in your country for a long time. He told me that your people are drab and dreary, made of sod and clay," she responds sullen.

"Do you believe him? Your father is angry that you didn't marry the Dauphin of France. He wants you to be a Catholic," I remark drily. "He's not going to praise our people."

"You told me that Prince William likes me. Why doesn't he tell me himself?"

"Because you cry all the time and he can't deal with women's tears," I tell her harshly. I decide that only the truth is good enough. "I understand you are desolate about leaving your sister and how much you miss Lady Apsley and your Mam. But your course is set. There is nothing anyone can do about it. Least of all Prince William. And has he behaved like Zeus to Callisto?" I ask her cryptically.

She instantly understands my reference to their wedding night and blushes crimson.

"Prince William is a kind man," I continue. "A brutal soldier, but a warm-hearted man. He took you to be his wife as a soldier, for the sake of Europe, to thwart the designs of King Louis. Of course you know that."

She nods, listening carefully.

"But he will not force himself upon you as long as you appear to not be ready for his advances. Right now you have not progressed beyond being a crucial matter of state to him. If you want to meet him as your husband you will have to behave differently. You have no other option. As I told you, he feels affection for you as his young cousin, respects you as a political ally in the Protestant cause, but that's as far as it goes. If you want him to become like William Bentinck to Anne Villiers you will have to give him an opening."

Unexpectedly she gets up from the bed, comes over to me and hugs me tightly. I am surprised by her uncharacteristic action and know instantly that mentioning the Villiers name has made her miss Anne's mother, her Mam.

"You mourn for her, don't you?" I respond, knowing she will understand my reference.

Mary sobs as I hold her the way I used to comfort Clara.

Part Thirteen

Mundanus

Chapter Twenty-Seven

The river Maas is choked with ice, so they will not be able to land where we have been expecting them. We've been without news for several weeks while the weather has been gloomy and violent. I have decided with Clara that I shall take The Twins with Hendrik to pick up Marianne and Helvetius as soon as they arrive. The children can't wait for a minute longer after having sorely and courageously missed their mother for over six weeks.

Finally Prince William's spies working at the munitions factory report to me that a ship flying Prince William's flag has been sighted some distance off the coast early on Thursday November 29, and they are expecting it to make landfall about seven miles south-west of The Hague. Carriages are being dispatched to fetch the Prince and Princess and bring them to Honselaarsdyke, his closest mansion near landfall, a two-hour ride east.

It has been sleeting steadily and Hendrik looks like an ice sculpture, with icicles hanging off his nose and whiskers. Across from us, Maximo is chatting constantly with overwhelming excitement, while Johanna is leaning into me, quietly staring out at the grey flat coastal landscape.

"It's a great present!" Maximo continues his conversation with no one in particular. He is describing the gift he made for his mother. "It is based on the clocks Uncle Christiaan has designed.

But I added a feature. It is a bell that rings when you set it to a particular time. Look Father!" He takes a square contraption out of his pocket. "I first thought of it when I was thinking of a way to detonate ammunition when you're not around. I thought of a little hammer connected to a time piece hitting some of your devil's element lighting the fuse of a bomb." I'm reminded of Clara's warning that Red Sulphur might carry a nostalgic longing for Hell. "I made it as a present for the Prince for when he returns. But then I thought I could connect the time piece to a bell," he shows it to me. It is a well-made box full of flywheels and ticking mechanisms. "Uncle Christiaan gave me the parts," he explains. I know his deep fondness for Christiaan Huygens, who I can't help but view with suspicion because of his love for Clara and her open return of his affections. But I am glad that Christiaan gives the excess of love he can't give Clara to Maximo. Our connection to the Huygens family is getting increasingly close now that Christiaan and his father Constantijn are helping us design a grand organ for Johanna in the munitions factory across the street.

Johanna is looking at the mechanical marvel with delight. She loves her brother's inventions as much as he cherishes her music. "That is gorgeous, Max!" she exclaims. "How does it work?"

Maximo winds the instrument with a key in the back. The current time is 10.15 hours. We left home an hour ago. He sets the clock to a few minutes past now. We wait until a little bell rings with a crystal sound at the indicated time. Johanna claps her hands with delight.

"What does it serve, Maximo?" I ask him, knowing that my Red Sulphur son sees technical implications well past ordinary humans.

"I though you could use it when you want to get up at a certain time so no one has to wake you."

"You made it for yourself!" Johanna exclaims teasing, knowing Maximo will sleep all day long if not awakened. Her brother laughs.

"Maybe Mother will lend it to me," he responds joking. Then he turns to me. "We should almost be there," he tells me. "In this sleet we probably ride at a speed of 4 miles an hour, so we should reach the beach in about half an hour."

A soldier stops us. Obviously the area around the landing site is being cordoned off. I know that the Prince doesn't want anyone to know about his arrival so that he has some time with his young bride before the grand festivities begin. I hear the soldier talk to Hendrik, and I open the window. Ice-cold air enters the cabin.

"I'm Giovanni Dolfin," I call out. "I'm coming to pick up my aunt and uncle, Doctor Helvetius and his wife." The soldier nods, obviously recognizing us. Maximo has become quite a celebrity among soldiers.

He salutes us respectfully: "They appear to be heading for Ter Heyde." He casts another look at Maximo and grins broadly, showing off all of his missing teeth. My boy smiles back with a comradery he has learned in the munition's factory, where he is revered as the miraculous chief engineer – no one thinking any longer of the fact that he is just 8 years of age.

"I will be telling my grandchildren about the day I saw you!" the soldier calls out to Maximo, as though the arrival of the Prince of Orange and his new bride is an entirely secondary affair his grandchildren will only hear about in the context of his momentous meeting with the great Maximo Dolfin. Maximo's military fame both astounds and worries me, but I can't help but feel a deep fatherly pride of my son and of my virtuoso daughter. I hug Johanna close to me and I note her fingers playing imaginary keys.

When we arrive, a bevy of soldiers on the beach is looking at the ship anchored a ways off the coast. Several oared boats – like wide versions of our Venetian caorline vessels – are returning from the ship, and we can already see how the first boat has a crew of four rowers and three passengers: a man dressed in military regalia, a woman, and a man holding up two large umbrellas in the way we use them as canopies for shade in my homeland and against sleet and rain in these parts. Behind them, two more vessels carry the other passengers.

"Mother!" both Maximo and Johanna call out simultaneously, pointing at the last boat. Their eyesight is much more acute than anyone's except for Monsieur Delamarche's. It takes a few more minutes before I can confirm their sighting. A sudden rush quickens my heart as I catch sight of the woman I love. I'm flooded with memories and I can't wait till Marianne and I can steal illicit moments. I feel in my pocket for the vial with the outcome of the experiments we had begun just before Marianne's departure: a mixture of caelum and the devil's element *phosphorus mirabilis*. The result has been a glowing greenish-blue substance that can light up a whole room with the power of its luminescence. The vial in my pocket shines brighter than an oil lamp. I wonder how Maximo will use it, knowing he will see totally unexpected technical applications; I haven't yet shown it to him. I can't wait to be back with Marianne in the laboratory. Beside Marianne and Helvetius I notice another man who I don't recognize, but for his costume that looks almost Venetian. I assume that I'm overcome by homesickness.

When the Prince disembarks, he walks straight up to us, surrounded by a guard of soldiers, holding the hand of his young bride tenderly. He greets me curtly and turns to the young Princess: "These are the most remarkable children you will meet in my country," he says with pride.

"Hi Prince," Maximo exclaims with his unceremonious manners. "Is that your new Princess? She is very pretty." The Prince grins broadly and translates Maximo's statement into English for his bride, who smiles shyly. I don't know if the red in her eyes is from the sea wind or from crying. "You beautiful," Maximo repeats in his best English. Now Princess Mary's face, ruddy from the cold, blushes brightly.

"Come with us to Honselaarsdyke," Prince William laughs. "Maybe your daughter will regale us to some of her incomparable music." The eyes of the young Princess light up. She must be a lover of music. Johanna curtsies with élan.

Then The Twins lose all interest in the princely pair and start jumping up and down waving at their mother's boat that has come into view behind a vessel, carrying a man I recognize as William Bentinck and two young women around the age of Clara when we first met.

Marianne waves back at them with abandon, using both arms. The princess looks at the waving figure in the boat while hearing the children shout "Mother!" at the top of their lungs. Tears roll down her face.

When Bentinck's boat lands, the two young women rush over to Princess Mary and embrace her, and I see her expression change to one of relief. Bentinck introduces the young Ladies to us and I can see that he is focused on Anne Villiers. Johanna goes over to the Princess and takes her hand while the Prince is talking to soldiers with his back to his bride. Princess Mary gives a forlorn impression. "I shall play something beautiful for you, Your Highness. You'll be very happy in our country." The simple words of the child – spoken in fluent English - lift the spirits of the lonely young woman who obviously was still a girl less than a month ago. An instant bond has been forged. My love for my children is boundless.

Maximo exclaiming a loud "Mother!" rushes over to her boat, and with total disregard for his clothes, wades in knee deep. The soldiers laugh at the incongruous sight of their hero acting his proper age. He jumps up and almost pulls Marianne overboard. They both coo like doves.

"Isn't she your great aunt?" I hear Princess Mary ask Johanna, puzzled.

"Yes, Your Highness," Johanna says, without any sense of contradiction, "She is our Mother." She lets go of the Princess's hand and runs to the waterline, as a loudly laughing soldier helps Marianne off the barge. Maximo is soaked and ice cold. I'm not worried, knowing my Red Sulphur children don't get sick. And indeed Maximo appears not to notice the icy conditions, and embraces his mother from the back as Johanna does so from the front. Seeing my beloved wrapped in our children leaves my heart with nowhere to go but Heaven.

And then she looks at me. I can't place her expression. It is a warning I must heed, but I don't know what for. Behind her I notice the man in Italianate clothing; his face is unknown to me but a lightning of recognition flares through me, searing my insides as the ground drops away. Marianne's steady gaze catches my precipitous fall, like a net used by high wire artists, preventing a white-out in my soul. The man's penetrating look is surprisingly neutral, as though he has rehearsed this moment many times.

"Giovanni!" Helvetius calls out to me in a boisterous yet respectful way after he has warmly greeted The Twins. He walks over to me and shakes my hand, obviously very glad to see me. Something in his expression is different from before. It is as though he admires me, which adds to my confusion. He doesn't let go of my hand, and I see the Italian-dressed man smile in a knowing manner. Marianne looks alarmed.

I feel left out. Some kind of circle of knowledge from which I'm excluded closes in on me, restricting my breath.

Helvetius turns around and waves to the Italian to approach.

"Let me have the honor of introducing fellow Adepts. Signor Ricaldo Rossini, meet my nephew Giovanni Dolfin the Seventh."

"I knew your grandfather," Signor Rossini tells me as he holds out his hand. My skin is crawling; I've never had a feeling this eerie before. I feel as if I have always known this man I've never met before. I look at Marianne for an explanation and notice the crescent scar on her forehead. This instantly replaces my sense of the uncanny with plain worry.

"What happened with you?" I ask her. She looks at a loss for words.

"She fell," Helvetius explains. I don't believe him. I feel compelled to walk up to her and palpate the scar with my thumb. It feels like bare skin over a hole in her scalp. Now I'm truly alarmed. Then I hear an unspoken voice in my mind: "I'll tell you as soon as I'm able." Looking around for the place where this communication originated, I see Marianne nod and Rossini grin broadly. I have encountered Magi before who could insert themselves into the minds of others and my unease reaches a dissonant crescendo.

Before I can say anything more the Prince invites us all into our various carriages to take the two-hour journey to Honselaarsdyke.

I'm sitting next to Helvetius while The Twins are all over their mother sitting across from us. Signor Rossini has joined William Bentinck and the Villiers sisters in the carriage following the princely equipage drawn by four horses. We close the convoy.

Helvetius is uncharacteristically talkative, speaking mainly of their meeting with Robert Boyle, which seems to have impressed him most. When he talks about the caelum I remember the vial in my pocket, so I show it to Marianne. It lights up the whole cabin; the children are delighted.

"Is that the outcome of the phosphorus and caelum experiment?" Marianne asks me with an undertone of 'I love you so much!'

"It is indeed," I say, expressing how much I adore her.

"Is it hot?" Maximo asks, fascinated.

I give it to him and he is astounded to be holding cold light in his hands.

"That could be made into paint and spread onto glass and we could have mirrors of light," he responds with Red Sulphur eyes. Now it is my turn to be amazed. His instant ingenuity is breathtaking.

"We could have windows inside and if we paint the glass on the other side with transparent colors we could light up the room with any shade we want," Maximo delights.

"I could play music all night!" Johanna exclaims.

"It would take a long time to make just a little bit of this tincture," Marianne warns them.

"Could I have some?" Maximo asks.

"We'll think about it," Mother Marianne responds. "For now put it back in your pocket Giovanni and don't show anyone," she tells me with emphasis, a slight tremble in her voice. "And children, don't talk about it! Please don't talk about it or you will never get any of it!" I wonder why she has to be so stern. She doesn't trust someone. Suddenly I understand: the Italian. The Italian is an adversary. We have to be careful around him. I nod to indicate that I understand her.

"Can I just hold it a minute longer?" Maximo begs.

"Until the bell rings!" Johanna chirps, pointing at Maximo's pocket.

When she receives the wake-up clock from her son, Marianne begins to cry. I realize that she has been under great pressure.

Prince William is proud of his glorious Court Honselaarsdyke, built almost fifty years ago by his grandfather Frederick Hendrik of Orange and his grandmother Amalia van Solms with funds from the Dutch capture of a Spanish fleet carrying vast quantities of silver from the New World. Many of the crowned heads of Europe have stayed here – as well as Prince William's crownless uncles Charles and James when his mother Mary Stuart was hosting them as a matter of course on the Orange fortune for many years during Cromwell's reign. It has red capped steep roofs with large dormers over two wings connected by a two-story gilded midsection of grand galleries, and an elegant front door with several broad steps flanked by regiments of lackeys dressed in festive attire for the occasion. The front courtyard displays the Prince's love of luxuriating gardens that he inherited from his French great-grandmother Louise de Coligny. Since he was a boy I have known him to walk around gardens with delight. It is the only time I remember him freed from his leaden destiny. By the time our carriage arrives, the princely couple has already descended, and the Prince is proudly showing his bride through the magnificent gardens before entering the mansion. I hope Princess Mary loves horticulture as much as he does.

Inside, the heavy Germanic imitation of classical Italian marble architecture reminds me of my dislike for the North-End Palace, also designed to the taste of Amalia van Solms. I wonder what Catherine de Medici felt about it when she stayed here forty years ago.

An excitedly chirping Johanna, who has discovered the clavichord spinet in a drawing room that has been remodeled in the comfortable Dutch style called 'cozy', wakes me from my Italian meditations. "Mother, can you please ask the Prince if I can play," she begs Marianne. Princess Mary overhears her and replies, "Please do, Johanna," as her first act of hosting in her new role as the Princess of Orange. Prince William smiles, delighted. I notice Signor Rossini regarding Johanna with a look I can only interpret as pride. I am puzzled.

We all sit closely together, the Princess in a seat of honor. Her mere fifteen years are visible in her girlish face behind the guarded mask. A wood fire crackles its accompaniment as my daughter lifts her hands up in the air and her inward gaze displays her listening to music we cannot yet hear. At first there is a rumble of the stormy sea. Johanna's music always tells a story. Then with light dissonant tones mixed with thrilling harmonies we hear her play the mood of the Princess. I see Mary's body move almost imperceptibly in the way of a dancer, while her soul takes on Johanna's musical rhythm. Signor Rossini looks transfixed, as if he is beholding a vision from Heaven.

I see how Marianne stares at him with the same puzzlement I'm feeling. Suddenly it seems to me as though pale blue light is shining upwards from her forehead and I'm reminded of the hole I felt in her skull. She closes her eyes and appears to be looking at an inner drama, the way our daughter hears music from other spheres. I know at this moment that Marianne has changed fundamentally, and I feel a harsh fear of losing her to a world I don't know.

Johanna is now playing a welcoming song placed like a thin veil over the Orange family anthem about fierce self-confidence, liberation and meditations on the nature of loyalty. Old Constantijn Huygens has taught her well. Our Prince looks emotional: a rare event in his limited repertoire of facial expressions. He bends over to his young wife and whispers something in her ear, probably a reference to Johanna's musical quote. Pounds of tension visibly drop off the Princess of Orange. When Johanna stops her recital Princess Mary whispers "You've indeed made me feel welcome. Thank you, dear Johanna." We all note the beginning of a significant friendship. Elisabeth Villiers looks jealous. I will have to keep an eye on her.

"You play like an angel," Signor Rossini says, in his terribly familiar voice.

"She plays what she hears," Maximo explains proudly.

"Any new inventions lately, Maximo?" the Prince asks, with genuine interest.

Marianne looks intently at Maximo; I assume she doesn't want him to reveal anything in front of Signor Rossini.

But Maximo is too excited. "Yes I do, Prince. I can show you when you're at the factory in The Hague!"

"Tell me about it," Prince William encourages him.

"That would be ill-advised," I intervene. "This is another of Maximo's inventions that will change the face of war. He should tell you in confidence." Now the Prince is truly curious and becomes like a young boy himself who is not allowed to unwrap his birthday present. For some strange reason I have a sense that Signor Rossini already knows about Maximo's invention and I see Marianne nod as if she reads my thought. Or maybe she implanted it. I feel the slow suffocation of nightmare enclosing me.

"We are among friends here," the Prince argues. "I've known everyone here for years," he adds, obviously disregarding the young women. Signor Rossini must be an old friend of his, a fact that calms me down a bit.

"I'm sure my nephew has his reasons when he advises you thus," Marianne comes to my aid in an unusually stilted manner.

But Maximo can't hold back any longer. "It is a timing clock that sets off a bomb so you have time to get away," he explains, and divulges the details he told me on the way in.

"And he made a wake-up clock for Mother," Johanna adds proudly. "Show it to His Highness, Mother, please." Marianne can't help but fulfill her daughter's request, and we all clap when the chime is heard at the set time.

"And instead of the chime the bomb goes off, right?" the Prince asks, delighted. "How much time ahead can you set it?"

"I could run it on a 24-hour clock," Maximo thinks out loud.

"I understand what you mean, William. These are the most extraordinary children I've ever encountered," Princess Mary acknowledges, using his bare first name. It is an intimate form of address I haven't heard anyone use with him since his grandmother Princess Amalia died. From Marianne's letters I had concluded on a state of enmity between them, especially originating from the young princess. Things must be changing.

"Madam Dolfin," a lackey at the door of the drawing room announces as Clara enters.

"A surprise for the children," Prince William announces to Princess Mary. "This is their mother, the maker of the miraculous textiles you've been wearing. I sent for her when we arrived. I thought you might like to meet her. And I'm sure The Twins are glad to see her."

Clara's face shows a mixture of happiness and a distress I can't fathom. Marianne goes over to Clara and embraces her. Their closeness, in spite of the dazzling complexity of their relationship, amazes me daily. The children cheer and Princess Mary tears up.

"Thank you so much for the beautiful dresses you made for me," the Princess tells her. "They were a support in difficult times." Clara curtsies but I note her distracted expression.

Suddenly she speaks directly to the Prince. "A calamity, Your Highness. Terrible!" Everyone in the room stops short. "What do you mean?" the Prince asks.

"I was just about to leave home in the carriage you sent over for me and one of your men from the factory came up to me. The entire inventory of glow cloth has been stolen. I don't understand. It was guarded by several soldiers. But it's all gone."

"Louis! Damn Louis!" the prince exclaims in a furious sentence accompanied by soldierly expletives not proper for civil society. "I've been receiving news for months that he has been sending agents to steal it. I had tripled the guard. How the Hell did that happen?!"

"Does that mean that King Louis can now make spinning bullets?" William Bentinck asks rhetorically, aghast.

We are all silent, understanding the terrible implications. Only the Villiers girls look non-comprehending, making it apparent that the prince has told his young spouse. I don't understand why Signor Rossini displays a complete absence of surprise.

"Unless we kill the textile," Marianne responds quietly as if she had foreseen this catastrophe.

"How?" Rossini asks too casually. I wonder if he is a spy for King Louis.

Marianne looks at him with superior contempt. Only William Bentinck seems to notice her expression and regards Signor Rossini with suspicion. All others are focused on the Prince to see what is to happen next.

"Is the textile alive?" Princess Mary asks with a heat of curiosity that appears to break through her melancholy.

"Yes Princess," Maximo explains. "It is made of the same stuff that created the world."

"God?" Princess Mary asks incredulous.

The Twins nod.

"It is closer to God than any other material," I elaborate.

"He keeps it right under His Throne. It is called Red Sulphur," Johanna specifies matter-of-factly.

"Magic!?" the Villiers sisters exclaim with witch-burning fervor.

"Alchemy," Prince William responds.

"But that is outlawed!" Elisabeth Villiers responds angrily, her Protestant piety deeply offended.

"Not in the Dutch Republic," I correct her. "Alchemy is a crime in England, not here."

Anne Villiers looks at William Bentinck for reassurance. I can see on the sisters' faces that they believe to have landed in the anteroom of Hell and are gambling their eternal souls by merely being in this godforsaken republic.

"Some Magi are evil," Bentinck responds gently, "Others use their power for good, like Doctor Helvetius, whose medicine is curing Princess Anne."

"Magic is *always* evil," Elisabeth Villiers hisses, but her words go unheard.

"We must return to our laboratory immediately, Your Highness. If your men can't locate the glow cloth, we must defuse it," Marianne insists, with an authority in her voice I have never heard before. Clara is also taken aback by her aunt's conviction. I wonder if Marianne is bluffing: I have never heard of diffusing Red Sulphur at a distance. Even Trismosin has never mentioned it in his diaries. Marianne is exchanging understanding glances with William Bentinck as Signor Rossini looks on with the discomfort of a man rarely taken off guard.

"I must go home as well," William Bentinck says, his usually modest voice slightly louder. "May I invite you to my residence, Signor Rossini? I believe the princely couple could use some private time before the Dutch Republic descends upon them. I know the people are already planning a grand festive entry into The Hague for Her Highness the Princess of Orange. Some time alone must be precious." Anne Villiers looks very disappointed while Elisabeth grins, apparently happy to have Princess Mary all to herself again. She casts a merciless look at Johanna, who is blissfully unaware of Elisabeth's vitriol.

Signor Rossini can't do anything but accept the gracious invitation.

Marianne looks satisfied.

It is dark when we arrive back home. Clara has insisted on being with us in the laboratory when Marianne explains her plans to defuse the glow cloth from a distance, even when we have no idea where it might be.

On the ride back Maximo has been speculating thousand-fold, coming up with one solution to the puzzle after the next. His quick mind goes over all the possibilities with lightning speed, disproving each one with sharp logic. Finally he comes to a firmly-held position.

"I don't think it is King Louis, unless the phantom sorcerer is working for him. The sorcerer can sneak by the guards. He would be invisible to them as he does. I think we have to attack the phantom sorcerer directly. Set a trap." His logic appears seamless and we are quiet for the rest of the ride, except for Johanna, who is humming beautiful music while playing imaginary keys.

When we arrive home both Venier and Monsieur Delamarche are awaiting us. They are equally distressed about the theft, and after warmly welcoming Marianne back, can talk about nothing else.

Marianne asks them to take care of The Twins while we go up to the laboratory. Maximo is already excitedly telling his theories to them while Johanna plays haunting music on the spinet. Helvetius goes to his study, and I admire his ability to keep himself in the background, even when it is not out of his innate shyness. His views of me have changed; I know that. But I'm not comfortable asking him why.

Once in the laboratory Marianne tells us about her suspicions about Signor Rossini being the phantom sorcerer and that she has come to the same conclusions as Maximo. She makes it clear that she has brought Rossini along to set a trap for him, but has no idea yet how to set it. I marvel at the emergence of a sonorous silver Magus voice that arises from deep down in her torso. I hadn't counted on the fact that Marianne could become even more ravishing. Yet here it is! I resent Clara's presence at this moment. But as if Marianne reads my mind and inserts a reply, I feel myself being mercilessly chided by her over these disloyal feelings. I try to banish them and fail miserably. Then she tells us the stories of the caelum: about her meeting with Robert Boyle when she revealed my identity under the influence of Signor Rossini; the anticipating qualities of the caelum in the laboratory; and about her experiment on herself that resulted in the opening of her third eye through a hole in her skull.

"But you didn't have to bring him home!" Clara responds, worried for the children.

"I feel safer when I know where he is," Marianne replies emphatically. "He can cast his phantoms everywhere. I agree with Maximo. He arranged this theft, probably during the days before our departure on the 28th. We have to find out where he went before he came with us."

"Don't tell me you think he conjured up a storm to delay you," I respond, incredulous.

"No, but he could foresee it and used his time well," Marianne replies with solid conviction. It is hard to keep a mind of my own in her presence. The only other time I had this feeling was when I was with my father in Venice just before he left. Sometimes I would enter into a conversation with him strongly convinced of one thing and end up feeling the opposite even more firmly. I remember it as a sensation of sinking in quicksand. That's exactly what I'm feeling right now. Marianne has expanded into a world with more dimensions than mine and I'm having trouble with this reversal of roles. She is the Magus now and I am just an aspiring adept. I attempt to reign in my competitive spirit and learn from her. One thing I'm sure of: I want to do the caelum experiment on myself.

"So I have explored several futures," Marianne continues in a matter-of-fact tone. "But in none of them can I find memories of what Rossini has done. He wipes his tracks clean every time he makes a move. I'm most worried about Johanna. There is something in his eyes when he looks at her as if he is seeing someone else, someone he wants for himself. I want to assign her protection to Monsieur Delamarche. With his eyesight he might notice presences the rest of us don't." Marianne sounds like a field marshal lining up her troops. Her intimacy with the Prince of Orange is rubbing off. I support her plan because it is obvious and simple. Delamarche would defend Johanna with his life. And his abilities to see clearly in the dark may have him notice traces in what to us is a world of invisible phantoms. I had noticed Rossini's fascination with Johanna as well.

"And how do you want to go after the textile?" Clara asks in her typical dry manner.

"There are two ways I can think of right now. First I want to enter into Rossini's mind and search his memories, and secondly I want to learn how to cast phantoms, so I can get to the glow cloth where ever it might be."

Clara is taken aback. "You have changed terribly, Aunt Marianne. I don't recognize you. I'm afraid you're treading the path I was walking with Venier in Venice. It is dangerous!"

"Not as dangerous as King Louis' army getting hold of Maximo's bullets!" she replies in a voice that will suffer no contradiction. The gentle Marianne of old has disappeared and has been replaced by a Magus with searing clarity of purpose. I feel a sense of loss while realizing that she may be in grave danger and wonder if her apparent self-confidence is just another trick conjured up by the phantom sorcerer, or worse, by Red Sulphur itself. But I can't fault her arguments. It would be disastrous if Louis XIV gets hold of Maximo's bullets. Becoming the Second Charlemagne would be in his grasp. He could indeed overrun Europe.

"If this is all true," Clara wonders out loud, "Why would the phantom sorcerer work for King Louis?"

"It is all just speculation," I say firmly.

"No, it is not," Marianne replies. "These are futures I have seen. When we put down anchor near the coast this morning I had a vision of the whole European continent under French rule. The vision was of a future far too encompassing to change. I just didn't know when in chronological time it was to occur. It could be tomorrow or in a hundred years. I surely don't want it to happen right now. It renewed my allegiance to Prince William, not just as his friend, but as his collaborator. He is the only one who can prevent my vision of French domination from happening as we speak."

We are silent. Clara is just nodding, absorbing her aunt's words. "But still," she says after some time, "what is the relationship between Rossini and King Louis? If he is the phantom sorcerer in need of Red Sulphur, there is nothing King Louis has to offer him. So why would he steal the glow cloth for Louis' bullets?"

"Once you know that, you know everything," a sarcastic voice combining the arrogant threat of an overlord with a brazen display of omnipotence booms out with vicious satisfaction. My skin crawls. I try to locate this disembodied voice in the laboratory, but it seems to reach us from everywhere at once.

"Rossini?" Marianne calls out into the void. I have the sinking feeling that the phantom sorcerer has overheard every moment of our conversation.

Marianne rushes over to the wall where ten years ago we had hung the glow cloth scrying screen for the purpose of making the panacea. The screen had revealed our copulating selves to us, as our passions were injected into the Medicine making it incomparably potent. We had decided to keep the giant scrying screen rolled up on the ceiling in case we needed to use it again. Over time I had forgotten about its existence. Now Marianne puts up a ladder and pulls down the screen with one grand flowing gesture. It flaps wildly like a sail against the wind, then hangs very still. The first reflections are of myriads of colors.

"You can't escape, so don't even try!" Marianne calls out to the screen.

Slowly Rossini's surprised face comes into focus on the other side of the glow cloth that slowly disappears, leaving behind a stage on which Rossini looks around desperately for an exit.

"Now the roles are reversed, dear Ricaldo," Marianne mutters with satisfaction. "Now we're going to enter your memories and there is nothing you can do about it." I realize that this was the trap Marianne had set for Rossini, thinking one move further than he, deducting back from a farther future than he had. My mind staggers, realizing that she had planned to be overheard, planned to seduce him to listen in to our conversations by making it seem she knew how to defuse the glow cloth at a distance. It had whetted his Magus-appetites and she had counted on just that. Thinking back I understand that our conversation tonight didn't reveal anything to the sorcerer he didn't already know. So Marianne had given up nothing, relying completely on Rossini's curiosity, counting on the fact that he never before had an adversary who could use the same powers to which he had access.

"Keep your mind in occultation Rossini; I'm coming for you," Marianne exclaims, with a glee I've never heard before from her. She is jousting with the sorcerer, and it exhilarates her.

Rossini's figure on the scrying stage fragments as he attempts an escape through an explosive scattering of his presence. All that remains is a dense cloud.

"Focus," Marianne instructs Clara and me. "Focus intently on the days before November 28. Let your minds think about nothing else!"

From the fog, a noblewoman's boudoir comes into view. Rossini is obviously vigorously fighting against this memory's appearance, since it blacks out at regular intervals, as if the earth is spinning at breakneck speed and night occurs every few seconds.

"You can't keep your memory away from the Red Sulphur screen. It will find you wherever you hide," Marianne says calmly.

Suddenly the boudoir becomes crystal clear as though it is with us in the room. We see the back of a nude woman sitting at her dressing table carefully applying makeup. In the mirror her high breasts tell us she is young, but we can't see her face. Rossini's point of view is from a distance behind her as though he's been staring at her for a long time. Then the woman turns around. I am startled. She looks very much like my mother in the Dolfin Chapel Virgin statue, yet she clearly is not. I don't know this woman.

"Louise de Kérouaille," Marianne mutters. "What is he doing in the boudoir of the Duchess of Portsmouth?"

"Who is she?" Clara whispers.

"She is King Charles' favorite mistress. Any man caught with her without his permission would be hanged. Why her? She is King Louis' lead spy at Whitehall. He holds King Charles in thrall by way of her."

Clara is about to say something when Marianne silences her with an authoritative gesture. We see Rossini's perspective moving closer to the Duchess. The room is filled with an intoxicating perfume. I feel how irresistible she is to him.

"He has to possess her," Clara says softly. Marianne and I nod. "There is something about her that is more than just ravishing. She feels like magic to him," Clara speaks as though she can feel directly into Rossini's soul. "He can't exist without her. His breath will stop if he can't be with her. He would do anything – anything!" I feel she is right and it solves questions as to Rossini's motives for stealing the textile.

"Where did you take the glow cloth you stole from me?" Clara rages with the force of a thousand cobras, her neck flaring. Rossini's vision shivers and shakes, goes in and out of focus. Suddenly the empty warehouse at the armory comes into hazy view. After some time it sharpens.

"Where did you take it?" Clara screams. The vision of the armory warehouse waves wildly like a stormy ocean and comes to rest in the same vision of the stone armory room. This time with all the glow cloth is stacked in neat piles upon the wooden shelves. Then night falls and the glow cloth vision does not return. Out of the dark, a wall of atrocious serpents emerges and hisses at us like the petrifying head of Medusa.

"He has cast a spell of protection around his deepest secret," Marianne exclaims, "Look away!" As I turn from the gruesome vision, I already note its cold venom freezing my heart. We stand with our backs to the scrying screen for what seems like an eternity until we feel the laboratory has returned to its original physical architecture. When I turn around I see reflections of oil lamplight dance upon the opalescent pearl texture. I take the phosphorous caelum vial out of my pocket and it lights up the room brightly in pale winter sky blue. The magic is gone.

I suddenly understand: the glow cloth is still in the warehouse! Rossini has made it temporarily invisible, hiding it behind a spell so he can move when we're no longer watching. I tell the others. "If it is still invisibly there we should be able to touch it," I conclude. Clara nods and rushes out the laboratory to the armory.

"What is the ultimate secret he is hiding?" I ask rhetorically after Clara is gone.

"It must be essential if he is willing to give up Louise de Kérouaille and the hiding of the cloth to us. It must have taken him a lot of power to protect the core," Marianne deducts. "His powers are waning. This must have cost him a lot. He will be coming for Red Sulphur again soon." She pauses. "Helvetius!" she expresses with concern. "He has always been the weakest link. A materialized phantom could just enter his study and take the whole bottle of the medicine."

"Or he could come after Johanna," I shudder.

࿇

In the armory Clara finds all the glow cloth stacked undisturbed on the wooden shelves. Our confrontation with the sorcerer must have broken his spell.

࿇

Clara has left for the weaving atelier early, after a hasty meal in the kitchen with Cook. She often leaves the house at dawn to prepare the wool and inspect the looms. She leads by example. Her workers idolize her.

We're at breakfast with the children, Venier, and Monsieur Delamarche. The thick oak table is laden heavily with eggs, cheeses, breads, porridge, ale, and especially festive buttered waffles with heavy syrup for The Twins to celebrate Mother Marianne's homecoming. The children are very talkative after having finished their chocolatl in one blissful gulp which made them gasp for breath. Both Delamarche and Venier nurse theirs in small delighted sips, having developed quite a liking for this bittersweet taste of the Americas.

"Have you ever seen phantoms?" Maximo asks Delamarche point blank. The latter is wearing his daytime heavy mesh eye protection to filter out the excess light.

"In my nightmares," he replies with a smile. "And when the ale gets the better of me."

"No, I mean real phantoms. Signor Rossini casts real phantoms. They can steal things. You know, I told you!" There is an undertone of a child's exasperation with the sluggish minds of adults.

"I have thought about it," Monsieur Delamarche tells us, suddenly serious. Marianne has asked him to protect The Twins, and he was greatly honored about having been given so vital an assignment. His soldierly past is fully engaged. "I will speak with Madam Clara if she can weave me an eye mask like gauze, with low thread count to get my eyes used to daylight."

"That might give you migraine headaches and spoil your night vision to boot," Marianne objects.

"I don't think so. I've now had this condition long enough to experiment. I want to make my vision more acute. I think I can train my eyesight to see the subtle world directly."

"What if she wove you an eye mask of pure Lunaria thread?" I propose referring to the active ingredient in glow cloth, made from the moon plant called 'Honesty', mixed with Red Sulphur. "That would infuse your already heightened eye sight with superlative glow cloth vision. I could make her a dye that is much more potent than the dye she has been using."

Maximo claps his hands, delighted with developing a new mechanical device.

"Do you think it would make you hear Heaven when you put it in your ears?" Johanna asks, intrigued.

"Just try it, Hanna," Maximo suggests. "That's how I do it."

"I would wear it over my heart," Venier responds to Maximo. He rarely talks, having become a great listener.

"What for?" I ask, still not liking him too much, incapable of separating him from Mantis' deeds.

"To make his heart see the demon before it enters," Maximo explains to me, exasperated over so much mental density. I feel like a dunce and I'm not used to being the least intelligent person in a room. It is disconcerting, especially when I've begun to believe myself quite the Magus now that Helvetius and others revere me as the great Theodore Mundanus.

"That's a great idea, Giovanni!" Marianne praises me proudly. I feel the last of my frozen heart melt and realize that I'd been filled with dread and my heart had turned to icy stone in the face of Medusa. "We can make the Lunaria dye during the next full moon."

"I want to come!" Maximo exclaims. Johanna nods emphatically. I realize it may be a good moment to initiate the children into their mystery, and show them the power of Red Sulphur as it lives outside of them.

Chapter Twenty-Eight

Initiations

We have a week to make the new Honesty tincture, since the next full moon is on Thursday December 9 at 4.00 hours. That means that I have to postpone my caelum experiment on myself to the following full moon, since I don't think having my skull blown open should happen in front of the children. So I will have to live with my acute sense of mediocrity for at least another month, an ominous prospect, since our next meeting with Signor Rossini in the flesh is foreseen for Tuesday December 14 when a magnificent state entrance is being planned for the new Princess of Orange. We know that the evil Magus has accepted Prince William's invitation to partake in the festivities. The Princess has asked us to be close by and for Johanna to perform an organ recital at the Great Church of The Hague where Clara and I were supposed to have married ten years ago. She has asked her to play her variations on the Orange family anthem. Constantijn Huygens and Johanna are found daily at the church for long and arduous practice sessions.

Clara has been enthusiastic about making a more potent tincture of Honesty and tells us that she wants to experiment with the large quantity of raw silk thread she's had brought over from Venice. It is a special kind of silk from Cathay, she explains to us, highly absorbent, able to take on the richest of colors. Maximo has proposed to use it for cannonballs with a higher spin rate than even the bullets he has made from wool glow cloth. This ammunition, according to Maximo, will be exceptionally accurate, reaching much further and loading faster than ordinary canon balls. He maintains that it will make the previous spinning bullets obsolete so it won't matter who has the old cloth. I am amazed at his ability to achieve quick technical progression and wonder what it means for the future. He has told his plans to the Prince by way of his bodyguards at the munitions factory, and Clara is forced by decree to comply. She hates to use the next miracle cloth for bullets and cannonballs, and stipulates that only half can be used for ammunition and the rest must go for beauty. The Prince has agreed begrudgingly but as a precaution in case Maximo's predictions are correct – and at this point no one doubts his technical genius – has ordered more silk of the same quality through his own channels.

Since Rossini most likely will instantly know what we are up to, Monsieur Delamarche suggests the sorcerer be put to death immediately. However, we all realize that no one will be able to catch him in the flesh if he wants to escape. At this point we can only arrest his image, not his physical body. We decide that Marianne must talk to the Prince before Rossini can get to Louise de Kérouaille and word gets out to King Louis. I will accompany her. The Prince will receive us right away, finding an improbable opening in his overloaded pre-celebration schedule.

℘

We arrive at Court Honselaarsdyke at dawn. Princess Mary is occupied with preparing the arrival of five more ladies in waiting who are about cross on the yacht 'Mary' now that the North Sea has calmed down enough for the slim vessel to make the passage. It is very unusual for someone in the Princess's position to bring over an entire household of her own country-women and Marianne has told me that Prince William is not pleased. Her meddlesome Confessor, a dour Anglican clergyman, is especially repulsive to him.

We find the Prince with William Bentinck, going over schedules and paperwork as though he is preparing for a military campaign. The atmosphere reminds me of the time Marianne and I visited him in his encampment at Bodegraven to ask for clemency in the case of Cornelis de Witt.

"But how can we prevent Rossini from casting his phantom at the whore to warn her? It would take several days to get a missive to my spies in England." the Prince asks after we have told him the whole story. He responds with a remarkable absence of surprise, as Marianne had predicted. He is an eminently practical man and trusts Marianne implicitly, having seen enough magic coming from our quarters to believe in the existence of alchemical sorcery. William Bentinck's face displays lightning-quick fluctuations of disbelief, awe, fear and ridicule.

"I suggest we ask Count von Waldstein to coordinate the interception of all messages going out from the Duchess of Portsmouth," Marianne says warmly. She has tried out several futures to find the right tone to use to the Prince. "The Holy Roman Emperor has an equal interest in keeping our secret from King Louis as do we."

"That doesn't solve anything. How do we get to him in time?" the Prince asks, a slight irritation rising up as Marianne had foreseen.

"I will use Rossini's own techniques. He can put memories in people's minds that didn't really happen. I will do something similar and communicate directly to Count von Waldstein. I will insert myself into the Count's thoughts and plant the conviction in his mind that he should intercept all communications coming from the Duchess of Portsmouth." Marianne speaks with a voice of powerful Magus - authority that won't allow contradiction.

"Don't use that voice with me, Madam Marianne. You don't need to insert yourself into *my* mind!" Prince William says, gets up and walks over to Marianne as if in confrontation. "How will I know your message has reached him?"

Marianne stands tall and replies with overwhelming certainty, "You send the message via conventional routes and check it out for yourself."

Prince William breaks out in a radiant smile: "You are the most surprising woman I have ever encountered, Madam Marianne Schweitzer-Van Os!" I have never heard him call her by her full name and am aware of his deep affection for her.

At this time anything can make me jealous.

When we arrive home around noon I feel inexplicably tired and have to go to my bedchamber to rest. This rarely happens to me. Usually I have a great deal of vitality all day long.

Instantly I fall into a deep sleep and find myself in Genoa. I am walking near one of the battlements at the harbor and see a flock of homing pigeons flying back to their nests to deliver messages from the many Mediterranean trading posts Genoa maintains. I look up and see one that looks like Marianne. I'm startled and wake up completely refreshed.

Marianne is up in the laboratory and I tell her my dream right off.

She sits down and says, "A homing pigeon indeed. If I only knew how to do it, I could deliver the message."

"We know that you're going to be a carrier pigeon. So that's nothing new, we don't the dream for that," I ponder out loud. "But I was thinking: what if we use the blood of a carrier pigeon and mix it with the Medicine and then as that pigeon flies home, you and I take the homing tincture and focus on Count von Waldstein." My words carry the full force of the utterly improbable, which in this context makes them eerily convincing.

"If we do it at night when he is asleep we have the best chance to enter his dreaming. The veil is thinner then," Marianne concurs with guarded optimism, immediately running with the speed of this idea. "So where do we find a homing pigeon before the night?"

"I hear that some merchants in Amsterdam keep pigeons here in The Hague for important messages," I remember out loud.

"Maybe the Prince can help," Marianne suggests.

We decide to send out Hendrik who returns with one of the pigeons the Prince keeps at Court Honselaarsdyke for important communication with his offices in the Residence. It will take fifteen minutes for it to fly back from here to Court Honselaarsdyke. That gives us a brief window during which we may participate in its activated homing instinct and find our way to Whitehall. If it works, Count von Waldstein will get the message more than a day earlier than through the Prince's courier and spy network. Knowing that usually the Count retires early, we decide to wait until 23.00 hours to take the homing tincture.

We get to work immediately because we need to draw a drop of the pigeon's blood and have the wound heal fully with the Medicine. I take a small vial with a pipette and fill it with the Panacea. Then I carefully puncture the bird in the belly, where it will be least harmful, and extract a drop of its blood, which I catch in the prepared vial. Then I dab its wound with the Red Sulphur Panacea. It heals before our eyes. Marianne holds up the vial that lights up pink.

"We should add a speck of caelum," she suggests. "It will make travel through the subtle realm more viable." I agree and add a quarter grain of the blue caelum powder we keep in a sealed vessel. The mixture now turns purple.

"Might we use the scrying screen?" I ask. "It may give us a head start. We could try and get to the other side of the screen and participate directly in the subtle world."

Marianne looks up at me, then walks over and kisses me passionately. "I've missed you so much," she whispers. "I've been looking forward intensely to working together in the laboratory again."

For the first time since her return, I sense an absence of imbalance in myself. My spine straightens and my feet feel larger. I take her in my arms, inhaling the jasmine sweetness of her breath, and feel her resilient body move in synchrony with mine. Our rhythms readjust like horses in a span as dance invigorates our hearts and lips get reacquainted. We sink down to the floor and clothes vanish as we enter the innermost thrill of our longing. Her salty skin is a spice of Heaven, her opening to me complete. My solid pent up longing rises to sublimation. We're enveloped in a moan of ecstasy. As I dissolve into her, a brilliant purple light from the homing vial spreads throughout the laboratory, acutely activated.

At 23.00 hours we lower the scrying screen. The house is quiet, everyone's asleep. I hold up the homing tincture and shake it, making it glow even more ardently. Then, with the pipette, I drop 5 drops under Marianne's tongue and the same under mine. We sit on chairs looking at the screen and Marianne begins to talk about Whitehall, describing it in great detail. She tells me about Count von Waldstein's beautiful Berlin carriage and the time he first mentioned Rossini's existence. She relays how excited he had gotten over the caelum and of his Bohemian boyhood fascination with what he called Vampires. I can feel my blood heating up as if I'm developing a fever without feeling ill. A storm is brewing and before the winds can blow me asunder I take the cage with the homing pigeon, open the window facing the open space above The Square and release the bird. It flies up, circles a few times for orientation above the Huygens mansion, and then sets off in the correct south-easterly direction towards Court Honselaarsdyke.

The scrying screen begins to sparkle and far in the distance a bird emerges in the center. It looks unlike any flying creature I have ever seen in nature. It appears most like a dragon, with a green snake body and the bony black wings of a giant bat. I'm reminded of the enormous Nagas that chased off the bandits before the birth of The Twins. But this bird has an air of benevolence and it seems to invite us to follow it.

"That must be the pigeon's arcane homing spirit," I whisper pointing at the primordial flyer.

"We have to get to the other side of the screen so we can ride it," Marianne replies. "I think we should lie down, so our bodies won't fall when we follow the bird." I agree immediately. In order to cross the screen between worlds we will have to leave our physical bodies behind. We lie on the floor next to one another with a pillow under our heads, so we can look up at the bird. I feel Marianne taking my hand.

Suddenly, without effort, we cross the barrier that feels like a soap-bubble-fleece of thin air. In the other world we rise high up, noting features of the dark land below getting smaller and disappearing from view. We are now on the back of the arcane homing spirit carrying us ever further aloft. It feels like riding Pegasus to the heavens. Above us a thick curtain of stars forms an elongated rectangular cloud like the Milky Way. While we are passing through the star-cloud it feels cool to the skin. On the far side we start our descent; the bird is no longer under us but it seems we have become birds ourselves, flying with mathematical accuracy towards our goal. It takes me a while to realize we have become one person, a single shooting star. We come to a full stop in a sunny meadow where a woman is telling a story. The scene is observed through the eyes of an eager young boy. We realize that we are in Count von Waldstein's dream, made from his memories of his beloved Bohemian governess. We enter into the woman and become her voice.

"The Duchess of Portsmouth is about to betray a great secret to King Louis of France. Have her followed and intercept any message she sends. Remember this!" We repeat it five times. From the governess' perspective we see a young boy with big eyes looking at her intensely, imprinting each word into his memory.

Suddenly we are back in the laboratory lying in front of the dark scrying screen holding hands.

Marianne has her eyes closed. I give her time to come back to the laboratory.

After a few minutes she opens her eyes. "Rossini has not noticed our journey to Whitehall. His powers are diminished and he is husbanding his remaining energies carefully. He has traveled to Louise de Kérouaille and told her about Maximo's new cannonballs and the higher grade glow cloth. She will send out messengers in the morning and Von Waldstein's men will intercept them. The Count has woken up and is preparing it right now. All possible futures tell me this."

"How can you be so sure?" I ask awestruck.

"When Waldstein began to investigate Rossini he sent his men secretly to his lodgings on Drury Lane. I had asked Waldstein to bring me any hair or nail clipping his spies could find in Rossini's quarters. Of course his men were instantly surprised by Rossini, who materialized in the middle of the room. They didn't see him enter. But one of the men had the presence of mind to hide a hair he found in a cap Rossini had been wearing. He managed to slip it out unnoticed. I now carry this hair close to my heart. It hones my access to futures of which he is a part."

I am startled by the inventiveness of Maximo's mother. My son's genius may be due to Red Sulphur, but the proclivities stem from his mother. I have traveled in places where sorcerers get power at a distance over their victims by taking their hair and torturing it. I'm sure I have never told Marianne. She found this out all by herself. I see with admiration how she is growing in leaps and bounds. But instead of it making me feel unsure of myself, this time it gives me an exhilarating sense of pride to be with this woman.

Johanna and Maximo haven't been able to sleep a wink during the night of Wednesday to Thursday. They've come to my bedchamber at 2.00 hours, waking me up with their infectious excitement. Clara moved to a bedroom of her own some time ago, since she leaves very early for the weaving atelier, just after the time Marianne and I finish in the laboratory in the early morning hours. When she wants my bedtime company, she wears a rose purpur garment, and I am instantly filled with an overwhelming longing for her. She has learned to be discrete, never seducing me in front of her aunt. Sometimes I see her leave the house in clothes of power and I never ask her why or for whom, keeping my intense jealousy to myself. She has a life of her own and we feel distant much of the time, except for the moments when she calls me to her bed and we ravish one another. While Marianne was in England Clara and I spent more time in bed together and grew closer in the intimacy of love's aftermaths. But the moment Marianne returned this closeness vanished. It makes me sad but there isn't much I can or want to do about it. When I look at Johanna and Maximo crawling all over my bed, tickling one another, I know I love them both equally and wonder why I can't be the same with my two spouses. But Clara has told me long ago that she knows her aunt is foremost in my heart and I couldn't but agree. Marianne is nature, Clara is magic.

"Get up, Father!" Maximo exhorts me, as Johanna tugs at my nightshirt. I have long given up disciplining the children outside of their schoolwork. Their spontaneity delights me too much. There is a knock on the door; Clara and Marianne always knock in order to avoid awkward situations.

"Mother!" the children cry out joyfully, completely indifferent as to which mother will appear.

Clara opens the door and is overrun by The Twins. They talk excitedly about the coming alchemical experiment, their first major exposure to practical alchemy. We will be using the Panacea that is much stronger than the tincture we used for the first Honesty dye since it came from both of the passions between me and my two lovers, mixed in with the deep familial love between Clara and Marianne. By having the children do the mixing, I expect that their Red Sulphur nature will make the tincture even stronger still. Clara is wearing a warm skin-colored bodice of high purpur thread count. I want to take her in my arms immediately and am grateful for the presence of the children. I look at her askance.

"We need the heat," she tells me.

"What do you mean?" Maximo asks her.

"We need to stay warm, wear warm clothes because we're going to be doing the main part of the experiment outside under the full moon. Come on, children; get yourselves dressed in your warmest winter clothes, as if you were going out skating." The children run out to their rooms to get dressed.

"I discussed it with Aunt Marianne. Actually, she suggested it. The more passion the better. And I like you more when I wear this. Otherwise you're just a boring old nuisance." Her tone is bantering and full of good humor. I want to pull her into my bed, but know better. Inspired by the children, I jump up and tickle her. She runs away, screaming with feigned anger, and bumps into her aunt.

"You seem to be having fun," Marianne says drily, looking rather imposing and composed. Standing next to each other I notice that they look less alike than they did when I first met them. Marianne's face is somehow wider than it was, her sharp intelligence more directly visible, while Clara's eyes seem to have become larger with grander dreams shining forth from them. Marianne's body is rounder and more softly maternal while Clara looks lean while amply curved, and muscled like a woman used to heavy physical labor. I can feel the entire range of my loving. "When you turtledoves are done we should be getting started," Marianne concludes and turns around with an unreadable expression on her lovely face. When she turns her back Clara sticks out her tongue at her aunt, suddenly being the age of our children. With some effort I don't laugh.

I am the last to arrive in the laboratory. To my surprise, I see Helvetius. I hadn't known he was to be present, but now that he knows that I am Mundanus it no longer matters. It is only fair that he know the whole story, except for my relationship with his wife.

He looks more excited than I have ever witnessed him to be. The children are explaining everything to him.

"So the dye is made of Red Sulphur mixed with a powder made from pearly Honesty pods," Maximo explains to his great-uncle-and-stepfather.

"Lunaria?" Helvetius asks.

"No, Honesty," Johanna corrects him.

"It is the same, Johanna, Honesty and Lunaria. Just different names," I explain, walking over to them and shaking Helvetius hand. Holding on to my hand, he looks at me with open admiration, which soothes my current insecurity.

"Thank you so much for inviting me to this experiment," he mutters *sotto voce* in profound gratitude, "You changed my life completely." I nod, not wanting to talk about it in front of the children, and feeling awkward about his sentiments based on just partial knowledge of the truth. I can't help but look at Marianne, gently press Helvetius' hand, and disengage.

"Here are the Lunaria pods," Marianne tells the children who listen with ecstatic transport in their eyes. "And here two stone mortars and pestles. Grind the pods while you let yourself become Red Sulphur. Invite Red Sulphur to take your hands and do the grinding." Maximo instantly understands; it is the way he spontaneously creates his technical inventions. "Go to the place where your music comes from," he explains to his sister. She nods, glad about the clarification.

As the children get to work, a strange halo begins to surround them, like the halos one sees in icons from Trismosin's days. It scares me; I don't know if we should subject our children to this. But both Clara and Marianne look calm. Only Helvetius has staggered back to the far side of the laboratory. "What is that light?" he asks, alarmed. I don't want to explain it too much by telling him about the Red Sulphur nature of the children, so I reply, "That is the light given off by the Lunaria pods when you grind them with Red Sulphur." This calms him down.

Marianne looks dubious about my lie but then concentrates on The Twins once again. Johanna is humming haunting tunes as the Honesty comes to life while it is being infused with the spirit of our Red Sulphur children. I realize for the first time, down to my bones, that these are the first Red Sulphur children to ever walk the earth; they are a new human mutation that has never existed before. We're standing at the great Abyss and witnessing as our children conjure up the naked powers of creation.

"Get me the phosphorus and caelum light, Father." Maximo speaks with great authority, fully infused with Red Sulphur spirit. My hands obey instantly, as though steered by a foreign power.

"Rossini doesn't stand a chance," Marianne mutters with certainty.

A sudden fear overtakes me as the Devil's light bathes the room in its blue green hue. My children are the unforeseen ancestors of a new race and I don't know how to parent them. I remember my Mother Mary in Dolfin Chapel, and send up a prayer towards the Virgin who birthed a Son like our twins. How did she feel when she realized her Son was gifted with the curse of powers divine? I shiver.

"I'm grinding moonbeams," Johanna sings in a voice that combines an ecstatic nightingale with a child at play. Maximo laughs, delighted, encouraging his sister to redouble their effort.

"You can stop now," I tell them.

"No Father," Johanna tells me with the same authority as her brother's, "We have to go on till their spirits fly loose." Maximo nods, grinding away with superlative zest. "Then we have to catch them," he adds.

Marianne seems to instantly understand that they are volatilizing the Honesty powder and gets two large funnels she fastens like hoods a few inches above the mortars of the children giving them just enough room to move their hands. I get what she is doing and connect pipes to the narrow mouths of the funnels and lead them both down to a glass vessel for collection of the volatile substances emitted from the ground powder. The Twins witness our activities with approval. The amount of white powder in the mortars diminishes, and we see a thin smoke rise up through the funnels, traverse the pipes, and enter into the glass vessel. At its bottom a clear fluid begins to condense. When all the white powder has disappeared and the smoke has settled into several drops of clear condensate, I remove the pipes from the onion-shaped glass container and quickly fasten a stopper in the neck. The children cheer. We have caught the spirit of Honesty.

The clock says 3.45 hours. We rush downstairs with the onion vessel. Our boisterous movements wake up the entire household. I ask Helvetius to send the servants back to their quarters and to allow only Monsieur Delamarche and Venier Solario to accompany us to the back yard carriage house, where Hendrik reigns. We stop in the small courtyard and view the moon looking like a giant Lunaria pod crowding out all stars in the cold crystalline silver sky.

I see that Monsieur Delamarche is not wearing his eye protection. He has taken it off and holds it in his hand. He looks at the children with a stunned expression, then he turns to me and whispers, "Signor Dolfin, I once was on a military expedition to the ice lands of the north. There I saw the northern lights they call aurora. The children give off that same borealis light with swirling rays of violets, greens and blues. What is happening?" His superior sight differentiates what we only perceive as a homogenous white halo. I have heard of the aurora borealis from whale traders but never witnessed it.

"They are a force of nature, Monsieur. I don't understand it; I'm in awe."

"Is that their Red Sulphur ancestry?" he asks. He attended their birth and must remember how the Red Sulphur presence in the room had been as nervous as any new father attending the birth of his children.

"Must be," I respond at a loss for words.

The bells from the churches around us ring the four o'clock hour.

Without asking, Maximo takes the vial of the Medicine, and Johanna grabs the onion vessel firmly and removes the stopper while Maximo quickly pours in the Red Sulphur fluid. Then with a speed that escapes our vision Johanna suffocates the spirits that rush up to the throat, by replacing the stopper. Then she holds up the vessel to the great Lunaria pod up in the sky and sings with piercing clarity:

> "Behold your daughter, mother Moon
> We have caught her in a glass
> and will shake her senseless
> Until you free her from our tortures."

I'm struck with the commanding violence of the incantation and witness with amazement how both twins carry out their shaking threat until the moon relents. Suddenly a silver sword of light flashes down from the moon, and inside the onion vessel, the dizzy moonlight-haze recedes, leaving behind a shining single drop of quicksilver. Mercurius has been caught in the bottle; our twins can make the moon and planets do their bidding.

Johanna sings a hallelujah of thanks that must wake the whole neighborhood and when she is finished I quickly herd our band back up to the laboratory. Helvetius is busy sending the servants back to their quarters and has to use his full authority as master of the house.

In the laboratory The Twins are behaving once again like ordinary children who have stayed up well beyond their bedtime, chasing one another excitedly in a game of tag. Both mothers have to call them to order, and they begrudgingly comply, looking a bit sour at the interruption. They appear as though they will be up for hours still – and within minutes they are fast asleep.

"Can you explain to me what happened, Mundanus?" Clara demands after she has lovingly covered The Twins with woolen blankets. "Alchemically I mean," she clarifies, to my relief; I'm at a loss to explain my children.

All eyes are focused upon me as the senior alchemist in the room. I wait a moment to let the inspiration flow and speak to my own surprise, "The ancestor of all metals is live silver, *argentum vivum*, much like quicksilver Mercury. It is a living substance that grows like fungus in the cracks of the earth and carries within itself the seeds from all the planets, Sun and Moon. Live silver is passive; it longs to be fertilized like an egg and grow into gold. The semen it desires is Red Sulphur, the spark of creation. Our children appear to have the power to tell the planets what to do. We ordinary humans are caught in a web of destiny, bound to live our lives within limits. The Twins seem truly limitless, free from all preexisting patterns, free to create beyond the borders of what is possible. They awakened the moldy ancestor of metals and caught him in is his primal condition, open to any future they wish to command. They've made wild, primordial Mercury docile. Don't ask me how, but that's what it looks like to me."

"So they can do whatever sorcery they please with this drop of activated live silver?" Marianne asks.

I nod. "They are free," I repeat with puzzled awe.

"Should we then use it for glow cloth?" she asks. "Or should we use it for a way to defuse Ricaldo Rossini?"

"Why not do both?" Clara asks, loathe to let go of her next magic cloth. "Since we can still steer The Twin's actions for now." She can't hide an undertone of hesitation. We all realize that we are caught in a new moral dilemma as we consider using our authority over our twins to acquire their magic.

"Shouldn't we ask them?" Venier breaks his silence. I realize at once that in this room he is the first to have taken The Twins as his equals from the beginning. To us they still appear as children, to him they are his protectors from demonic Mantis and people who truly understand a life possessed by forces other than oneself. We are still under the illusion that we need to protect them and can steer their fate as their parents and teachers. Venier has none of our prejudices; he can see past their current incarnation as children, directly to their gigantic spirits. We all realize that he is right. Now that we have allowed them to become initiates into their Red Sulphur destiny, they have become adults at eight years of age, while paradoxically being whimsical little children at the same time. We can't turn back time to a moment before 4.00 o'clock this morning. They have crossed a cosmic threshold, and we will have to deal with that.

"Signor Rossini must have seen the moonlight flash from where ever he resides," Monsieur Delamarche says practically. "They may be the most powerful beings in the world, but they are still children in danger. I will not leave their side until Rossini is dead," he declares in a voice that allows no contradiction. Venier nods vehemently.

We agree to wait until the children wake up to decide what to do with Mercury's potent spirit in the bottle, and transport the sleeping twins to their room after having placed a third bed so Monsieur Delamarche can be with them at all times. Our confidence in him is complete. Venier will sleep in the adjacent room; he is sure that his experience with Mantis will help him in detecting Rossini's potential phantom presence. The knight, who the children still call Uncle Billiards, carries Johanna to the bedroom with solemn dignity, while I hug Maximo to my shoulder like a common father holds his ordinary child. Marianne follows the procession with the captured live silver. Monsieur Delamarche will guard over that as well. Helvetius and Venier stay behind in the laboratory with Clara so she can fill them in on all the details they need to know.

༄

The Twins - followed by a tired Monsieur Delamarche who stays respectfully outside my bedchamber -wake me as the church bells chime eight times. They are all over me again; I want them to go and bother their mothers and let me sleep some more, but they are merciless. Their loud mirth wakes up all the participants in this morning's early lunar transmutation and finally Cook leads us down to the kitchen where we gather for pancakes, waffles and ample chocolatl for all members of the household including the servants. Christmas has arrived more than two weeks early.

An hour later we are together in the laboratory, some of the adults looking bleary eyed, the children boisterous and bright. We have brought in chairs from Helvetius' study, and sit around like at a meeting of the Royal Society.

"We have gathered here …," I intone, taking the solemn lead. Maximo bends over in uncontrollable giggles over my officious voice. "We have gathered, gathered, gathered," Johanna sings. I'm flustered. How do I father children like this? One moment they have the powers of gods, the next they are brats. But they are right in making fun of me, I must admit.

"You're right," I tell The Twins. "No gathering. But we need to decide what to do with the Mercury you caught in the bottle." Monsieur Delamarche has put it on a small table next to him. It seems as though Mercury is anxiously awaiting our verdict like a bead of silver sweat.

"We're going to make better glow cloth," Maximo says, puzzled. "That's what it was for, wasn't it?" He looks at Clara, who can't help but nod. Marianne stares at her with an icy gaze. Johanna catches it instantly. She is very sensitive to disagreements between her mothers, who are like one person to her. "What is it?" she asks, looking from one to the other with alarm.

"We could also use it to take care of Signor Rossini and remove him from our lives forever," Marianne says firmly in her new voice.

"He isn't worth it!" Maximo utters, with disgust. "I won't spend this precious stuff on him. Never!"

"But he could harm you!" Monsieur Delamarche counters.

"No, he could not," Maximo replies with complete conviction.

"Red Sulphur would not allow it," Johanna adds, invoking their parentage.

I'm painfully aware that at this moment I'm a secondary father, trumped by the First of All. I wonder if they are as conversant with Red Sulphur as they are with me, their human father. I'm sure they don't jump all over him in his heavenly bedchamber. With a sense of humor, I note that I am jealous once again.

"How can you be so sure?" Venier asks shyly. He has been tricked by Mantis often enough to distrust demons and other spirit-beings. "Signor Rossini is a vampire, your mother told me. One of the few things I remember from when I was Brother Wenceslaus at the monastery in Bruno is that all the monks were terrified of them. They sneak in at night and suck the blood of children. I'm sorry for being so blunt, but how can you be sure?"

"My blood would kill him," Maximo replies authoritatively. "My blood hates him. My blood can make him shrivel to less than a worm. To me he is less than an ant and I don't mean to insult worms or ants. I can't wait to encounter him, and he knows it."

We are all in stunned silence. Maximo's words are spoken with the force of a king commanding a vast army. They carry no trace of his child-nature. He speaks in the voice of Red Sulphur.

For the first time I notice a disunion between The Twins. Johanna doesn't look as sure as her brother. They usually speak in one voice. "But what if he knows tricks, Max? What if he can do things we haven't dreamed of? Maybe he is made of Red Sulphur just like we are. I think we should be careful." Her caution diverges sharply from her brother's brash bluster.

Maximo looks taken aback. He has never experienced an essential disagreement with his sister and doesn't know how to handle it. He instantly becomes a child again, and looks at the floor fidgeting, unsure of himself. He is confronted with an initiation even more powerful than the one at 4.00 o'clock this morning. At this moment Maximo is realizing that he and his sister are two people. I see a sense of loneliness come over him that he has not felt before and I go over, touching his cheek with my hand to console him. A tear rolls down his face. Johanna rushes towards him and hugs him tight. Yet the shift is irreversible. Maximo gets up as if to leave, but Clara holds him back. She is always the tough parent among us.

"Don't go, Maximo; we have to talk about this. We have to decide how to use the live Mercury." Her voice is strict and he obediently sits down. His twofold nature, human child and primordial force of nature, couldn't be more glaring.

"Let's split it in half," Johanna suggests, her resilience at this moment greater than Maximo's. "Could that be done, Father?" She turns to me.

"It will be difficult," I admit. "The moment we take off the stopper he will try to escape. He is in his most volatile condition. It will be safer to do either one thing or another, or we might end up with nothing at all."

"So we only have just one wish?" Johanna implicitly quotes the famous fairy tale about the spirit in the bottle. "Not three?"

I smile about her childhood certainty that fairy tales are true. But then again, maybe she is much wiser than I am.

Maximo seems to return to his usual cheerful self, and we can see that he is bubbling with ideas.

"What are you thinking, Maximo?" I encourage him.

"I still think that our blood is poison to him; I'm sure of it. I think that if we make a tincture of our blood," he points at Johanna, "he would lose his powers."

I look at Marianne and we remember our journey to Whitehall steered by the blood of the homing pigeon. If Maximo is right about the effect of their blood on Rossini, the tincture itself could certainly be made. And if it were to act in any way like the homing tincture, it might conjure up their primordial Red Sulphur nature as it had the archaic homing flyer with the bat wings. Marianne nods.

"That's a good idea, Max," Johanna chimes in, apparently having forgotten the distressful moment of discord some seconds ago. I marvel about their ability to move from one instant to the next like in a discontinuous dream where one moment may have nothing to do with the following.

"And then how do we get it to him?" Monsieur Delamarche inquires, instantly seeing the implications.

"There may be a way," I wonder out loud, turning to Marianne. "But it could be dangerous."

"You mean if we would take the tincture made with The Twins' blood and travel to Rossini's lair and ambush him in the world behind the glow cloth?" Marianne guesses my thinking. I nod. The others look puzzled and Marianne quickly explains our journey to Whitehall to deliver the message to Count von Waldstein.

"Did it work?" Maximo asks with curiosity, his engineering nature aroused.

"I think so," Marianne replies. "But we're waiting for confirmation from the Prince's network. I suppose we'll hear on Tuesday," she concludes referring to the grand celebration for the Princess of Orange when we will meet the Prince again.

I have an instant visceral disgust of taking an extract made of my children's blood and sense the onset of nausea. "If we'd do it, let's wait till after Tuesday to see if our message truly got across to the Count," I propose.

Marianne understands my hesitation and agrees, obviously knowing my postponement has nothing to do with the impending confirmation, which she is convinced will occur. She has traveled the futures and knows. I'm distressed with the increasingly convoluted nature of my life and feel a strong need for the same caelum concoction she has taken to open her third eye. I want to wait with an open confrontation with Rossini in the world of Red Sulphur until after I have taken the caelum during the next full moon.

"So that means that I can use Mercury for silk glow cloth?" Clara drily asks us all, while masking her emotions carefully.

"Yes!" the children exclaim in one voice. Marianne and I nod. "Can we help?" Johanna asks. Clara hugs her tightly, happy for being a mother of such children and to be making the next generation glow cloth. "We'll wait till after the celebration," she says. "Your father would say that the spirit of celebration will enhance the transmutation of the silk." I smile, loving my family.

ଌ

As we ride to the Great Church, I find myself proud of our beautiful Hague, seeing it with radically different eyes from when I first came here, miserable and shivering, eleven years ago. I can see its stately new buildings and understand why its reputation as one of the finest, cleanest, and richest cities in the world is well-deserved.

The regal procession will pass through these same brick-paved streets along the bright, clear canals, accompanied by young virgins singing and strewing herbs. It will ride under triumphal arches hung with inscriptions and adorned by emblems. I'm sure the young Princess of Orange, in the open golden carriage, will be enchanted by the loving adulation that is about to rise up from the vast masses of people who have come to the Residence from all over the Dutch Republic. I am convinced she is going to immediately like the Dutch as strongly as her new people already admire their Princess. I have been hearing murmurs from women about Princess Mary's gentle sweetness, and from men, satisfied assessments of her timid obedience to her husband. I can feel a general pride among the people that their worshiped Prince has married a Princess of the Royal blood, bringing their Viceroy, already a grandchild of England, one step nearer to his grandfather's throne. Everyone realizes that this is a terrible blow to the pride and designs of Louis XIV, which makes the populace giddy with elation.

We first see Signor Rossini again when we are all gathered at the North End Palace. From there we will ride directly to the Great Church to await the official ceremonies and give Johanna a chance to install herself behind the organ. Old Constantijn Huygens is proud of his young protégé who sticks closely to his side. Christiaan Huygens looks rather sickly and is wrapped in warm blankets. I try not to notice the intimacy between him and Clara. William Bentinck tells us what a pleasure it is to see us again under these delightful circumstances: code for the fact that Louise de

Kérouaille's messages to King Louis have been intercepted by Count von Waldstein. Marianne and I funnel our pleasure over this news into the general high spirits. I don't think Rossini notices. He looks very tired. I know he will soon attempt to steal Red Sulphur. Maximo walks up to him and I'm too late to prevent the encounter.

"Hi, Signor Rossini." Maximo speaks to him in his usual fearlessness. "Are you feeling unwell?"

Rossini looks at Maximo with a disconcerting kindness in his eyes.

"Thank you for asking, Maximo. Yes, the climate does not agree with me here. It is very different from my homeland."

"Maybe you should go back there then," Maximo concludes with impolite directness.

Signor Rossini smiles sadly. "Maybe I shall indeed, Maximo. Probably sometime soon." I don't understand the way he looks at my son. It seems that my children move something deep inside him. I'm worried that he is imagining killing them for their Red Sulphur nature – of which he is obviously aware – and that he has remorse before the deed.

From nowhere, Marianne appears behind our son.

"Your grandnephew wishes I were gone," Rossini tells her with a big smile. "And I wish I could convince him otherwise." They stare at one another for a few seconds and I realize that they are each exploring potential futures with lightning speed. "Your skills improve rapidly, Madam," he remarks with good humor. "Soon you'll be a danger to yourself." Then he turns to Christiaan Huygens, who instantly believes he has known Rossini for as long as he can remember and begins a conversation about the nature of time and the precision of clocks.

Maximo follows him. "Tell him how in the end all time runs out, Uncle Christiaan. He needs to understand. " The boy's bluntness takes even the unflappable Signor Rossini aback, but before he can respond, Maximo joins his sister and Christiaan's father in a conversation about music.

I'm shaken by the fact that Maximo is facing off against the powerful dark Magus and don't think my confrontation with Rossini can wait the month till my caelum experiment.

&

The Great Church was built more than a century ago. A community of stodgy steep roofs rises behind a proud red brick tower; the grey stone nave billows up from their midst in high-windowed majesty. It epitomizes the solidity of its burghers. In each place God takes on the particular face of his local people.

My children had asked to travel with father and son Huygens and our equipage follows them with Helvetius, Marianne, Clara and me. Rossini and Bentinck close our small procession. Bentinck had requested to stay close to the Magus and has opted out from being part of the celebratory ride of the princely couple.

My two women sitting across from Helvetius and me are ravishing in their blue and blush power gowns, Marianne looking like a vision of heaven and Clara like the shell from where Venus rises forever. I am of two hearts, two longings, each one utterly oblivious of the other.

As the carriage comes to a stop before the Great Church, Helvetius says with complete confidence in my Theodore-Mundanus-abilities, "I trust that you have found a way to protect the children." To him, I am the great Magus who knows the mysteries of creation, while he is unaware of the fact that his wife's abilities by now far outrank mine. I wish I had his faith in me. But I play the part and nod solemnly. The women smile, amused.

Inside, two arched galleries of classic pillars hold up a roof that aspires to the heavens from which the church must have gotten its "Great" epitaph. In Protestant fashion, the old wooden pulpit on the right hand side is the only adornment in what is otherwise a sparse atmosphere. The iconoclast Protestants have destroyed all the rich imagery of our Roman churches to build a sober home for their Spartan God. The organ stands at the far end under mostly transparent windows; though some of them with rich stained glass cast aberrant splashes of color over the otherwise solemn grey atmosphere. Our Johanna sits down behind the large pipes, a glowing fairy in a land of stone. Old Constantijn takes his place beside her, and for a few chords she pipes Heaven directly into our hearts. The silence after it is magical.

Rossini has been placed to my left, an awkward silence keeping us apart.

Maximo, to my right, asks me loudly in obvious provocation, "Is it true, Father, that some people crave Red Sulphur like others gin?" He is on a tear and I don't want to stop him. His bluntness actually feels like a relief. I look directly at Rossini to underline his words and do not answer. There is a noticeable fidgeting in Signor Rossini as in a thunder-god hesitating to flash his lightning. For a moment I fear. Can we effectively shield ourselves from his thunderbolts?

"It appears your son mistakes me for someone else," Signor Rossini finally responds in a dignified tone.

"No I don't," Maximo replies in harsh defiance.

"Then who do you take me for?" the Magus asks Maximo directly. The church seems to resonate with his words.

"A vampire," Maximo hisses. It sounds ridiculous and I hold my breath.

Suddenly there is a strange flicker in Signor Rossini's presence, as if for a fraction of a second he isn't there.

"You're a phantom!" I exclaim, utterly surprised. My heart stops one beat, two – three. I'm terrified, trying to garner the hatred needed for his destruction. But I find I can't hate this man who has devoured a child. He looks at me with an expression I can only read as profound affection. My heart starts beating again and as blood rushes up to my head my brain is fully scrambled. To the consternation of us all, Rossini displays a tired, sad smile, and disappears.

"Everything we've thought about him is true," Maximo says calmly. "But how do we find him?"

As Lackeys announce the arrival of the princely carriage, Johanna intones the first of her many variations on the Orange family anthem.

Chapter Twenty-Nine

Storming Heaven

Another full moon approaches; the days of Christmas have passed; the new year is 1678.

For some days Johanna's variations that had raised us all to the key of love and freedom were on everyone's lips. Her prodigy status rose sky-high, and then to Johanna's great relief, receded back to public inattention.

Rossini's disappearance had not been noticed by many people, and those who did notice wouldn't believe their eyes and quickly forgot. When events are thus far from the ordinary, people dismiss them as momentary aberrations and return to their daily awareness. The events had happened in the front of the church kept open for special guests arriving in the grand procession. We were the only ones up front, so we could be visible to Johanna. It calmed her anxious mood. From the back, the disappearance must have looked like a trick played on the eyes. Only William Bentinck, who had been with us, close to the phantom, remained in a state I could compare to mine. The soldier who had seen the dreads of many war campaigns, a man familiar with death, had no register in which to place this haunting disappearing act. To his credit, he didn't dismiss the impossible, and told his Prince at the first opportunity the next day. Marianne, Clara and I were requested to come and meet with Prince William after the days of Christmas.

Meanwhile, Clara began the process of creating glow silk from the drop of the spirit of Mercury our children had caught in the bottle. Together with them she placed the drop in the small egg of the athanor furnace with a batch of the highly absorbent silk. Johanna told me that the flash of lightning coming off the material when they opened the athanor egg had been blinding, and she played it for me on the spinet with rushes of chords that were almost out of control in their explosion, like lightning striking at close range.

Clara had asked Marianne and me to be absent so she could have this particular experience with her children only. To her it felt like a next step in her art and she wanted The Twins present at its inception to the exclusion of us. She believed that the purity of her closeness to them, unobstructed by the complex relations between the three of us, would make the transmutation most forceful. I had to agree. An absolute clarity in her relations to our Red Sulphur children could only enhance the atmosphere inside the athanor. Marianne and I had reluctantly consented, realizing that the value of our curiosity could not compare with the precious nature of the experiment itself.

The responses of the silk were comparable to those of the wool from which the original glow cloth was woven: the initial batch could be used as a sourdough starter to leaven larger quantities of silk, a process that could be foreseen *ad infinitum* as it had been with the wool.

Marianne and I were waiting in fascinated expectation for the outcome of the new textile woven from the transformed thread. But only the children were allowed to follow their mother's progress. Maximo spent increasing hours with Venier discussing the next step in the capture of Signor Rossini's physical body, while Johanna kept informing us about each progression in the creation of the new material. She made us hear the events in the weaving atelier – from where all the workers were sent home for Christmas with full pay plus a bonus, a radically innovative economic act – in colorful chords of abstract music of a kind I'm sure no one had ever heard before. She allowed us to be present in the unfolding of the new magic cloth.

At times Maximo provided us with a precise verbal narrative.

"I try to follow Mother's fingers as she weaves, but I can't. I don't think even Uncle Billiards' eyes could. They go quickly like the lightning that comes off the cloth. This is lightning-cloth. Often I have to close my eyes or I will get a headache. But it seems not to bother Mother. I don't think she sleeps anymore. And when she looks at me her eyes shine like the lightning cloth itself." Johanna accompanied his words in the highest register on her clavichord, producing an eerie twang of the ethereal.

And indeed, Clara was in her atelier day and night. She had Cook give her meals to The Twins, who brought them to her workshop, where the three of them supped together.

Finally the unveiling day arrives. We're in the laboratory with Monsieur Delamarche, Venier and the family as Clara, with the help of Hendrik, carefully fastens the lightning cloth on the same rod from which the glow cloth scrying screen had hung.

When we stare at it after it stretches taut nothing happens.

"Just wait," Clara whispers, her eyes in mystic surrender. I can't help but be a bit disappointed. My expectations had risen to a fever pitch and I believed we might have found the medium by which to follow Ricaldo Rossini to his lair. So the absence of even the slightest tinge of the unusual makes my heart sink.

Johanna had insisted that her small transportable spinet on which she practiced in the bordeaux-red best room was brought to the laboratory, so she might accompany the initiation of the lightning cloth.

Suddenly twangs of the highest note sound in slow intervals like a heavenly flock of bells. Then the snowy reaches of mountains in winter come into view as the light of the cloth gets ever brighter, until it gathers into a single flash of palest blue lightning that makes the room vanish and our bodies disappear. An electric world inside a blue spark envelopes us, and I notice all my hair standing up. The smell of the air itself has changed as if it were no longer made of the volatile substance we usually breathe, and the taste of it turns into cooling azure. It has the high-mountain lightning scent of amber rubbing silk. When the visions of ourselves reappear in space, we are like soap bubbles with a filmy membrane of our transparent exteriors clothing a visible vacuum. We seem to ourselves like angels in an electric heaven.

"Too much light!" Maximo exclaims, covering his eyes.

When I look at Monsieur Delamarche I notice that he has removed his mask from his hyper sensitive insect eyes and is gazing directly into the lightning-lit-scape washing out all solid features.

"This isn't light, Maximo," he explains. "The atoms have turned inside out and we are inside their core. These are the original dancing sparks." I understand that he is right. This is the inner light of nature we call *scintillae*: the original scintillating sparks of creation that give life to each atom. Alchemy tells us that before the world was made, the All was full of God. He had to make room for His creation, and withdrew so that Space as we know it could come into being. In this newly-formed cosmos His creative essence was left behind: a sea of invisible creative sparks that ultimately cooled down, coagulated and crystallized into the encrusted atoms of our physical world. The alchemist could free these original sparks of creation by melting each atom in his furnace. From these sparks that we call the interior light of nature, *lumen naturae*, the essence of creation was slowly garnered: Red Sulphur. We are looking back straight to the origin of time through the eyes of our Creator.

Johanna's music now is close to inaudible. I didn't know a clavichord could produce such subtle sounds. It is as if the blades barely touch the brass strings.

"What do you see, Uncle Billiards?" Maximo asks, his hands still in front of his eyes.

"This is called aurora," Delamarche struggles to explain. "It is the memory of the beginning of time. It sometimes plays like music in the skies of the Northern lands where the ice lives forever. There are purples and greens, yellows, blues and violets. Yet they truly are the opposites of colors. Negative light, if you could call it that; an elemental force that removes all colors before it like a white-out storm of snow." Monsieur Delamarche stops, at a loss to further describe the paradoxical nature of this primordial element that renders the world visibly invisible. I am very impressed he has gotten as far as he has, and realize he is describing a presence we had first noticed as halos around The Twins when they were creating the drop of original Mercury. His explanation that these halos are actually negative light, eliminating the visual realm altogether, makes paradoxical sense.

"Is it a kind of invisiblizing light?" Johanna inquires calmly, stopping her music for this playful invention of a new word.

Monsieur Delamarche nods adamantly. "Except that it is not light at all," he adds.

"It's like Robert Boyle's vacuum pump for light instead of air," Marianne obfuscates the matter further. She quickly explains Boyle's pneumatic engine to the children, who are perfectly satisfied, displaying a remarkable absence of surprise. It seems that making these phenomena increasingly obscure, we have achieved clarification.

"Look!" Clara points her transparent finger at a presence that is rapidly growing into disconcerting closeness. Venier screams, as Mantis' presence overtakes the environment. It seems we were all absorbed inside of Mantis, our world tinged a swampy green.

"Open your eyes, Max!" Johanna yells, hoping her brother can repeat his destruction of Mantis in the same way he had when she was held at gunpoint by Wenzel Seyler. But Maximo is blinded and can't come to our aid.

Suddenly I notice a shaking from deep within the invisiblizing medium, like a glint off a transparent ocean contorting in storm. Venier's scream turns into a paroxysm of rage, driving out Mantis by shattering his world. I have never heard such piercing fury before, driven directly by the accumulated pain of his terrifying hostage years. It blows away the emanations of the lightning cloth, which now hangs taut and still in the laboratory.

It is cold this early January night. The moon is almost full as Marianne, Clara, Helvetius and I get out of our carriage at Court Honselaarsdyke, where the princely couple is spending their honeymoon.

To my surprise, we are welcomed into the drawing room by an ebullient Princess Mary with the Villiers sisters in tow, Anne looking happy to see us. Elisabeth Villiers has a morose expression on her face as if we are interrupting an intimate occasion – as if it were her honeymoon! William Bentinck is smiling in the background, looking the happiest of them all. I assume his courtship of Lady Anne is progressing well.

"I know my husband needs to talk to you about matters of state," the Princess says warmly to Marianne. "But I wanted to see you before dinner. I am so very happy! I just wanted you to know. I am grateful to you, Madam Schweitzer, and wanted to express my gratitude in the presence of my husband. Your support of me has been invaluable. One doesn't broach such personal subjects over supper."

Marianne bows slightly in acknowledgment, Helvetius beams like the lightning cloth, and Prince William has an air of deep satisfaction. "Madam Schweitzer never ceases to surprise us," he says in a rare moment of public compliment. I'm afraid we'll have to carry Helvetius out on a stretcher in a swoon. He can be flattered to death.

Elisabeth Villiers looks downright hostile. Might she be a spy for the Duke of York?

"Let's get the matters of business over as soon as possible," Prince William continues in his usual clipped soldier-like manner. "I'm hungry."

I can't help being flattered to think we shall sup with the couple during their honeymoon. Prince William could have given us an audience at a less intimate hour of the day to discuss the matter of Rossini. I can only imagine that he must wish to express his own gratitude to his friend Marianne for her positive influence on his bride. The Princess' attitude has reversed completely from brash anger into conjugal love. With a sour sense of distaste for his fawning I have to admit that I'm as proud of Marianne as is Helvetius.

The young ladies-in-waiting file out behind their Princess. I wonder if her entire retinue will be at dinner.

William Bentinck takes the lead and retells Rossini's disappearing act in the Great Church. "Before my own eyes!" he concludes.

When the Prince asks for an explanation, Marianne explains the phantom notion to him. He takes it in the same way he might a report of a battle, displaying a dispassionate careful attention, a quickly calculating mind and an utter lack of surprise – almost like The Twins.

"Where do you think he is now?" He asks us the obvious question.

"Maximo is sure he is still with the Duchess of Portsmouth and that he sent his phantom to travel with us on the ship home," Marianne responds. "He is smitten with her."

"It is hard to believe," the Prince replies pensively. "I've had lots of conversations with him and he looked entirely like a person."

"I had the same impression, Your Highness," William Bentinck comments formally. "He stayed at my home, slept in my guest room. If I hadn't seen him disappear I wouldn't believe it myself."

"Why does Maximo think so?" the Prince inquires, obviously holding my eight-year-old son's opinion in the highest esteem.

"He says that there was a sufficient break in time for Rossini to travel to the mansion of the Duchess and prepare himself to cast his phantom when he knew the storm was going to delay your ship," I relay Maximo's words.

"How could he have known we would be delayed by storm?" Helvetius asks puzzled.

"He can see into the future to some extent," Marianne replies, matter-of-fact.

Now the Prince is truly fascinated. "Are you sure of this?" he asks her.

All Marianne needs to do to convince him of this improbability is nod.

"Does anyone have a better idea than Maximo's?" Prince William inquires.

We are all silent. "I'll have it checked by my men in England," the Prince closes the conversation as if it concerned an ordinary strategy meeting.

"It will be hard to verify because he can make himself invisible where he is and visible where he is not," I counter. I think we had best check it by way of the lighting cloth when we encounter him in a world where he can't hide. Prince William looks to me for a solution to this conundrum.

"We can encounter him in the same way we delivered the message to Count von Waldstein," I suggest.

"Magic?" the Prince asks. I nod.

"How?" Helvetius inquires.

I don't know where to begin. "I'll explain later," is all I can say. I'm glad the full moon is on Saturday, in two days, so I can do the caelum experiment on myself and be a match for Rossini's powers.

"You have three days," Prince William tells me calmly. He turns to Clara. "And how is the progress on the new ammunitions cloth?" he inquires eagerly.

Clara is weighing her words carefully. I know how much she hates it that her art is being used for killing. Since her misadventure with Venier she is particularly sensitive to the sinister side of Red Sulphur, such as the phantom world of Ricaldo Rossini. She has talked about this to me often, relaying her fears that our children might be seduced by the same powers that had swallowed up the vampire Magus. As Clara extends the silence in the room to a significant pause in the conversation, keeping our Captain General waiting without mercy, I think about the trials I will soon undergo.

Marianne's skull-exploding caelum experiments sound gruesome enough, but they become entirely unpredictable when we mix the caelum tincture with a drop of the twin's blood and the tincture of the homing pigeon. Marianne will take the full concoction with me, certain that the extra caelum will improve her vision of future.

"The cloth is more than we had hoped it could be," Clara finally begins to speak. Just in time, as I can see that the Prince's patience is beginning to run low. A field marshal in the habit of being obeyed operates on a short fuse. "I am convinced it will create a medium for the ammunition that will make it travel faster than ever before with an accuracy that will astound us. It will seem that the ordinance will travel through parallel space, raining death as if in a dream. I hate to think of the havoc it will wreak. My conscience weighs heavy with the murder I am about to cause," she concludes with obvious disgust.

"You are a tender soul, Madam Dolfin," the Prince responds, with a sad smile displaying his own gentle side. "But we can't let the garden of Europe be overgrown with French weeds. A second Charlemagne will enslave us all. King Louis is mad with ambition. My battle against him may bathe us in blood, but there is nothing more precious than freedom; not even life itself."

"Let's not spoil the evening with politics," Helvetius suggests.

The Prince smiles at him. "You sound like the incarnation of my grandmother Amalia. And you are right. It is better to celebrate your achievements, Madam Schweitzer. Let's join the Princess of Orange and her many, many Ladies," he adds with a grin, giving credibility to the rumors that he doesn't seem to mind spending his honeymoon with a bevy of fawning young English Ladies.

This experiment is carried out in secret: just Marianne and I, assisted by Gerda. The day after our visit to Honselaarsdyke, on Friday January 7, we go off to one of the farms Gerda has purchased for her large flocks of sheep. The moon will be full on

Saturday at twenty hours and a quarter. The preparation of the tincture is to occur in her new state-of-the-art laboratory built in one of the barns. The ceiling is high and the walls a moldy green. I have given her a generous supply of the Panacea, and a strong smell of the spices and plants Gerda has used for recent experiments pervades the air. Red pepper and cardamom, turmeric of the Hindu, and the root of valerian from the swamps at the far end of the field behind the barn mask the lasting odor of a long line of cows. Purple foxglove hangs from the ceiling, used to strengthen the heart. Gerda has mixed the Medicine with most of the herbs described by Culpeper some 50 years ago and has come up with dramatic cures that make her constantly have to skirt accusations of witchcraft. Her childless condition doesn't help, women without offspring always being suspect. In her quiet way she is elated to show us around her impressive domain, worthy of a serious adept. She had two chimneys built, one sloping up to the side wall over a fireplace for the production of cured charcoal to feed the hooded furnace diagonally across with a predictable source of heat. Next to the fireplace a large grindstone wheel resting in a water basin awaits the sharpening of tools. I note at least five distillers heated simultaneously by the thick stones over the large charcoal-heated belly of the furnace. Two assistants are constantly at work to keep it at the right temperature. They treat Gerda with hushed respect. I marvel at the fact that it has only been eleven years since I met this gifted young peasant woman, who has now turned into a full-fledged alchemist. She goes over to a shelf near the grindstone wheel and returns with a two straw figurines of a little boy. "These are effigies of my brother Peter," she says. "I have drenched them in a mixture of the Medicine and the spit of my hatred toward the phantom sorcerer." Venom drips from her eyes. "He will never dare enter a room with this figurine in it. I assure you. Put it as a protection in your house so he won't be able to enter any room." I'm deeply impressed with Gerda's alchemical ingenuity.

"We'll put one in de children's room. And one in Helvetius study," Marianne replies with gratitude. "The sorcerer will never dare touch them or steal the bottle of the panacea Helvetius keeps in his medicine cabinet." She goes over to Gerda and embraces her.

It is eerie to notice Gerda standing next to Marianne without a noticeable age difference. Naturally in robust health, Gerda never uses the medicine on herself. I realize acutely how the lives of my family members are unpredictable alchemical experiments fueled directly by Red Sulphur. I am 53 years of age, but I look barely older than Gerda does at 30.

"I think we should add an essence of the Devil's element," Gerda suggests. "I have ground and mortified a small dose of phosphorus and mixed it with the Medicine. I have been using it for folks whose blood is too cold because they're old. I tried it on Klaas," referring to her old father-in-law. "He was getting sluggish and melancholic this winter and so I made a powder from the Devil's substance I prepared from horse urine. It works just as well as human urine and you don't have to let it rot. I don't do well with the stench of putrid piss," she remarks calmly in her peasant tongue. "I ground the powder for two nights by full moonlight and one night at the new moon. Then I mixed a dose you could barely see without magnification with medicine mixed with Lunaria-leaf dust to attract the moon's attention. I let it sit for several days and then decocted it again till it was pure white powder. When I gave that to Klaas with a large serving of gin, his blood began to boil and he lost all signs of melancholy. You only have to give it once and it leavens the blood for months. It had some unexpected effects," Gerda says with a grin. "Klaas can see much better in the dark and no young wench is safe in his presence."

I laugh and ask, "But why should *we* take it?"

"I'm well aware that your blood is hot enough," she replies, looking at Marianne mischievously. My beloved blushes crimson, like a young maid in springtime. "But night vision may be very helpful and you'll need much less sleep. None of us can keep up with old Klaas, and the girls he hires for his pleasure leave exhausted."

"How do you think it will mix with the caelum, The Twins' Red Sulphur blood, and the essence of homing pigeon?" I ask Marianne, who looks dubious. "Can you explore some futures about this?" She closes her eyes and I can see them roll up to her forehead under closed lids. By now I know to watch for the almost imperceptible twitches of her eyeballs as they rapidly explore the world of vision. She is silent for some minutes. Gerda has never seen Marianne practicing prophesy and looks puzzled. I take her over to the charcoal-making fireplace so the sound of the sparks will mask my whisper, and Marianne is not disturbed. In a few words I sketch out Marianne's new abilities. Gerda listens without surprise, instantly grasping the time-altering potential of caelum – the inner spark of Heaven that stems from the eternity before time came into being. I also ask her to send home the charcoal makers. There is enough fuel for our experiments. As she does so with a subtle authoritative wave of her right hand and the laborers leave, Marianne turns to us from her position next to the furnace. When we are alone she says:

"It will both increase the power of the concoction and make it more unstable and unpredictable. It gives us deeper penetration at a greater risk. I think we should use it." I so love her boldness and am instantly swayed. "It will be very volatile and become a gas so we must inhale it like I did when taking the caelum tincture at Whitehall."

"One more thing," Gerda says calmly. We both turn to her, curious what she's going to say.

"It's not really my place, but I have another alchemical suggestion. The phosphorus tincture that heats the blood has already been prepared." She points with a swing of the head to a shelf full of vials on the long side of the laboratory near the fire pit. "I suggest you take that first before activating the blood and caelum tincture during the full moon tomorrow night …" Her voice trails off, allowing the implications to linger. Then she grins,

"Of course I will have other matters to attend to elsewhere on Friday night." She obviously enjoys the embarrassed look on our faces as she leads our souls towards the heat. I find myself gazing intently at Marianne, already sensing the explosive phosphorescent nature of our impending dance of desire. She stares right back at me, her eyes unflinching.

"So that's it then," Gerda concludes drily.

During this Saturday it has been snowing lightly. Marianne remarks on the curious fact that when she did her caelum experiment at Whitehall there had been flurries as well.

"It seems as if caelum likes an *albedo* landscape," she tells me, referring to the snow-white moonlight phase of the work when the material turns bright like a silver mirror and mysterious presences arise from behind the looking glass.

Gerda brings in a large straw mattress. She spreads it out in the center of the laboratory and bows at us with uncharacteristic panache, as if she were imitating Monsieur Delamarche when he was still the jaunty knight. "May your experiment have wings," she remarks with a sincerity that belies the humor in her eyes as she unabashedly guides the ram to the ewe. She fluffs up the straw and leaves. When she is gone I suddenly feel scared. Marianne notices.

"I am too," she says, "and it will get worse. This is the most volatile experiment we have ever embarked upon and all futures are contradicting. Fate has not yet decided its course."

We instinctively sit down on the mattress and look at one another. I feel the iron in her resolve. It steadies me. I take a vial of the Devil's phosphoric essence dissolved in alcohol and instinctively shake it, though it is probably not necessary. Gerda had given Klaas 7 drops, based on the number of beats she could hear her heart pounding in her ears when she opened the vial. When I open it I hear 12 clear drumbeats before my heart settles. I drop this number for each of us into two thimbles of gin.

"Cheers," I say, and we simultaneously swallow it down in one gulp. Within moments I am blinded by glare, like flint hit by steel, and my head erupts in a flash. Marianne falls over backwards onto the mattress, grabbing her forehead, where the opening in her skull makes for a perfect red spot. I feel no compassion as my heart turns to ice. The world stands frozen as time stops between beats. This ambiance is unrecognizable: a sphere without motion, burning with frost in a silence of death. I'm locked in an unchanging state between breaths. All I feel is mild curiosity. I see Marianne contract in spasm and wonder if her feet are cold. It seems the outside snow has entered the laboratory covering it with a quicksilver frost. The walls appear liquid, dripping with disparate reflections like in a distorting hall of mirrors. My heart is a crystal as I view the world with dispassion. In a shift I observe without interest as a shy glow dawns, like a pale rose cloud of flickering stars. Suddenly an eruption of unbearable brightness blinds me once more and I fall over backwards into the same spasm as Marianne while the mirror of my soul shatters. Then darkness.

I am woken by a kiss of hot ginger burning my palate. A tongue explores me as I move through ripped shrouds of memory, not knowing where I am. All I know is that I like this kiss and don't ever want it to stop. A fragrant body embraces mine and in a flash I realize it is Marianne … though at the same time I see her body in twitching contortions next to mine. Her embrace is thick with passion as she writhes on top of me while the Marianne beside me quivers in spasms. I know I have to shake off this enchanting vision of flesh and move my physical body over to the real Marianne's while feeling languid with the seduction of this succubus. My entire being wants to give in to the voluptuous suction of the demon's presence, but clarity arises out of the fog and I know I need to get to the contorted body next to mine. A love for Marianne sparks briefly, rising up from a fire down deep.

I have to make my way down to what's real, to the fires below! Urgency rises as the pleasure increases and the demon redoubles her passion. I groan, close to surrender. Marianne's body twitches briefly; I notice her breath and push the apparition-flesh away like a heavy encumbrance. Air enters my lungs and I realize that I hadn't been breathing since I was woken by the succubus who took my breath away. My love lies rigid by my side: I have to move towards her and focus on the air she exhales! Inhaling her breath, I feel myself moving closer, drawn in by the life of her lungs. The succubus loses density and starts to evaporate as my lips touch Marianne's, and I transpose the kiss of the demon to the physical world, dispelling the magic. My beloved wakes with a startle of fear, pushing me off. After moments of being repelled, the mists lift and she bounces back into my arms like an object falling to earth. Searing heat envelopes us – life takes us back.

"The dose was too high," she concludes softly in her dry experimentalist voice; we laugh, drawn together like magnets.

"We need to hold off and use it for the experiment tonight," I respond with regret, feeling the inexorable pull of my body towards hers.

Marianne nods, "Strong forces," is all she manages to utter. Silence holds us very still, as the steel counter-forces of our wills polarize us far enough apart from one another so we don't have to melt into fusion. The effort is exhausting, so I rise and offer her my hand to get up as well. Standing, though a bit wobbly, makes our resolve more steadfast, and we set out on our laborant's chores, preparing the charcoal for tonight's transmutation. We need to constantly resist a potent pull of rubber ropes, encountering the overwhelming attraction to one another in each step we take.

It is 15.30 hours; dusk's shadows loom large. The sun is to set at 16.30 and the moon will rise at around 18.00. We will start the caelum and Red Sulphur blood activation at moonrise.

ꝏ

By 18.00 hours it has stopped snowing, but the cloud cover is thick enough that we have to decide moonrise based on the astral ephemeris and the nautical precision clock Christiaan Huygens has given to Clara. I feel a twist of jealousy in my gut and grin that it is as predictable as clockwork.

"Clara loves him, but not like she loves you." Marianne reads my thoughts with kindness. "You make her suffer … *We* do." I know that my mood is a distraction from the upcoming experiment. I will need all my focused attention. Marianne penetrates by way of my eyes to the back of my soul and my jealousies vanish to vapor. I straighten my back to regain equilibrium.

Maximo and Johanna have mixed their potent version of the caelum tincture with drops of their blood I have carefully extracted from their arms by way of a fresh leech planted on the inner heart-side elbow. The Twins grounded the leeches engorged with their blood together with the droplet of the homing pigeon's vital fluid in a stone mortar and heated the resulting paste in a cast-iron pot until it was completely calcined to less than a grain of dry powder. Marianne and I are to dissolve this powder in the Medicine through the heat of the double boiler –called Mary's Bath – while raising Moon-goddess Diana from her dark lair as she bathes naked deep in her heavenly forest.

It is bitter cold out and pitch-dark, although I imagine a faint halo rising from behind the horizon. The meadows around us are bitten with frost, and our wooden shoes crackle on the crisp snow-clad earth. Marianne shivers and grasps my hand, transmitting her fear and resolve. Our exhales rise up in steam clouds. I notice terror clutching my muscles: how will we survive this ordeal? I've known alchemists gone mad with the mere vapors of their experiments, and we are ingesting the spirits directly in much more concentrated essences. I squeeze her hand tight as we sink into brooding. Marianne is the first to shake herself loose: "There is work to be done," she utters in a deep alto voice, as she resolutely turns back to the barn. I stray a bit longer in the thrall of melancholy, then cast it off with a gesture of my right hand as if waving away an annoying insect, and force a gust of cold air down deep into my lungs. Marianne is a few steps ahead, leading the way as she often does, adjusting more quickly to changing conditions. The fields around us gleam like a silver shroud as Diana's moon forces her way towards us through translucent clouds. The Huntress awakens from her slumber below the earth. Two hours until her gown is pure silver, never finer than in that very instant. I feel the vial of powder in my pocket, take it out and show it to the goddess' great single eye. At that same moment Marianne looks back at me, then up to the moonrise horizon, and the three of us know what needs to be done.

Inside, we carefully shovel red-glowing charcoal over to the belly of the furnace, which sits patiently ready to ingest heat like a fire-eating dragon. We step back and look at one another. I notice the glistening on her pale blonde skin, a view that always enrages my passions. Now, combined with the potent elastic pull of the Devil's element, it is irresistible and I force myself to the opposite end of the laboratory, where I focus on sharpening my knife on the grindstone wheel. The blade of many travels quiets my mind and steadies my hand. Through careful contemplative action the sharp edge of the blade appears to vanish into infinity, able to split hairs. When finally I look up, Christiaan's nautical clock shows 20 hours, a quarter before the full glory of Diana's moon.

Arms extended, we meet in the center between the charcoal pit and the furnace, pressing the vertical palms of our hands against one another in order to counteract the magnetic pull, as in a well-rehearsed minuet. Immediately a fluid force starts circulating through us, hot and phosphor-green like a steady swarm of fireflies buzzing through our veins. The attraction becomes unbearable; resisting it demands great resolve. I push myself off her palms far enough to break the circuit, and take my knife to divide The Twins' minuscule amount of white powder in two on a silver plate, as silver is the seed of the moon. I note myself mirrored in the high-polish surface and reflect momentarily that this may be the last time I shall see this face, since both the visage and the vision are about to be irreversibly altered. I don't allow the flash of fear to reach up to my hand, so the blade remains steady in its task. Marianne places a teardrop of Medicine over each mountlet of powder, and we watch them absorb the white dust like glass micro-spheres of whirling snow. I take two tiny glass pipettes, suction up each drop using both hands, and turn the small vessels upside down as Marianne places stoppers over their mouths. We place the vials in the upper pot of the double boiler, and wait for the moon to be full.

When Christiaan's clock shows us 20.15, we lift out the boiling hot glass receptacles without feeling the heat on our bare skin, and walk outside, my right hand holding Marianne's left, each with a stoppered pipette in the other. In a shared trance, we take off our clothes on the silver, snowy meadow, impervious to the cold around us, all laws of decency vanished. In peerless synchrony the pipettes come undone; we put their mouths into ours and inhale the volatile vapors down our lungs and legs deeply into the earth underfoot.

The result is instantaneous. Our bodies disappear as the invisiblizing light comes over us with the sound of a grand whoosh of air. I hear a whirling of storms in the distance as the medium in which we find ourselves shakes, heavy with turmoil; dark lighting is visible at the horizon. The moon hums quietly, becoming the steadfast point in seething turbulence that scatters the vectors of time until total stillness remains in the shape of a giant Throne. We stand at its foot, holding invisible hands, awaiting the Verdict. We have joined our Creator in His shuddering Alone-ness. I realize that we are with the timeless Father of our Twins. The force of his nod blows the cap off my skull, and my brain lies directly exposed: red froth boils the gelatinous grey walnut pit, turning the tubing to writhing serpents. I've become Medusa, knowing the same is true for Marianne and I should not gaze in her direction. In a sudden instant I know what needs to be done as a perfectly honed sense of direction guides every subtle movement of my invisible body.

The rupture of time has completed, and the silver light of Huntress Moon reappears while the entire cosmos takes on the single body of Marianne.

This time I know it is truly she and not a succubus illusion; her unmistakable fragrance exudes towards me, becoming the air I breathe as our bodies are bathed in a bed of warm snow and the only sense remaining is touch. The rippling music of her silk skin plays my heart in rapid variations of pitch. The universe undulates. We ravage ourselves into each other until the sigh of Creation from the onset of time is heard once more, and we face the ultimate silence. The world begins in a glaring hot cloud as great as the timeless Throne itself.

As the waters of the Ocean recede to the horizon, the elements of both God and Devil lie down in exhaustion.

Part Fourteen

Clara

Chapter Thirty

Honselaarsdyke, August the 16th, 1678

I received the message from the princess of Orange early this morning. The request was that I come to Honselaarsdyke at my very earliest convenience. I am in the middle of a desperate effort to produce enough lightning cloth for the production of Maximo's bullets and cannonballs. Prince William is engaged in a losing struggle to oppose a peace agreement that is being forced upon him by everyone, including the Grand Pensionary of the Dutch Republic. The Prince is the only one left resisting King Louis' dictated peace agreement which amounts to surrender by the Dutch Republic. King Charles had betrayed our Prince, as was to be expected. Charles' loyalties were leaning increasingly towards Louis. Only the fierce opposition of the English people prevented him from becoming a Catholic like his brother the Duke of York. Aunt Marianne told me that the Prince knew that he was fighting a lost cause, but he couldn't let it go. He felt, and accurately so, that his heart was the only rampart against the Charlemagne ambitions of King Louis. Yesterday he fought desperately to take the town of Mons, engaging the Count of Luxembourg in a great and bloody battle everyone had been dreading. I was to supply him with Maximo's ammunition and we were working 'round the clock. So the Princess' missive came at a very inconvenient moment. Since she must have been aware of this I realized that her request was extremely urgent.

At the Honselaarsdyke mansion, I am welcomed by a man with a long narrow face and a sharp beak of a nose. Dark curly hair with strings of grey hangs limply down his shoulders. His black velvet skullcap, wide rectangular white collar, and black flowing garb signify a minister of the English church. Half-closed eyes look at me with palpable aversion.

"Her Highness is about to put a request before you which you will have to decline," he tells me without formal greeting. I let the affront pass, knowing that Dr. Hooper, Princess Mary's chaplain who had come over with her from England to guarantee her proper devotion to Anglican dogma, was known to be rude.

"Thank you for telling me." I return his haughtiness and halt the conversation.

"You are performing witchcraft for the Prince. In my country you'd be burned at the stake."

"I'm glad to be here then," I retort lightly. His dismayed mouth stretches like a flat horizontal line between his sunken cheeks.

"I will not have you endanger the eternal soul of Her Highness," he hisses. "You will burn in Hell, but not in her company."

I don't have to wait for the afterlife to be acquainted with Hell. I've know the burning demonic fires intimately during my lifetime, and his threat holds no sway over me. I look at him intently and matching his rudeness, I tell him, "Well, at least I know what company I shall be keeping in the great Beyond. And we shall not be friends there either." His eyes open wide at my curse and I am well-pleased with myself. For a moment he is taken off balance, overtaken by the fears he tries to instill in others.

From a door to our right Anne Villiers comes in to greet me warmly. I'm delighted; of all people in the Princess' retinue, I like her warm heart most of all.

"Madam Bentinck," I say, genuinely glad to see her, especially after the grating encounter with her vituperating countryman. "I have not seen you since your wedding, and then barely - just for the fitting of your gown."

"It was so beautiful, Madam Dolfin," she tells me, flush with girlish enthusiasm. "Everyone agreed that it was the most beautiful wedding dress they had ever beheld." Dr. Hooper's dragon eyes spit fire. "It protected me. It made me feel as though I was alone and in private with my beloved husband among the hundreds of people in attendance." I realize how important that must have been for sweet shy Anne Bentinck-Villiers. "I've just received word from my husband at Camp St. Denis," she blurts out in the instantly established intimacy between us, "The battle at Mons has been bloody and very great, he said. He requested I assure the Princess of the perfect health of His Highness. They shall be coming home tomorrow." After a brief silence she says to no one in particular, "I don't know why they went into battle. They were so completely outnumbered…"

I notice how pleased I am that the Prince of Orange is safe. I've always had mixed affections around Prince William ever since I met him over a decade ago, when he was a boy no older than the current age of his Princess, and his devotion to Aunt Marianne had made me uncomfortable. Since then he had forced me to use the beauty of my cloth to rain death upon his enemies and for a while I despised him for this and for the harm it might do to our twins. But now I feel a sigh of relief hearing he has come through this battle unscathed. I realize that I am firmly on his side, knowing he is right in fighting King Louis with all the might at his disposal. The Sun King is casting his dark shadows all over Europe.

"Did your husband tell you that, about the numbers?"

"Before they set out they knew it. But the Prince had this great confidence that even with an inferior number he could defeat King Louis' vast army." I'm reminded of a conversation Mundanus had with the Prince at Maximo's ammunitions factory across the street. He warned him that Maximo's bullets were just faster and more accurate, not magical. He had tried to make the Prince take heed and not become reckless by the effects of Red Sulphur. I'm painfully aware of those dangers. I had felt invulnerable with Venier in Venice with disastrous results. The Prince had listened politely to my husband. I feel weighed down by our Red Sulphur magic. Maybe the despicable Dr. Hooper's witchcraft allegations have some merit.

"Let me take you to the Princess. She is awaiting you eagerly in her boudoir," Anne Bentinck invites me. I follow her with the enraged Dr. Hooper in tow, his flame-throwing eyes searing my back. I'm glad I'm wearing protective fabrics.

Her Highness' boudoir is dominated by a massive dark oak four-poster bed with elaborate exotic carvings. It must have been brought here from a great distance - the Indies, I suspect. From the far corner of my eye, I note Elisabeth Villiers glaring at me with the same passionate hatred as the dour priest, who immediately goes over to her side. The low overhang of her eyelids and the cast in her eyes makes it obvious why my countrymen call her "Squinting Betty." She squints like a dragon - though I hear some men find it alluring.

One look at Princess Mary's glowing countenance reveals her state to me.

"How far along?" is all I ask, with a directness that takes all in the room off guard, which is my intention.

Her face is flushed. "About 7 weeks," the Princess replies in great excitement. "I want you to make me dresses of your best cloth for all stages of my pregnancy." I'm happy for her. She's not yet 16 and to her this is all a fairy tale. But when I look deeper into her eyes I note disquiet. I remember that last December, the infant of her young step-mother the Duchess of York had died suddenly, and Mary is worried about her pregnancy, even though her genuine happiness overrides her anxious affections. The Stuarts are known to miscarry.

"Can I speak to you in private?" I ask her, disregarding all protocol.

"There is no reason to speak to Her Highness without her chaplain present," Dr. Hooper says with conviction. I see that the Princess is torn. She looks over at her confessor in consternation. Elisabeth Villiers squints knives at me.

I don't want the young Princess stretched taut between us, so I decide to speak my mind right now. "Your Highness, you know that we are in full production of your husband's ammunition and you wouldn't call me over at such time to make you pretty dresses. What is the real purpose of your request?" Princess Mary looks distraught.

"I told her about the protective nature of your fabrics," Anne Bentinck-Villiers comes to her aid in a gentle voice.

"Witchcraft!" her sister caws.

"Do you think your fabrics could protect my baby?" she asks me, throwing caution to the wind.

I have never thought about this. I suppose the lightning cloth could keep harmful spirits at bay and protect her from the fevers so common in these swamplands. The fabric is suffused with the panacea that heals the plague. So I don't know why the cloth couldn't protect our Princess from the shivering ague that makes women miscarry.

"Employing a witch to so-called protect you will land your baby's soul in Purgatory if not Hell. Nothing is worth that risk!" the pious priest exclaims with utter disdain.

"It caused me no harm," Anne Bentinck intervenes softly.

"Just wait till you get pregnant!" Elisabeth replies with stunning cruelty. I have to end this.

"Yes, I believe our alchemy can protect you from the dangers of many illnesses, though maybe not all. My fabrics are infused with the same medicine that keeps your husband strong and controls his asthmatic condition. I'm sure the Prince would concur."

"Your Highness," Dr. Hooper implores anxiously, "Don't be seduced by the evil ways of this barbaric country. There is good reason why alchemy is illegal in civilized nations. It harms the soul and relegates it straight to Hell!"

I've been reflecting on this since the first time the courtiers talked about my witchcraft at the Hofburg in Vienna. I've discussed it with Mundanus and Aunt Marianne. She had told me that at the English court the superstitious invocations had been even more adamant, especially in the Lady Mary's immediate circle. We hadn't decided how to respond, since we know for a fact that far and wide all over Europe and the Colonies women are burned at the stake. Others are thrown into rivers with stones attached to their feet, only able to prove their innocence by drowning. These accusations are serious matter. Only in these more tolerant Lowlands does reason outweigh the old beliefs. I hear the voice of my grandfather fulminating gently, but with iron resolve, against these mindless customs, themselves more evil than of what they accuse the hapless women. One thing is certain: reason does not help against accusations of witchcraft that are fed by a blind fear of the bottomless Abyss from where devils rise at nightfall. I know that dread myself when confronted with the sinister interest of the Phantom Sorcerer in the blood of my children. The only difference is that I know the magic to reside at the Red Sulphur heart of matter itself, active in everything we touch. I notice a pang of fear and the flint of resolve.

"Your Highness," I direct my words exclusively to the young woman with the shivering soul, "when my uncle was first given the medicine he believed that it couldn't possibly exist. Its properties repel common sense. It garners the mysterious powers of nature. Your chaplain is right to warn you. Our minds do not understand the powers we involve when we apply the Medicine. Alchemy indeed engages magic. But it is the magic of nature, not of the Devil. Your sister the Lady Anne would have been dead without it. It is a magic that saves lives. How can that be evil? Do you believe your sister's soul will go to Hell because the medicine was allowed to save her?" Princess Mary is holding on to one of the richly carved posts of the exotic bed looking diffidently at her confessor.

"The afterlife is eternal, Your Highness. This life is only a brief breath," he replies with conviction.

"Is my sister going to Hell?" she asks him directly.

"The Lord may forgive her because she didn't know she was given a witchcraft concoction. But you are making a decision. That is an altogether different matter. Your soul and that of your unborn child are in the balance."

I didn't expect his voice to have a mellifluous register. His threat has an aspect of seduction beyond the brimstone he wields. I suddenly have a vision of a fierce rope tow over the future of the young princess and her offspring. I realize that this future child holds Europe in the balance. This child she carries will immeasurably strengthen Prince William's position and will bring him and Princess Mary a step closer to becoming King and Queen of England. The child will ally the Dutch Republic with England, combine their riches, and erect a serious citadel against the would-be Charlemagne. The battle our Prince has just lost would have been victorious if King Charles had sent troops. The political implications of this pregnant moment can hardly be overestimated. If Dr. Hooper has his way, not only will the Princess be devoid of protective clothes, but if she were to succumb to the ague fevers, he would prevent her from taking the Medicine as well. Then I hear the voice of my grandfather Maarten van Os. I let myself be steered by his words. "There is much in nature we do not understand, Your Highness. Most forces are unknown to us." Distractedly I notice the bright August sun hit a floral pattern on the wall, lighting it up with serpentine vine shaped patterns. Princess Mary looks at me with keen interest and I know that my words need to carry her. Dr. Hooper's beak looks vulture-like, ready to sweep down on carrion. I know that he has been trying to sap the fierce independence of the Princess' spirit since her pregnancy became apparent.

"But we know what our Faith tells us," the bird of prey intervenes. "We shall not succumb to the voice of the Devil. We know that the Afterlife awaits us and we have to avoid the fires of eternal damnation!" I can see the effects of the immovable certainty of his words on the Princess. It seems to push her back against the bedpost. Anne Bentinck instinctively reaches for her hand; her sister Elisabeth's eyes spit fire. "Alchemy is the Devil's handiwork. It has recourse to the help of demons. We know how the Devil seduces by promising life and good fortune. Think of the tortures to which you will subject your infant for all Eternity!" I can feel how feeble my grandfather's faith in the uncertainty of knowledge sounds, when compared to the conviction of dogma. I remember Grandfather taking me out to the courtyard in the back of our house. I had been frightened by one of my mother's spells of crying and had fled to his bedchamber. He pointed up to the stars and said: "Look at the incomprehensible work of God. Behind the firmament resides the force of creation. Look at the stars and you know that there is so much more darkness than light, so much more invisible than visible. You may not understand your mother's tears. But each star tells us that God believes in us. We are made of the same material as those points of light and the love you feel for your mother is what the stars are made of. Just look at the lights." I sat on his lap, leaned back and looked up at the great expanse, and thought I could see the kind face of God behind the stars. It didn't surprise me that His face resembled Grandfather's.

"It is the same love that created the Medicine as grows your child. God placed his secrets in the heart of nature and calls upon us to discover them like eggs for Easter," I declare.

"Some eggs grow demons, Your Highness. That's why we have to be vigilant and put our trust in the wisdom of the Church."

I take a white lightning cloth stole I carry over my shoulders to protect myself from the summer heat and place it over Princess Mary as a thin film of starlight. I know my weavings can say more than words.

"That's her witchcraft," the shrill voice of Elisabeth Villiers caws in alarm, and I can see the chaplain move in our direction with hatred in his eyes, ready to rip my fabric to shreds. Anne Bentinck steps in front of the Princess, briefly interrupting the swoop of the vulture.

"It feels like a cloud of angels," the Princess whispers softly to no one in particular.

The fabric shines with the light of the face behind the firmament and I can see the countenance smile. For a brief moment love outweighs the forces of dread.

"Please make me dresses," Princess Mary begs me gently.

ꟹ

When I finish the gowns and send them to Princess Mary, they are refused. We know that Prince William has returned from his bloody battle for the protection of Europe in the despondent state of a man who has been robbed of his mission. He spends his days hunting in the company of his soldier friends, caring little for his pregnant wife. I am certain Dr. Hooper has destroyed my lightning cloth stole.

The work at the atelier comes to a halt. As part of the Nijmegen "peace" agreement Prince William has had to concede to stop the production of his magical ammunition. The armory is dismantled and I made the unilateral decision to destroy the lightning cloth I'd made for the bullets and cannonball, while Maximo independently has broken all the molds. French pawns take up residence in the now empty armory across the street from our home to make sure no ammunition is being produced.

Christiaan Huygens has returned from Paris for a brief visit. His position at the French Royal Academy is becoming increasingly untenable and the pressure on him to leave is rising by the day. Since I am being considered a crucial enemy of France, every step I take is being watched by at least ten spies, and my chances to meet with Christiaan have diminished dramatically. If we flaunt our relationship, he will not be able to return to Paris.

ꟹ

Dressed in Venier's clothes, I leave the house by myself. I like wearing men's dress. The blue and peach doublet hides my form and makes me very aware of my breasts. The round gold buttons barely contain the tight stretch across my chest. It is strangely exciting, making me feel virile, as my hand clasps Monsieur Delamarche's rapier, with its shapely hilt hanging off my hip. My dark brown wig with its waterfall of curls looks manly and proud like a mane. Damask gold breeches flow into Mundanus' high leather boots he wore on our first visit to the North End Palace. I'm ready to conquer the world. Even the street looks different as I cross it in the guise of a young man. Men keep a respectful distance and some ladies of my station glance at me with seductive approval. What might it have been like had I been born a man? With my twins, I can see how Maximo owns the world as a matter of course, while Johanna is tentative, remaining hidden behind a polished exterior. They are equally gifted beyond measure but Johanna's bearing is less confident than her brother's. Most likely I would not have been a weaver and my spirit might have found a manly outlet. Possibly I would have been a portrait painter, or a sculptor of stone. I know I would not have been a soldier, though I could have liked fencing. I might have conquered many a heart for sport. I notice how my footstep falls louder on the pavement of the square, tapping out my proud manly strut. The grand Square itself looks different, as though the mansions look smaller and less imposing. Would I have wished for this? To be a man? A beggar moves toward me carefully, trying to provoke my kindness and generosity in an elaborate ritual of submission. I hand him a small coin and he calls me Master. It is strange to be Master. I'm aware of the muscles in my arms, ready to draw my sword. It makes me indeed a master of the streets. Around me are the trees of the rectangular Square, created by Constantijn Huygens from the lot he received near the Court Pond from William's grandfather and Amalia van Solms. He created a classicist square along the tractates of the great Italian architect Vitruvius. Mundanus makes fun of it all the time, pointing out that everything is just a bit wrong, making it a cold stilted copy of the contained exuberance in the classical Italian architectural masterpieces. Nowhere around me do I see

King Louis' spies. I threw them off my track, making me feel more buoyant still. Would I have loved Mundanus if I were a man myself? Socrates was surrounded by young men, loving them into wisdom, so why not Mundanus? My head is twirling with questions and I wonder what it would be like if I had just dreamed being a woman for all my life and found myself a man upon waking. It is a mixture of eerie attraction and profound confusion. My toes feel the straw in my boots, reminding me that they are not my size, and I slow my pace. In my heart I notice a sharp pain. Far in the distance behind me I hear faint sounds of the organ we built with old Constantijn Huygens in the armory so Johanna could practice her music. It is the only thing left in the otherwise empty building. We had asked the Prince of Orange, who owns the building, if Johanna's organ might stay and he had consented. Now the French inspectors get to hear Johanna's heavenly music daily, something that fills me with resentment. The music stops. I've probably gone too far away. There is a sudden urge to return but I keep it in check. I must be feeling guilty about my decision to give myself to Christiaan. I smile. I've tried to do so before but have never been taken by this shy man who has worshipped me for over a decade. I feel like an exile from my family as I venture out into a world that does not include them. My manly feelings recede as I approach Christiaan's doorstep. He doesn't know I'm coming. We've corresponded and he has expressed his sadness that we can't meet here in The Hague now that I am viewed as an arch-enemy of France, as the author of the rain of death upon her soldiers. I feel my rapier, left over from an earlier age when battle was close-up and not yet a distant hailstorm of anonymous bullets and cannonball. My hand on the elegant hilt can sense the waning age of chivalry killed by my far-reaching bullets. It may not yet be fully realized, but I feel I am standing at the dawn of anonymous mass killing, and suddenly I loathe myself and my illusion of manhood. I have supplied the world of men with their weapons so they can unleash the demons of Hell upon one another. I despise King Louis, but he is right to consider me as a purveyor of death. My mood of exile increases. I now feel estranged from myself, no longer knowing who I am. The nasty Anglican minister is right; I deal in witchcraft. As I erect a witch's stake in my heart and burn in the fires of self-recrimination, I walk up the stairs to the Huygens home, noticing from the corner of my eye that an obvious French spy is staring at me. I feel hot guilt and turn my head, looking the enemy straight in the eye as a punishment for my wrongdoings. I know that he does not recognize me. His handsome face is a question mark.

A maid opens the door and I tell her that I have a message for Master Christiaan from Doctor Helvetius. I am shown into a room to the right of the hall with two massive marble staircases leading up to the living floor. I've never been treated as a stranger in the Huygens' home before and relish the moment, looking at the building with alien eyes. Mundanus is right: all the cold gleaming marble feels off. There is too much effort in it, too much emphasis. In Venice I have seen marble dance, playful like the waters of the Grand Canal. Here, even though the morning sun shines in through the windows on this late summer day there appears to be a Spartan rigidity in the unbending stone, as if the Nordic winter ice has frozen the white marble, at home in Carrara but in exile up North.

The door opens and Christiaan's older brother Constantijn the Younger enters. We've met on occasion and I know him intimately from the stories told me by his sister Susanna. Besides being a famed maker of telescopes, he is a master organizer, able to oversee grand ventures with ease, deeply involved in the Orange family enterprise of statecraft and a trusted Secretary to the Prince. At 50 he lives with his wife and son in his father's house.

I feel a sudden playful urge to see how far I can push my man-being charade.

"Sir," I say in the deepest register I can manage, "I've come to see your esteemed brother Christiaan with an urgent missive from Doctor Helvetius," I intone.

"Well Madam Dolfin," he replies unfazed, "how early is this carnival? I much like your guise. It is quite fetching. I'm sure my brother will be most taken by the inverted charms of your manhood." His tone is full of amusement and his reference clear. Whores frequently dress as men to titillate their customers, I have been told. Constantijn the Younger has a sensual round face with a long brown wig like the one I'm wearing. He looks at me with discerning eyes that reveal little of his inner workings, much like the look of a card-playing master of bluff. His sister Susanna had told me that Constantijn keeps extensive diaries and that if one doesn't want matters to go down to posterity one better keep them from her ever inquisitive gossip-loving brother. The grin fades from his face and unexpectedly, he thanks me: "It is most thoughtful of you to come to us in disguise. Your status with King Louis is rather low, shall we say. Thank you for protecting my brother. I will go up and tell him you are here. I was just about to leave. Maybe my wife and I could have supper someday soon with yourself and Signor Dolfin." Not awaiting my response he turns to go back upstairs and apprise his brother of my arrival. His invitation sounds like an act of politesse not to be taken literally.

I ponder what it is about Constantijn I don't like – I can't quite put my finger on it, but it must be related to his incisive perspicacity behind a closed face. He's so different from his younger brother who is open and clumsy, at least around me. It must also have irked me that I had no effect on Constantijn whatsoever, taking me back to my days before the irresistible Venusian fabric, when my life went unnoticed. I must still be feeling insignificant without the magic. I hadn't been aware of it and it makes me cross with Constantijn, who is actually quite handsome. … Oh no! What is it with these Huygens brothers and their splendid minds?

Before I can answer my own question, the door opens, and Christiaan enters with a broad smile on his face. "Sir!" he exclaims with uncharacteristically loud gregariousness, possibly intended for the servants. "I'm so glad you bring me word from the venerable

Doctor. Won't you please come upstairs to my study?" I realize that he wants me to continue the charade until we are in private, and I'm happy to oblige. I use all my newly gained masculine charm and praise my ancestors who made me tall. I almost stand face to face with him and I see him inhaling my perfume while looking approvingly at my attire. I understand the ladies of the night; it is indeed quite effective. Just to make sure I open my collar to show off a shawl with a haze of purpur I wear under my martial garments. I feel desire rise and I want to kiss him. He clearly has the same wish and we bounce up the stairs. I do, that is; I notice how he is out of breath after the fourth step up.

"Are you still weak?" I ask him when he closes the door of his dark wood study behind us. Books are everywhere. It looks like a laboratory of the mind rather than a library. Abandoned yellow copper telescopes hide in corners, and the smell of tobacco infuses every particle of the air I breathe. I'm reminded of the air around Grandfather when I used to sit unobtrusively on a low stool, watching him and Aunt Marianne do inexplicable things. I saw their movements like a dance and felt my body whirl with their rhythms. I pick up a book from his desk, not so much to look at it but in order to have something in my hand. It is a heavy Latin tome about optics. "Are you not taking Uncle Johann's medicine?" I inquire, pretending to be interested in the Book of Optics by Alhazen. Christiaan has told me about it and I know it to be the central reference work in the field, which must be the reason it lies prominently on his otherwise remarkably uncluttered desk. The surface is in stark contrast with every other place in his study. It tells something about the workings of his mind, creating a small space of clarity in the mysterious world of time and space. I notice the quiet tick-tock of several clocks displaying the exact same time. A rough drawing of the moon of Saturn and its rings that must have been made in the era when he first discovered it hangs next to a large upright pendulum timepiece.

"Alhazen was a great mind," he replies, non-committal.

"Why are you not taking the Medicine?" I ask him point-blank in order to cut off one of the long oratories on optics Christiaan employs to hide his attraction to me. He looks like a schoolboy caught in the act, and I melt. I walk over to him, take his face in my hands, and gently kiss his lips. He tastes like a tobacco pipe, very different from Mundanus, who chews mint leaves before he comes to my bed. I stroke his cheeks and see that his eyes have receded since last we met, the darkness around them enlarging as an encroaching cloud of death. His hair is still his own, long and curly and a mustache adorns his lips setting off the sensuous nature of his mouth over the mischievous dimple in his chin, giving him the appearance of determination and pause.

"Your health worries me, Christiaan," I say softly, noticing a deep concern for this man who has cared for me with no demands over so long a time. I want to feel his touch and caress his skin. It is the soft skin of a man who is not exposed to weather, living an interior life of study and contemplation. His hands cup around mine and I can feel the callouses left behind by his toolmaking. The telescopes and clocks around are primarily fashioned by him. His fingers are strong and I desire them on my body.

"I know, dear Clara. Susanna tells me so in every communication we have, hoping it will induce me to take your uncle's medicine."

"So you're not taking it?" I ask him, almost incredulous. I thought we had been able to convince him. I'm suddenly reminded of the dour Doctor Hooper who rules the life of Princess Mary.

"For what reason?" I implore.

"Because I know it will change me. Because I know it works. Because you're not growing any older, and I don't want to leave the natural order."

"Prince William is taking it, and he ages normally," I argue.

"But I would have to take a much larger dose to make it work," he explains dispassionately, as though he were describing an experiment in natural philosophy. "My ailment is not chronic, as is His Highness' asthma. I have a wasting illness devouring me slowly. I'm eaten alive like a lobster - leisurely, over a good glass of wine." His attempt at levity falls flat, giving me an indication that he is not at all lighthearted about his health. I wish I could take the medicine in my mouth and kiss it into him. I pull him tighter towards me and long to insert myself into his physical well-being with a remedy of my own. I kiss his eyes, his cheeks, and then I linger in play with his shy tongue tasting like pungent tobacco. He tries to disengage, but I move my hands behind his head and feel his thick curly hair while pulling him close. My newfound manliness gives my arms extra force as our breaths fuse in a kiss. I feel pressure on my breasts held back by the tight jerkin pushing roughly against my nipples that desire to be free and felt by his skin. His hands obey my demands and our embrace sheds all restraint, as we give in to a longing that has been brewing for a decade. Impatiently I fumble at removing my male attire till it irritates me to the point that I have to call in his help to undo me. His fingers are about as clumsy as mine and I'm sure he has never removed men's clothes before, other than his own. Our common inexperience adds a delicious adolescence to our passion. I wear my Venusian undergarments and his already uneven breathing now pants in staccato rhythms of unbearable desire. We are naked and plunge into a funnel of carnal love that carries the seal of permanence. This is for life. As I feel his abandon inside me I leave behind the memories of who I was and drown in a sea of senses. He sinks into my body, and I no longer know where my flesh ends and his begins.

Afterwards we lay very still.

There is a hard knock on the door. Someone on the other side is out of breath, as if he has been running up the stairs.

"Open up, Christiaan!" I hear Constantijn the Younger's voice. "This is very urgent!"

We quickly disengage and Christiaan covers himself with a dark-blue silk scholar's robe. He opens the door slightly to keep me out of view and slips out. As I struggle with the buttons of my unfamiliar attire I hear heated talk outside the door. By the time I am mostly dressed Christiaan knocks on the door and enters, followed by his brother, who looks at me with obvious distress. I suppose it is related to the compromised condition in which he has found us, though I know him not to be a prude. I think of their sister Susanna's words and realize that this occasion will certainly not slip by Constantijn's diarist habit. Christiaan and I will be part of gossip history. Or maybe he will spare his brother. While thinking all this with some consternation I'm suddenly aware of the content of Constantijn's words directed at me.

"I was just at the Inner Court," he bursts out, referring to the courtyard across the Court Pond a few minutes from here, where the States General of the Dutch Republic gather and the Viceroy Prince has his offices, "They are looking for you all over, Madam Dolfin. His Highness has received news that your daughter has been abducted for ransom by King Louis' men."

The ground gives way from under me, and Christiaan catches me as I fall.

"How do we know it was King Louis?" Christiaan asks as he holds me up. I feel his arms around me and I focus on a point on the ceiling to hold me steady. I want to hear Constantijn's response while at the same time the world recedes like the wind as I don't want to know what I'm hearing. My whole being resists. This can't be true!

"A ransom note was found," Constantijn replies hesitantly.

"What does it say?" I blurt out through the fast-building fog.

Constantijn hesitates again.

"Tell her, Brother," Christiaan commands him, as he moves me over to a chair and sits me down with exquisite care. Distractedly I notice that I love him.

"It says that in order to get her back Signor Giovanni Dolfin needs to go to Paris to release her."

"On what terms?" Christiaan asks gently, as if his voice tries to guard me from blunt reality.

"No terms. He just has to come to Paris and present himself to the court of King Louis. No harm will be done to your daughter.

In a separate personal note signed by the King Louis de Bourbon himself he assured His Highness of this."

In the ways of Europe's monarchies, the Stuarts and the Bourbons are cousins. Prince William is a Stuart from his mother's side. In my anguish I feel a simultaneous sigh of relief. These personal notes outweigh political treatises. They belong to more intimate family matters. Louis must know the personal significance the Dolfin family has to his cousin-adversary. Then the fear for my daughter is instantly replaced with a fear for Mundanus. In a flash I realize that this is the work of the Rossini, who has notified King Louis of Giovanni Dolfin's true identity.

I regain my balance and become alert once again.

"And the note didn't say anything about what Signor Dolfin needed to bring?" I insist emphatically. I see a quick flicker in Constantijn's mind as his eyes squint briefly.

"There was a strange drawing on the ransom parchment we can't decipher," he replies in an uneven tone of one who is not used to being ignorant.

"I assume that it is an alchemical drawing and I'm sure my husband and aunt could understand its symbolism." I'm convinced the drawing is a symbol of Red Sulphur.

"I shall return to Paris today," Christiaan says with certainty.

"I will join my husband on this journey," I respond gratefully. Christiaan's instantaneous willingness to risk his livelihood and his membership of the French Royal Society for me by potentially associating himself with my husband, his longtime rival for my affection, moves me deeply. I suddenly feel like my husband: I love two men equally. "Could you have the note sent to us, please," I ask Constantijn.

"His Highness wishes to speak to you, your husband and your aunt today," Constantijn concludes the conversation. I feel an acute pain in my heart as molten lead gushes in through a vital breach.

Maximo is beside himself. I have never seen him in paroxysms of rage. He looks like an adult, his 9-year-old boyhood having receded entirely behind his Red Sulphur nature.

"I will destroy him," he rants. "I will poke out his eyes and tear him to shreds." His hoarse voice rasps like washboard and I can hear that he has been screaming for a long time.

When I enter the house, still in disguise, having been brought by carriage from the Huygens' mansion, Maximo barely recognizes me. Mundanus looks in my direction, quickly guessing the reasons for my charade, and regards me with pain and disapproval, as if I caused the abduction of our daughter. I feel my back lengthen and stare straight back at him with un-averted gaze. Then the pain in my heart makes me relent, and I walk up to him and embrace him as if I truly were a man. As my arms enclose his back I feel tears arising from deep within him as he is fighting back a wail of sorrow. Then I give in to my own despair and sob.

Aunt Marianne is holding on to the flailing Maximo. He suddenly calms down and looks fully entranced. Venier recognizes it instantly and says in a gently voice: "Give in to it, Maximo. Let Red Sulphur take you wherever it wants to go." Maximo and Venier leave the wine-red living quarters downstairs, and I follow him. Venier makes a small hand gesture, indicating that Maximo has to follow his possession like a sleep walker. I realize painfully that Venier is much more conversant with the state in which Maximo finds himself than am I. With sorrow I see the door close behind them.

Monsieur Delamarche sits in the corner of the room. Uncle Johann is attending to him with sniffing salts. He moans in barely audible utterances. He was with Johanna when she was taken.

I walk up to him with cold anger. She was under his care.

"Speak, Monsieur Delamarche," I tell him bluntly. "What happened?" As Delamarche begins to whisper softly, I exclaim, "Speak up!"

"Calm down, Clara, please. He can't help it," Mundanus tries to soothe my hostile tone.

"We entrusted her to him!" I respond with intransigence.

"He came looking like Signor Dolfin and told me she had to come with him to see you," Monsieur Delamarche finally says.

"The Phantom Sorcerer took my form and tricked him," Mundanus says. "It could have happened to anyone. He can conjure up any shape. And now that Rossini knows who I am he can just dress his phantom in his memory of me. He tricked Gerda once when he came to her in the guise of her brother Peter. Monsieur Delamarche is not to blame."

I instantly see that Mundanus is right, but I can't let go of my anger. I need to blame someone and don't know what to say, so I glare at Monsieur Delamarche, who casts down his eyes. I look about me and note distractedly that I don't like the wallpaper. It is too red. I hadn't noticed it in the decades I have lived in this house. It reflects my mood and I realize that I'm in the same red rage as is Maximo.

"I'm going to kill both Louis and Rossini," I exclaim impotently.

Aunt Marianne comes over to me and touches my arm gently. In her eyes I see quiet sorrow. "I know what you're going through, Clara. But we have to keep a cool mind."

"She's not your daughter," I hiss viciously. "You don't know what I feel!" This has never been spoken out loud: that we each love our own child more than the child of the other; that our children are not twins but half-siblings. The silence in the room tastes like the sulfuric ice of the Underworld.

The bell chimes in the front hall. We hold our breath, dreading any news that might arrive.

We hear Mina open the door, and all pour into the checker-tiled entrance hall to the house.

A messenger from the Prince brings the parchment ransom scroll and a request that we be at the offices of the Prince of Orange within an hour.

Mundanus takes the scroll and we all stand behind it as we read the ominous text and stare at the image above the words.

A red sun rises over a city at dawn on the far side of a river. In the foreground is a landscape of barren trees, a yellow-and-blue-flowered intimation of springtime arising shyly from the grass. It is painted with the precision of an illuminated manuscript.

"There is no doubt," Mundanus proclaims. "It is the last picture of the Splendor Solis called *rubedo*, the emergence of Red Sulphur."

"Why would he have used Splendor Solis?" Aunt Marianne asks. "He could have used dozens of other Red Sulphur images. Why does he use a picture by Salomon Trismosin? We never told Rossini about your ancestry."

"He needs no explanation. He can find things out in sorcerers' ways," I say, despondent. "He wants you to bring the Red Sulphur in exchange for our daughter. How come neither of you anticipated this? You both can see the future - why not this one?" My voice is bitter. What's the use of all their alchemy if it can't even protect my daughter? "He surely is a much better sorcerer than the two of you combined!" I know I can't trust their powers to guide me during this most horrible disaster in my life. My own death is nothing compared to my daughter's!

"He must have lulled us into a false sense of security, I suppose," Aunt Marianne admits ruefully. "We thought we caught him with the Duchess of Portsmouth memory. But maybe he just allowed this as a strategic sacrifice. Maybe he was one step ahead all along."

"I don't think so," Mundanus corrects her. "I think he made this plan up long ago, and then spent a lot of effort to keep this secret in deep occultation. That may have been the core he was protecting when we caught him in the glow cloth."

"All this speculation is useless. All we know is that we've been outwitted. We need a real strategist. We have to take the Prince of Orange into our confidence," I posit in a tone of voice that doesn't tolerate disagreement.

When we enter the Prince's official Viceroy Offices across from the Hall of Knights where the seven provinces of the Dutch Republic are currently meeting in parliament, we find him crestfallen. I'm moved that Prince William be so distressed about Johanna's disappearance, but it is quickly established that he has barely registered her abduction. The Princess of Orange has caught the shivering ague fever so often suffered by delicate visitors to these morass lowlands, and her pregnancy is in serious danger. From the window we can see ducks and tall white swans on the Court Pond floating around a tiny tree grown island. The late August midday sun lights up the wood paneling in this place of power, where the fate of our republic is being decided on a daily basis. As we enter, Grand Pensionary Gaspar Fagel, Johan de Witt's successor, is taking leave, his portly body sweating profusely in the summer heat. I had never seen him before and instantly like his genuine modest demeanor that contrasts sharply with Johan de Witt's supreme authority. He looks at me with pity and wishes me a strong faith to get me through these trying days. His words are simple, true and moving.

"Is she not being administered my uncle's Medicine?" Mundanus asks with surprise. I resent that he hasn't followed my encounters with the Princess. I had told him that the dresses I had made for her protection had been returned by Doctor Hooper, but he had been too absorbed in his alchemy with Aunt Marianne. The fury, mixed with extreme worry, must be visible on my flushed face, but I keep silent.

"That bloody Hooper has poisoned her mind. He has convinced her that the Medicine is witchcraft and she has been demanding that I too should stop taking it for the sake of my soul and that of our children to-be. I'd rather be damned than listen to that sick pretext for a man."

"But she may miscarry," Aunt Marianne exclaims in dismay.

"I can command armies, but I can't force my wife to do what is best for all of us. I told her it is a matter of state. If she loses the child our position in Europe will be much weakened."

I find it a heartless comment and am ready to take on any man. My masculine demeanor has carried forward from this morning even without the charade. I instinctively feel for my sword and am slightly surprised that it is not there and I'm wearing woman's clothes. Someone here needs to be a man and be blunt!

"She insists that she will not risk the soul of her child," the Prince adds, despondent.

"Then force her!" I exclaim with passion. "There is not going to be a child if she does not take the Medicine." Aunt Marianne looks taken aback. One doesn't talk like that to His Highness. But to me he is no Highness, just a weak, fumbling boy incapable of making a firm manly decision. And then I no longer care about his troubles, thinking only of my Johanna in the claws of the phantom sorcerer. I know that my aunt and husband are going to be pale and mealy-mouthed, and swallowing down my tears decide to take the lead.

"But that is your business," I add crassly. "We've come to speak of another danger. And that danger is not just to my daughter. King Louis is on a mission to get hold of the most powerful force in the world. If he gets it, he'll be Charlemagne. It is called Red Sulphur and the picture on top of the ransom document is a symbol for it." I suddenly realize that if we let him know that Mundanus possesses incomparably large amounts of it, William will demand it for his own purposes and I'm instantly sure that he will employ the most heinous tortures to achieve his goal. Aunt Marianne may be his closest friend, but his mission to thwart the imperial aspirations of King Louis comes first. I have to move differently than planned. The fact that neither my husband nor my aunt had foreseen this eventuality makes me realize that I have to make a tactical retreat.

Prince William looks very intrigued, all his personal worries forgotten. "You mean the gold-making material you use for Maximo's ammunitions cloth and Helvetius for the medicine? I thought Theodore Mundanus possesses it. And no one knows where he is."

"I know how to find him," Aunt Marianne intervenes with a sonorous voice. I realize that this is indeed the only way to go. The Prince would never torture her personally. "I think it is Rossini who abducted my grandniece and he is using my family to get to me, and ultimately to you, Your Highness," she adds formally, making it clear that this is not a personal matter but one of state.

The Prince utters a profane curse in the direction of Rossini. "Where is this Mundanus?" he asks finally.

"In Paris," Aunt Marianne replies. "But the King does not know where. He needs me to reveal his whereabouts."

"So why did he ask for Signor Dolfin only?" Prince William asks, puzzled.

"I can't read his mind. But he must realize that one of us knows and he supposes it is Signor Dolfin. The question is: how do we get Johanna back without giving up Mundanus and the Red Sulphur? My niece is right: if King Louis can torture Mundanus into submission, he will provide the King with the powers of Caesar."

I realize that my aunt has checked her strategy against many parallel futures and must have found that this would be the one the Prince could endorse.

William of Orange instantly transforms into a field marshal devising a battle plan.

"If you give me Mundanus' location I could have him warned and arrange for his escape. We will have the exchange of Johanna and Signor Dolfin occur on our southern border between the northern provinces and the Southern Netherlands." The Southern Netherlands are currently occupied by King Louis.

"I would suggest the same," Giovanni responds. "I'd rather have myself than my daughter in danger."

"With the exception that I shall warn Mundanus myself," Aunt Marianne adds. "I'll go by separate carriage. My niece goes with her husband to take Johanna home."

"Why is that?" the Prince inquires neutrally.

"Let's not insult one another," I interject. "We all know that you need the Red Sulphur just as much as does King Louis. It would be exchanging the wolf for the fox and Mundanus would never go for it." I sound appropriately like the desperate mother of the abducted daughter so I can say anything I please. Inside myself I feel the spreading of an eerie calm I can't explain.

Prince William smiles briefly. "Of course you are right, Madam Dolfin. Were he not to cooperate, I would send Mundanus to the rack. King Louis has the upper hand in Europe at the moment and if I could change the balance of power, I most certainly would. But what if the King catches you?" he asks Aunt Marianne, with genuine apprehension well beyond his soldierly concern.

My aunt looks at him with deep affection and remains silent. Her silence spreads throughout the room and the peaceful scene on the Court Pond.

We shall wait till next morning to leave for Namur, a Dutch city close to the border of French occupied territory, so Prince William's emissaries will have a chance to ride to Paris ahead of us and propose the exchange between Signor Dolfin and Johanna to King Louis. Aunt Marianne is to ride to Paris in an inconspicuous carriage used by the Orangist spy system.

It is evening. We haven't seen Maximo and Venier since we've returned from the Inner Court. They have ensconced themselves in the laboratory and we all know we should let Maximo stew in his Red Sulphur nature. As with a sleepwalker, it is dangerous to wake him in mid-trance.

When he finally comes down, he carries a bag with him. His eyes look tired and he is crying, so we know that he's back to being a child.

As Maximo sinks down to the floor of the wine-red room, Venier tells us that Maximo has been working without interruption at inconceivable speed, as if he were following directions.

"He hasn't stopped since morning. I had no idea what he was doing. I could recognize that he was possessed by Red Sulphur, so I let him be. I couldn't see the movement of his hands. They went faster than my vision could follow. He spent over two hours grinding some blue substance with a pestle until it all evaporated. Then he added something glowing and compounded it with something barely visible left behind in the mortar. He ran down and got bread dough from Cook, and then wrapped tiny amounts of his mixture in little balls the size of a pea. When he was finished, he collapsed. After he came to, I asked him what it was he had made; he told me he didn't really know and that we should go down to ask his father," Venier concludes. "It is in the bag."

Maximo holds the bag tightly between his legs. I ask him to open it for us. He does so obediently. In it we see the little peas Venier has talked about, wrapped in wool together with some amber stones and pieces of silk textile.

"What do you remember, Maximo?" Mundanus asks him gently, knowing that his day in the laboratory is like a fast-fading dream.

"I took some of the caelum you gave me, and for some reason I began to grind it until all of the husk had disappeared and only invisible essence remained behind. Then I did the same with the Devil's element until it had become invisible, but I still knew it was there. I kneaded the invisible stuff into the dough and then I searched for silk and amber. I haven't tried it out yet so I don't know what it is for," he finishes in the voice of a child who can barely keep his eyes open. "All I know is that it is more explosive than gunpowder."

"The *lumen naturae*!" Aunt Marianne exclaims in awe. "He has penetrated to the essence of the *scintillae*!" Mundanus nods, apparently having come simultaneously to the same conclusion.

"And by using the sparks from the *elektron* he can ignite the phosphorus, which in turn unleashes the powers of the *lumen naturae*!" Mundanus adds, completely overwhelmed by our Red Sulphur son's discovery. Yet, I have no idea what they are talking about. Maximo sits up, nodding. I can see in his face that even though he understands their explanations as little as do I, he knows instinctively that they are right.

Mundanus and Aunt Marianne are looking at one another in complete bafflement.

"What is it?" I ask.

"We've been trying to do this for the past years. The caelum we made was only a gross presentation of its actual subtle form. In one single day Maximo has approached the essence of Red Sulphur much closer than what we have been able to do in a decade."

"I still don't understand," I insist, my head spinning.

Monsieur Delamarche and Helvetius have come down from Helvetius' study and have listened in to this strange conversation.

"Can you explain it, Uncle Johann?" But he just looks at Theodore Mundanus in awe and remains silent. So I turn to my husband. "Tell me!" I order him in the tone of an army captain.

"The alchemists of old tell us that the powers of our Creator are everywhere in nature. They are the essence of every atom. The visible atoms are the body of this power. But at the heart of that body lives the invisible essence of pure creation, the *scintilla*. What your aunt and I have been able to do is to undo most of the physical husk of the *scintillae* but we have never been able to get to the pure essence itself. That's why it still had color, blue. But Maximo has been able to take away the last of its enclosure and set free the essence itself. He has made the subtle body of Red Sulphur. The last step needed to make the Red Sulphur of Trismosin is to compact a vast amount of subtle scintillae together so it forms something that has the appearance of gross matter, but isn't truly. It is very dense subtle essence of creation. We don't know what the invisible essence Maximo has caught in dough will do, especially if it is mixed with the essence of phosphorus. The phosphorus could ignite it and the essence of creation could start expanding as it did when God made it. That would cause a giant eruption, completely unpredictable." Mundanus stops, awestruck.

"Will it work?" Venier asks.

"It could incinerate us all. Or it could rupture space itself. I don't know. I sure wouldn't want to try it," Mundanus concludes with conviction.

"Then why the amber?" I ask.

"Amber is called *elektron* by the Greeks, because they found it on the shores of their seas and believed that it came from pieces of the sun that broke off when it disappeared under the earth at night. One of the names of the sun was *elektor*, the bringer of brilliant shining light. So they called amber *elektron*. When you rub amber on silk, it magnetizes the amber and sparks can come off. This power of amber has been called the *electric* force. Maximo intends to have the electric force spark the Devil's element, which in turn will ignite the essence of Creation and set it off like cosmic fireworks with the powers of the Sun god himself. I wouldn't touch it." Mundanus grows silent and can't be induced to say another word.

I stare at the peas in Maximo's bag where he has concentrated all his Red Sulphur rage over the abduction of his sister in tiny balls that are the essence of cosmic destruction. I despair over having electric children with the powers of Apollo, the Sun god.

"I want you to take them, Father," Maximo tells Mundanus in a voice that has suddenly returned to its Red Sulphur nature, sounding as if it comes from deep down an echo-well of wrath. "If they do any harm to you or Johanna, I want you to destroy them." When he speaks in this voice he is uncontradictable, his will much greater than ours.

"I will sew them into your undergarments," I follow Maximo's orders. Mundanus nods, as if under a spell.

"But what will happen when you use it, Maximo?" Venier asks. He is impervious to Maximo's Red Sulphur presence, having known possession intimately. This confuses Maximo, who instantly becomes a little boy again and begins to sob.

"It may give you the power to part the sea and lead you out of slavery," Helvetius intones unexpectedly.

"Or incinerate you," Aunt Marianne repeats Mundanus words. She takes Maximo in her arms as he cries like a baby. We stand around them, rocking together, Maximo's face against Aunt Marianne's cheek, while I'm holding a bag of explosives.

I see Mundanus' eyes drift off and roll up in his forehead. I had seen Aunt Marianne do the same when she was investigating futures. I know my husband now has these same capabilities.

Suddenly he returns to the present: "The Princess of Orange is about to miscarry. You have to go over there at once, Helvetius. You will not be able to give her the Medicine because Dr. Hooper will block you. But you have to be there to help the Prince. This will happen in the next 24 hours." Mundanus rarely calls Uncle Johann by his Latin name - only when it is a matter of the greatest medical emergency.

With a slight bow Helvetius nods in profound respect, asks no questions and goes up to his study to fetch his physician's valise. As he takes his leave he says, "Whatever you decide to do, bring back Johanna safely." Mundanus has tears in his eyes. I take Maximo's bag to go over to the atelier and sew the magic peas and pieces of elektron into Mundanus' silk formal undergarments, where they will not be discovered when he will most certainly be searched by King Louis' men. Aunt Marianne takes Maximo up to her bedchamber so he can rest close to her body until she leaves in the dark of night.

ഇ

Mundanus and I leave at four in the morning, thus giving the Prince's messengers a 14-hour head start. They'll be going much faster on horseback than we will travel by carriage. Aunt Marianne has left earlier, to voyage in disguise along a separate route. Old

Hendrik has insisted on being our coachman. He is very distressed over the abduction of Johanna and has been liberal with his gin. I feel that Hendrik may be too old for this trip, but I don't have the heart to tell him. His overwhelming loyalty is a constant blessing. He has promised to avoid the drink.

I have worked all night on the sewing of Mundanus undergarments so they will be comfortable for the long ride. It was good for my hands to be busy. It gave me time to reflect about this horrible moment in my life. It is peculiar how it coincides with my realization that I love both Mundanus and Christiaan equally; differently, but with the same intensity. I need to talk about this with my husband. Not that I need his forgiveness, or even that I care about his judgment. I don't. But I want him to know that I understand double love now, like the feelings he has had all along for both my aunt and me. However, these considerations fade behind my profound anxiety over the fate of my daughter. My personal life pales into insignificance when I compare it to the life of my child. How much rather would I be in danger myself, die myself, in order to have her safe.

We are several hours into the ride. I have slept and upon awakening am pondering my realizations from last night. And then I realize with a shock: King Louis will never go for this exchange. He knows, or at least Rossini knows, that he has much more power over us with Johanna than with Mundanus. I know that Giovanni feels the same way as I do. He'd rather die than have her suffer. The exchange is not going to happen. As this realization washes over me, with the stench of a sewer suffocating me with revulsion, I sit up, startled.

"What is it Clara?" Mundanus asks me with a gentle concerned voice.

"He's never going to let go of Johanna," I say in a strangled voice. "He wants you both in his power." In the morning light I see him grow pale and know instantly that he knows this for a fact to be true. He has seen this future.

"Why did you go along with this travesty?" I demand, suddenly in full command of myself. "What else do you know about this future?" Furies rise throughout my being.

"That's all I know," he responds timidly.

"And Aunt Marianne knew as well," I say aghast.

"I don't know. We didn't speak about it. But she knows futures better than I, so I suppose she does."

It is hot in the carriage; the late summer heat is unseasonably fierce. We have crossed the great rivers on our way south and are on rocky post-coach roads. The metal of the wooden wheels clashes loudly with the sandstone rocks and we sway and hobble furiously as Hendrik tries to keep maximum speed.

"So are you going to give him the Red Sulphur then?" I speak loudly to have my words be heard above the raucous of the carriage.

"I didn't bring the Red Sulphur," he replies softly so it barely can be heard.

"Aunt Marianne has it," I conclude.

He shakes his head.

"You left in at home?" I exclaim, incredulous. He would not willfully risk the life of our daughter in this way. But he nods. I have a vision of my daughter being put to death, and I lunge towards him to scratch his eyes out. But he has anticipated my outrage and catches my hands in a steel vise grip. I have never been this furious in my life. I feel betrayed by the man I love and the woman I trusted. They are playing with the life of my daughter as though it were a game. Then everything grows eerie quiet. The noise of the carriage disappears and I know what it is like to *hate*. I hate this man across from me who restrains my hands so I won't maul him. My heart is cold and hollow. I look at him with venom.

"You wouldn't do this to our daughter. You would bring the ransom. You would give up everything for her as would I," I lie to myself out loud. "Mundanus would never betray his daughter. Who are you? Are you Rossini? Are you one of his phantoms?"

He steadily holds my gaze. I can't read the expression in his eyes, but I know he is not a phantom.

"What do you have to say for yourself?" I pierce him with my voice like a sword.

"If I give King Louis the Red Sulphur it will be Rossini who gets it. It will make him all-powerful and the results are too horrific to contemplate.

"So you are willing to have our daughter die," I conclude. "You are a coward, Mundanus. You're not a man. You're not standing up for your child. What limpness is that? I thought you would do anything to protect her. And this is not about Rossini getting the Red Sulphur. It is about the bloody mission Trismosin has sent you on. You know that King Louis will convert all of the Red Sulphur into gold. Even Rossini couldn't prevent that. He could finance all his wars and built his palace in Versailles. You want your mission from Hell to continue, leaving your daughter dead in its wake. You are not a man, you are a flaccid louse. The great Theodore Mundanus is a phantasm." I try to hurt him as deeply as my words will cut.

He sits motionless insofar as the bumpy ride allows and waits for my storms to pass. They won't, I know. They never will. I despise him. Finally he speaks:

"I will probably not survive this. But together Marianne and I have enough power to get Johanna to safety. Maximo knows this too. That's why he provided me with the explosives."

"Which you'd never use," I remind him.

"I would if it could save Johanna. It would probably kill me, but it could save her," he replies coolly.

"What is that power that could resist an army of the most powerful King in the world combined with the forces of a sorcerer who has steadily outwitted you?" My rage diminishes slightly and I feel a faint curiosity arise.

"When Marianne and I took the combination of caelum and phosphorus mixed with the blood of our children, the density of our presence in the world we at first only saw behind the glow cloth got stronger. We now can enter that world at will without the scrying screen. We can bend people's minds so they will not see us and we can overpower their will. Rossini can do this too but he is weaker because he has no access to fresh Red Sulphur. In order to keep these powers you have to constantly imbibe the original *scintillae* of Creation so you can stay close to the Source and bend time back to its origin. Red Sulphur is the essence of creation and it lends you the powers of God."

"But you're risking our daughter's life!" I insist. "Your powers are untested."

Mundanus remains silent. Then he nods. "I am risking her life; you are right. But the risk to the world is much greater if King Louis and Rossini get hold of the Red Sulphur. Many people will die."

"It is our daughter you're speaking of," I yell. "To Hell with the world! It is Johanna!"

"Johanna would want me to take this risk," he says calmly. "She is the daughter of Red Sulphur and she knows what it means for it to fall into the wrong hands."

"She's a child, for God's sake! She's nine years old!"

"She is that too," Mundanus concedes. "But not just that. She is also a direct descendant of the Source of Being, endlessly much closer to that Source than are we. You saw that yesterday with Maximo: he did more in a few hours than Marianne and I accomplished in a decade. Our daughter isn't just a frail child. She is the direct offspring of Heaven. She is as close to an angel as anyone has ever been."

"Wenzel Seyler could have killed our angel," I object.

"But he didn't. Maximo was there. I believe that's the reason why Maximo made the explosives for us. They are to protect her in his stead."

"So you're asking me to put my faith in your untested powers, to trust your alchemy. You want me to entrust my daughter's life to your magic?"

"Our daughter *is* magic," Mundanus concludes, and refuses to say another word. The noise of the carriage is suddenly unbearably loud.

For hours we sit in brooding silence. We stop to change horses. Hendrik will pick up our horses on the way back. We barely have time to gulp some ale and rush down a tepid partridge. And we're off again.

"Christiaan is on his way to Paris," I say in a non-committal tone, once the meal no longer ferments in my stomach causing a slight nausea.

"That's kind of him," Mundanus responds cautiously.

"I love him," I add to hurt his feelings.

"I know," he replies.

In order to torture him some more I loosen my bodice and show off some of Venus' purpur cloth.

"You don't have to be crude," Mundanus moans, the telltale signs of desire displaying on his face and other parts. He can't keep his eyes off me. I release more of the magic textile and reveal the upper foothills of my bosom. I notice sweat on his brow.

"Stop it, Clara," he utters, hoarse. "I'm glad you've found Christiaan Huygens. I hope he treats you well. He is a worthy man. And God knows I don't deserve any claims on you." He is panting by now, his passion barely restrained.

"I want him," I add cruelly. I hate my husband for putting our daughter at risk. My desire to punish him waxes like a tropical storm. Then to my own surprise I lean forward and kiss Mundanus with raw eruptive desire. I devour his mouth and sob with fury as I all but tear off his clothes ready to rape him. The pain I feel needs immediate quenching, my burning heat wants to be doused by his seed. As he draws the curtains of the carriage we disrobe in a trance – I ravish him with searing hatred and viciously strangle his manhood between my thighs.

After it ends, I despise him still. Love takes ferocious turns.

Chapter Thirty-One

September 1678

After 40 hours of the fastest possible ride along a circuitous route at close to 6 miles per hour, we reach the confluence of the Meuse and Sambre rivers at Namur at nightfall. A group of French soldiers, surrounded by Prince William's troops, awaits us on this pre-assigned spot. As we expected, we are told there shall be no exchange between Johanna and Signor Dolfin. They want him to change to another carriage but to the consternation of King Louis' men I vehemently refuse to leave him. Screaming at the top of my lungs in perfect courtiers' French I make it abundantly clear that I'm not going anywhere without him until I have my daughter back. Our drama unfolds on the modern cobblestone pavement along a 90-degree corner of quays aligned with prosperous merchant homes rising some five stories above the rivers. In the distance I see the ancient fortified city walls and distractedly notice that this is an attractive town. Curious citizens stare at us from a safe distance and Prince William's men don't intervene.

Mundanus walks up to the leader of the Frenchmen, a sergeant-at-arms of small stature dressed in a grey uniform coat down to his knees, with bright red pants and a broad red belt. His face has the blunt brutality of a man used to killing without remorse, yet his proud mustache twitches nervously. He obviously doesn't know how to deal with outraged women he is not permitted to rape or kill. I understand him. Just having come down from a horrific fury I pity any man.

I see Mundanus whisper something in the soldier's ear. The sergeant looks startled and frightened. I wonder what is going on and stop screaming. Then Mundanus says loudly in French so everyone can hear, "Sergeant, I would really appreciate it if my wife could accompany me." He instantly concedes. I don't know what happened but I'm grateful to Mundanus for the outcome. The sergeant breathes rapidly like one who has come to the surface after almost drowning.

As we enter into the French equipage Mundanus signals to Hendrik to go to the nearby inn and water the horses and take care of himself. Then he has to bring the news back to The Hague that both Mundanus and I are on our way to Paris.

This carriage is much less comfortable but faster than ours. It has no suspension and hobbles painfully over the unpaved roads and muddy paths.

"Thank you for doing that, Mundanus," I tell him as a peace offering. "Seeing what you did with that soldier makes me feel a bit safer. Maybe you *can* set her free. Tell me what happened." Having witnessed Mundanus' superior power over the mustachoed man gives breathing space to my strangulated throat.

"When I saw how afraid he was of your screams I realized that something must have happened in his life that makes him terrified of women. I could sympathize with him because your fury during the ride had given me a fresh respect for a woman's wrath." He smiles. I don't know how to look back at him so I keep a Regent's mask of neutrality. "I realized at that same time that I can't live without you and that you *had* to come along with me to Paris. Not just for your or Johanna's sake, but for mine as well. I was willing to do anything to keep you close to me. Suddenly I entered into a Caelum world of vision. I saw the sergeant's scabbard tremble, and then behind the rough hand touching his sword a small boy's hand appeared. With my eyes of vision I saw him being chased down a sandy road by other peasant boys much bigger than him. He feared for his life; it was over a girl. I recognized his dread and addressed it directly. I whispered softly in his ear, 'Nothing bad has to happen if you do as I say.' I noticed how his scabbard trembled even more. I was holding his raw terror in my hands and mercilessly squeezed his heart like a sponge. Then I hissed, 'The woman is coming with me. Just tell your men.' After he ordered them to let you join me I let go of his heart."

I can see that he is well-pleased with the powers his newly acquired Caelum vision can work. I feel safe for the first time in two days and lean into him; he strokes my hair. His scent calms me while he speaks. "I've realized that I love you not for your magic garments but for the resilience of your spirit. You're a formidable adversary, Clara. I've been thinking of the young girl who looked up to me as her Savior and must admit that it flattered me then, even if it made me feel uncomfortable. But you have no childlike trust anymore. You're the mother of my daughter, fighting for her like the tigers I've seen in the land of the Hindu."

I remember why I love this man.

A long road lies ahead and I have no idea where we're going.

We soon enter occupied territory and take leave of Prince William's men, who have accompanied us until then. Mundanus' powers make it so we're being treated very respectfully by what are now our jailors. At regular intervals the carriage stops for refreshment and relief. I barely notice my environment, as I spend most of my time sleeping on Mundanus lap, completely exhausted from my extreme worries about my daughter. Mundanus has assured me that in no vision of the future he can discover any harm done to Johanna. She seems to still believe that she is with her father.

After two days more of riding we can see Paris in the distance. Mundanus points out the landmarks to me. I see a white church on a hill far away. But our road keeps Paris to our left as we cross the Seine River by way of two ferryboats (there is an island in the middle of the river.) Then we are entering the town of Louvecienne.

"Where are we going?" Mundanus asks out the window. But no manner of pressure on the soldiers through his Caelum powers can make them speak. They must have been sworn to the most complete secrecy. Finally we enter upon the largest construction site I have ever seen. Thousands of workers haul stones, and many buildings are half-finished. A whole town is being erected.

"Versailles," Mundanus whispers. "We're going to see him personally. He hates Paris and spends as much time here as possible, overseeing the building himself." He can't help but have a tone of awe in his voice. This project is the largest architectural event ever to take place in Europe, and it takes his breath away.

"But I thought we were going to the Louvre Palace in Paris," I utter, confused.

"I've been told that King Louis is always worried about a revolt of the nobility as it happened when he was a child. In Vienna Von Waldstein mentioned that the King intends to move his whole court here when the building is done so he can control them more easily than in Paris. Waldstein said that the King spends much of his time here now together with a core court, the architects and his mistress. He is overseeing every detail of the building. Waldstein mentioned that King Louis is always followed by a small orchestra, who make music wherever he goes. Maybe Johanna is playing for him here in Versailles."

"Is that good or bad?" I ask him anxiously. The thought that Johanna is performing like a trained monkey for this brute of a man disgusts me. I look out over the vast construction project and marvel despondently over the magnificent ambition of this would-be Charlemagne who believes himself to be Apollo the Sun god.

"I don't know how to assess it. Johanna steals everyone's heart with her music. I hope it's true here as well. His mood in Versailles is better than in Paris. So maybe it is better to see him here. But the futures are unstable like an unmade bed. He hasn't made up his mind." Mundanus looks out and absorbs all construction out the window. "It will take years before this is done," he mumbles. "They have already been building here for over 15 years! This King certainly is tenacious."

"Tell me about him. All I know is that he is a ruthless tyrant and wants to rule the whole world. But there must be more to him. He's bankrupting the state to create something beautiful." As an artist I recognize beauty and I'm afraid the King is a fellow artisan. I need to hate him, but surrounded by the force of his imagination, with thousands constructing magnificent architecture, I waver.

The same must be happening with Mundanus because he tells me, "They say he's a good musician and plays the guitar. He's apparently an excellent dancer and organises great ballets; he's a magnificent rider, on par with Prince William, and like him, he loves hunting. Waldstein says the King is very gregarious, always involved in outings, fencing, putting on shows, and in playing parlor games, billiards in particular. He's been surrounded by the great playwrights like Moliere and Racine, and he loves all kinds of art."

"If he weren't the Devil he sounds actually likeable," I ponder out loud against my better judgment.

"No, he's definitely not likeable. A man with absolute power is never likeable. He is feared. He is awe inspiring, but you never like him. That's dangerous. Then he catches you unawares and you're dead. I wish we had brought Delamarche. He knows the court inside-out," Mundanus ends wistfully.

The horses ride in front of the main section of the palace. New construction is occurring on the giant terrace on the second floor in the back of the palace. The entire floor is being converted into the largest single hall I have ever beheld; the noise is loud and shrill. The King must love all this building to be willing to live at the centre of it, like a conductor surrounded by an orchestra of stone-deaf masons.

I'm trembling, filled with an unspeakable desire to hold Johanna close to my body.

The carriage rides along the right wing of the palace to the left of the back terrace. We stop by a side entrance and are ordered to alight. We're now surrounded by tall, bearded guards with shiny metal breastplates covering dark blue garments under sandy-colored vestments, dark wine-red pants, black leggings and shiny black shoes. They look imposing – as they are supposed to. I notice that I look at their clothing with instant precision in order to center myself. An unfinished hallway with vaulted ceiling leads to an open door by which we enter the palace. The guards separate me from Mundanus and I know instinctively that no matter how loud I scream, it will not be of any help this time. I cry, suddenly not knowing if I shall ever see Mundanus again. My heart drops down a well as I stand in this cold deserted room of grey stone surrounded by my valises, abandoned in a way that leaves no doubt that I have not been invited and am now on my own. I feel hollow.

Looking around me I realize that I am in an as-yet-uninhabited part of the palace. I have no idea if someone will come to get me so I decide to sit down and wait. It is no use wandering around through all the construction. I hear the loud banging of hammers and stonemasons' chisels. It appears as if the hammering is taking place inside my skull. A stale smell of urine contrasts sharply with the creation of beauty I saw on my way in, giving rise to an acute sense of dissonance. Grey stone bare benches line the walls. I'm in the reeking anteroom of Hell, not knowing if I'll ever see my daughter or my husband again, and I crumple unceremoniously onto the hard seat looking down at my green travel coat. The smell of my fabrics calms me and I pull the purpur shawl from under my overcoat and caress my face with it, noticing how spots turn dark from my tears. When I look up I see a man with curly brown hair and a bright red cape over a golden vest, brown knee length pants on top of white legs in light brown spurred riding boots flaring out flamboyantly at the top into white lace collars, looking at me in the way men do when they're beguiled by my fabrics. I'm instantly aware that I'm not powerless here and unbutton my overcoat to reveal more of my purpur gown. He stops breathing and is fully engrossed in my Venus apparition. The purple tassels hanging down from a wide belt along his waist to the top of his thighs barely cover his instant salute. I smile sweetly and remain silent and alluring, rearranging my blond curls flowing out from under the stylish red silk bonnet I fashioned to impress Christiaan Huygens. I'm sure he has never seen a creation like it, shining imperceptibly with an under-glow of purpur. His eyes seem to take up a larger than natural section of his face, his gaze stunned like that of a man stumbling unawares upon a bathing goddess.

"My name is Clara Dolfin," I speak in my most elegant French honed carefully by the French Lyceum young Lady Regents have to attend. He looks surprised. So he must know who I am and that I come from the North where the Barbarians live who don't speak in a civilized tongue. French arrogance is legendary. Everything about this place is wrong: from its overwrought grandeur to that damned Charlemagne riding his country to ruin. I straighten my back and encourage my textiles to drive him to distraction. I need to take my vengeance on this preposterous jester. All my rage over Johanna's abduction surfaces, and I smile sweeter than honey.

"I am supposed to lead you to the suites of Madame de Montespan, who is expecting you," he stammers clumsy, as if his tongue has to climb arduously over a tall hedge of teeth.

Everyone has heard of Madame de Montespan, the King's titular mistress who rules his bed and is the most powerful person at court. She is a legend all over Europe. The only thing more legendary is the King's purported sexual prowess. Stories abound how when she is not available he takes the maid. A disgusting man. Madame de Montespan is said to be one of the great beauties, eclipsing all others. At the court of the Sun King, beauty combined with rapier wit is the ultimate currency for women. Monsieur Delamarche knew her during his last days at the Louvre court in her very early 'reign' in 1667 when she first drew the King's attention. He told me that she had sardonic humor and could decimate a person with a single word. The King was attracted to that because her humor didn't spare him either, and she was openly disparaging about him to his face. Her daring made her irresistible, combined as it was with the stunning beauty of the great Helen of Troy. When Delamarche talked about her, his face would have signs of a transport he otherwise only displayed towards Aunt Marianne.

The jester in red tells me his name, which I instantly forget. Several servants, dressed in bland clothing as grey as the bare room we're in to make them invisible among the many-colored principals, enter to carry my valises to God knows where. On the way up the stairs I encounter women with low cut necklines, bare bosoms shown off as matters of trade. They look at me with curiosity, obviously knowing where I am going, making me a person of interest. The power structure here at court is very clearly defined by one's proximity to the Sun King, and Madame de Montespan is his Moon, having given birth to 7 of his children, the surviving ones having been adopted by him. Christiaan tells me that there is now a fierce rivalry over the affections of the King with the governess of her children, the formerly penniless widow Madame Scarron. It is rumored that since the latter had grown up in Martinique in the West Indies she has knowledge of secret heathen love practices. Christiaan had said that the animosity between them added spice to the life at court. Recently she had been elevated by the King to Marquise de Maintenon, making La Montespan extremely jealous even though she had suggested it herself. Yet she still appeared to be the governess of La Montespan's offspring, a powerful position making it possible to speak to the King as an equal about matters of his children. He liked being in her company. Christiaan tells me she is much kinder than La Montespan, though a bit on the pious side. He likes neither of the women, and his dealings with them were minimal, even though both were intellectually powerful women with an interest in the new science. Armed with this knowledge, I follow my nameless guide up the freshly hewn marble staircase adorned at regular intervals with golden effigies of the Sun King or his emblems. The man disgusts me more with every step I take. My sober republican upbringing abhors the opulence of monarchs, especially one who feels he has been sent to earth by God himself to rule us all. At the top of the stairs to the right I hear the sounds of happy children's voices, and I flush with hope that I shall see my daughter. Nothing else matters to me and I stop being aware of my gold and marble environment. I almost overtake my guide, who speeds up to precede me to the open doors of what must be the nursery. In the background I hear the noise on the giant veranda at the back of the palace that is being transformed into a great hall. Through the windows I notice structural elements of the unfinished architecture. Close by the door the voices of children at play compete with the constant hammering of the workmen on the veranda.

"Madame," the jester says in a most deferential tone, "Madame Dolfin is here." He obviously addresses a woman I see from the back. I look around the room but see no signs of Johanna, not even a harpsichord. My heart drops back down from its hopeful beats. The children have stopped their play. The eldest is Johanna's age; tears come to my eyes. They look at me with the genuine curiosity of the young. A young girl is wearing the same velvet blue dress with a shade of purple and plum as her mother, who has still not turned to look at me. I notice that she is wearing more fabrics than necessary on this warm September morning. Usually women do this to hide their bodies and I begin to suspect that having given birth two years in a row, this year and last, has left its effects on her body. There is too much brocade in her gown.

When she turns to me I behold the setting sun. Her round face is of a vanishing beauty, her eyes darting, not pervaded with the supreme self-confidence she has been known to possess. She has clear signs of a double chin and is well beyond what men find pleasingly plump. This is a woman on the losing end of a battle for the affections of her King known for his affinity towards youthful triumphs of the flesh.

"Madame Dolfin," she says as she turns her head in a voice that is deeply melodious. "We've been expecting you."

"Where is my daughter?" I irrupt instantly. My voice sounds shrill and the children recoil.

"I am not at liberty to tell you that," she replies in a tone that conveys genuine regret. We meet as mothers. I take a reluctant liking for this embattled woman who has exchanged her beauty for offspring. Her face reflects the waning interest of the King, a moon in its final quarter.

"Françoise," she calls out to the other room in an intimate voice, "Could you please come here, and take the children." She could have transmitted this message by way of one of the invisible servants.

The woman who enters, though 5 years La Montespan's senior, looks much younger and naturally maternal, with kind eyes hiding a calculating nature. The Marquise de Maintenon is not only La Montespan's rival in the eyes of the King, but also in the affection of her children, whose hearts are the battlefields of their increasingly open hostilities. At the same time these women have an intimate closeness, La Montespan having been for many years Madame de Maintenon's protectress at court. I am glad that I have been well informed by Suzanna, Christiaan's sister, who has constantly insisted on receiving all the latest gossip from the court in Paris when her brother was on home visits.

"This is Madame Dolfin," la Montespan waves her hand in my direction. "I need to speak with her in private." Marquise de Maintenon nods back in a way equals behave together. I realize their relationship is extremely complex.

"I've come to get my daughter," I say to the governess whose power at court is in ascendance. Maybe she will respond. But Marquise de Maintenon's face closes towards me and she does not reply. She just gathers up the children and leaves with them to her connecting quarters.

When we are alone La Montespan invites me to sit down.

"I can help you," she opens without further ado. "You know why you're here," she adds as a matter of course.

"In fact, I don't," I reply in an icy voice. "All I know is that your people have abducted my daughter. You have children; you know how I feel. That's all I know and all I care about."

We are seated on chaise lounges, facing one another over a low informal table with a silver pot and children's toys.

"Do you care for a cup of tea?" she asks. I nod, and she calls over a maidservant.

"What can you do to help me get back my daughter?" I ask bluntly.

"I hear that you have access to an elixir that rejuvenates people," she says in a neutral tone as if this were just a polite inquiry.

I don't reply.

"You had your daughter at 13?" she asks me in the same tone, void of inflexion.

I remain silent.

"My information tells me that you are 30 years of age, yet you look no older than 22. I repeat my question: do you have access to the elixir of youth?" There are audible claws in her voice this time.

"How could you help me getting my daughter back?" I reply, certain that only my maternal ferocity can stand up to this grand cat.

She smiles sweetly, a sign that I aggravate her. "All right then, Madame Dolfin. I shall go first. I can offer you a private midnight supper with His Majesty. I often choose his companions for the night. You may sleep your way to your daughter's release." It sounds crass and I'm revolted, yet it is not unexpected. I have packed my irresistible clothing. I can't help being nauseous. I know that I shall have to take up this midnight assignation and then outwit the King. I will never submit to his caresses! But he is the jailor of my daughter and I need him.

"And in exchange you want the elixir," I reply stoically, not betraying a spark of emotion.

She nods, picks up her silver cup and drinks the tea. I do the same. The tea from Cathay unfolds its inimitable tang on my palate and I'm reminded of Mundanus, whose ancestor Marco Polo was the great explorer of those regions.

"I will consider it if my husband gets freed as well," I posit.

"That may be too much to ask, Madame. Your husband owes our King some favors only he can fulfill. I can only give you access to your daughter." A faint smile plies itself across her countenance. "Your husband will have to fend for himself."

"Where is he?" I demand.

"On his way to the Bastille. They have some questions to ask him and they have the necessary apparatus for inquiry there." I'm distraught. Mundanus knew that he was going to be tortured, but I kept that certainty out of my mind.

"If he is tortured there is no deal between us," I say.

"You will have to make many choices, Madame. Between your daughter and your husband; between her release and your body. Maybe I should give you some time to think it over. My servants will guide you to your quarters. But if you want to see His Majesty tonight, I shall need your reply well before dinner. After that there will be little chance because the celebrations around his birthday will start tomorrow." She gets up, indicating the audience is over.

As she faces me her almond eyes look very sad. "You are young and very lovely Madame. You would greatly please the King. You look remarkably like Mademoiselle de la Vallière, the King's first mistress. You will have no trouble winning over his heart, or at least his flesh." When I don't reply she continues, "Madame Dolfin, we are women. We get what we want with our bodies. Our body is our weapon. The only one we have. We live by our wits." Now she looks very sad and I feel a flicker of compassion.

"I will consider getting you the elixir of youth, Madame," I reply, and bow.

She nods back at me, and entirely against my will, I feel sisterly toward her. I know for sure that no matter what I do for her, she is about to lose everything.

Just before midnight I am led to a small room behind the King's bedchamber. The King goes to sleep in the Royal bed in front of the favorites at the court – who fight for the right to be present and pay exorbitant sums of gold for the privilege – at around 20 o'clock in the evening which is the end of his official day. Then he gets up at 23 o'clock and begins his private life at night. He first visits the Queen in her bed, and then gets up to devote himself to a dissolute life of pleasure. He is a man of great stamina, about to turn 40 years of age, at the height of his powers, both virile and imperial.

I notice a harpsichord spinet in the corner of the room, and my hopes are raised that I might see Johanna. A small round dining table, with sumptuous gold settings for two, stands in the center between the two doors of the windowless room, one leading to the Royal bedchambers, and one, I am certain, leading to a bedroom of delights. The space is lit with uncountable candles and the yellow light dances spritely off gold and many mirrors. The King loves his reflection. As I stare at the harpsichord I realize that I will do anything to get my daughter back. I feel my body cringe in revulsion. A spasm contracts my womanhood and cold fire crackles throughout my skin. But I feel prepared. My mind returns to the women of the night I had seen in Venice who sold their bodies so their children might have food. I had felt a sense of security then, being with my husband who could protect me. Now he is in prison and I am like those women, about to be ravished by a repulsive man driven purely by his lust. I close my eyes and wish I could wash myself already.

When the pendulum clock strikes midnight, the King enters. He is wearing a long elegant dark wig, setting off the pale skin of his egg shaped face to his advantage. His lips are full and sensuous with a trace of a mustache adorning the center of his upper lip. His long nose with visibly raised bridge leads up to eyes carrying each an individual expression. The right side of his face lights up with amused self-satisfied arrogance while his left is both weary and romantic at the same time. His bearing is forceful and straight; I can imagine him as the exceptional horseman they say he is. The sheer power of his presence takes me by surprise. I have met powerful men in my life, but this man stems from a universe in which he exists all by himself, basking in the reflected glory his subjects beam back at him. He mistrusts men and feels more comfortable among women. I have been told that he always remained very close to his mother, even when she was his principal adversary.

"They are right," he tells me with a sonorous voice after having accepted my deep bow. "You are a beautiful young woman. And a mother, no less. I love young mothers." His mood is gregarious.

"I've come to intercede on behalf of my daughter and husband," I say right away, having decided to approach him as an equal, a manner he apparently craves from women. He both demands and despises subservience.

"For the moment, let's not entertain the obvious, dear Madame. You're here with me because you are lovely." He wants to unbalance me like a knight in a jousting match. "But if you don't wish to amuse me, let's bring in your daughter to play the harpsichord. She has been my primary musician here at court and I intend to keep her here for that purpose. She is currently preparing for my birthday concert on September 5. You're invited of course," he concludes his opening attack.

I parry by removing the neutral shawl covering my magic textiles.

The King leans forward displaying an unseemly desire. Now *he* is off guard.

"I intend to take her home. She can give the concert to please Your Majesty, but after that she's coming home with me." I raise my arm, letting the gossamer voile fly.

"You will do nothing of the sort," he responds, with a faint stumble in the back of his voice.

"In that case, we have nothing to say to one another," and at the apex of my impertinence, I get up.

A big grin spreads all over his face. "You have courage, Madame. I like that in a woman. Please sit down, I beg you. Let's call in your daughter to give us a brief concert." This time I'm the one falling off my horse and I can't prevent tears from welling up. He looks at me with delight. He enjoys women becoming emotional. He rings a bell and from the pleasure door a servant emerges.

"Bring in the child," he commands.

When Johanna enters I instantly see that she has been drugged. Her eyes are in a twilight state. I run up to her and take her in my arms. She feels like a rag. I am outraged.

"What did you give her?" I demand, barely containing my fury as I rock my absent daughter in my arms.

He looks genuinely surprised. "What do you mean?" he inquires.

"They've given her some kind of poison. They stole her spirit!" I look deeply into Johanna's blue eyes but can't find her anywhere. Now I despair.

"What do you mean?" he asks again. "She always looks like this."

"Rossini?!" I yell out. "Is Rossini here?"

"Ricaldo Rossini? Yes," replies the King, entranced by my textiles. "He's been here many times. He is a regular guest at Versailles." I know the King only replies because I have now taken off all covers and display the full measure of my beguiling gown.

"Probably not," I hiss, knowing that the phantom sorcerer controls even the King.

His Majesty collects himself and shows displeasure. I don't care. I'm worried sick over my daughter and realize I have to get to the vial of the Medicine to counteract whatever potion Rossini has given her. I hold her close to me and make a move to leave the room with her. The King rings the bell. "Take Madame Dolfin and her daughter to Madame's room," he concedes. Against my will, I feel gratitude. I twirl to make the textile magic spark and enslave his heart as I imprint my will on his. I have conquered the King … and I instantly realize that I am in the grip of *superbia*, the pride of hubris that destroyed me in Venice with Venier and Mantis. I know that I am under the spell of the primordial Red Sulphur Being, who seems as upset about the condition of His daughter as am I. The man across from me may fancy he is the Sun King, but Red Sulphur created the sun. I follow the servant back to my room.

Some hours after I have given her the panacea, Johanna shows signs of reentry. I can see in her eyes how the clouds recede and clarity of spirit finds its way back.

"Mother?" She sounds surprised. "Where am, I Mother?" is the first thing she asks upon return.

"What do you remember, my darling?" I ask her as I gently rock her.

"I remember that Father came to fetch me from the armory where I was playing the organ. He took me to a carriage, and now I am with you. That's all I know." I feel commanded by the Red Sulphur spirit to tell her the truth. We are like two parents worried sick about our daughter.

"You were taken to France by the phantom sorcerer. He abducted you."

"Signor Rossini?" she asks without alarm. She is returning to her unflappable self.

I nod.

"But it was Father who came to fetch me," she responds, puzzled.

"He took on your father's guise," I say, at a loss to explain this sorcery.

"Like when he took on Gerda's brother Peter's shape?" she asks. "When he was a Vampire?" I am astounded by her quick wit and am acutely aware that she is Red Sulphur's daughter. She issues directly from the Source. I am not her mother, just the woman who carried her to term. But instead of this awareness alienating me from her, it opens me to loving her for who she truly is: a being in her own right, not a part of me. Together we are in an unprecedented cosmic drama. No wonder Mundanus could not gauge the future. At every moment Red Sulphur is at liberty to choose *any* future it wishes since it is forever undeterminable, free of all predestination, far beyond the temporal chain of causality. Aunt Marianne had explained this when she told me about Robert Boyle's caelum experiments when the material adapted seamlessly to unexpected futures. Now I understood.

"The King wants to make you an offer," Madame de Montespan tells me after I have come at her request to her second floor apartment next to that of the King in the right wing of the Palace. It is 11 o'clock in the morning. I have taken Johanna with me, refusing to let her out of my sight. Marquise the Maintenon takes her to the nursery adjacent to Madame de Montespan's quarters. I follow them and demand that they bring in a harpsichord so I can hear her play and will know she is all right. I don't let go of her until the harpsichord is brought and the children gather around her as she plays exuberantly. Only then do I consent to leave her.

"You can take your daughter after the birthday celebrations, and your husband will not be tortured. His Majesty's conditions are that you present yourself to him fully nude, without any of your magic garments, and submit to his wishes for the night of his birthday."

"I'm going to be his birthday present," I remark drily.

"You could call it that," Mme de Montespan smiles.

"Why do I have to present myself to him nude?" I ask.

"You know the answer." Her voice is curt. I realize that the King must have spoken to Rossini, who has advised him in this matter. Without my garments I am vulnerable, like Samson after having been shorn by Delilah.

"Now we have to attend to the matter of our agreement," La Montespan continues.

"I shall need an alchemist's laboratory," I respond. "And you have to procure Lunaria pods for me that shine like the full moon."

"That can be arranged," La Montespan agrees. "I have someone who can assist you with everything you need. The King's birthday is in four days. I want to take the potion before that."

"I must warn you that the outcome is unpredictable. If you take the potion between now and the grand ball, you might be too sick to attend the celebrations." By now, I am aware of the reasons why the core court is gathered here at Versailles, and the full court will arrive over the next two days. The celebrations for the King's 40th birthday must be incomparable to any other festivity ever held. It is King Louis' custom to strive to outdo everything that has ever gone before. The fireworks shall be superlative, created by the same men who made the victory fireworks of August 1667 in The Hague when Aunt Marianne, Mundanus and I made the Medicine.

"The most powerful moment to take it shall be during the fireworks on Monday," I tell her. "And it should be made as soon as possible. It was a full moon last night on Thursday so we still have a very strong moon tonight." I speak with great authority, as if I actually know what I'm talking about. My only knowledge of the creation of the Lunaria Red Sulphur comes from Aunt Marianne's account. I have actually never performed it myself.

"We shall leave within the hour for Paris, to Villeneuve-sur-Gravois, where I know a woman who has an alchemist's laboratory. Her name is La Voisin. We will attend Father Guibourg's mass at her home tonight and afterwards you can make the potion."

"I shall take my daughter," I tell her. "That is not a matter of negotiation."

"I don't know if the King will allow her to leave Versailles," she replies apprehensively.

"That is your problem, Madame," I respond, determined. "If you wish you could ask Signor Rossini to use his influence with the King. He is an old friend of His Majesty, I'm sure." I gaze intently at her face hoping to read signs of recognition. But her mask is perfect. Our stoic Regent educators would have been impressed.

"We shall leave in an hour," is all she responds.

Johanna and I wait by the same side gate of the unfinished part of the right wing ground floor where Mundanus and I had arrived. Remarkably, there are no guards around us. It is the first time I'm being left alone. I get the sense that someone is vouching for me.

When Madame de Montespan's elegant carriage pulls up, and the lackey opens the door, I stare into the sweet smiling face of Ricaldo Rossini.

"I took your advice," La Montespan says amiably. I instantly experience an overwhelming desire to kill him.

"You had better wait with killing me, dear Clara." Rossini reads my intentions. "There shall be plenty of time for doing so." His tone is friendly, and to one who was unaware of the complexities it might sound kind. "For the time being you need my presence for the sake of Johanna. If anything happens to me, you shall never see her again." His threat is spoken with breathtaking nonchalance.

"You poisoned her," I hiss.

"Good morning, Signor Rossini." Johanna speaks with mysterious politeness. I sense the Red Sulphur timbre in her voice and feel protected by my daughter. Rossini must have heard it as well because he flinches slightly. We are in the carriage under the tutelage of Johanna's Red Sulphur parentage, and the phantom sorcerer knows it. La Montespan, of course, is unaware of the undercurrents of this ride, and chats about court gossip while the three of us study one another during the entire journey.

"Did you travel well from The Hague, Signor?" Johanna asks with exquisite innocence, after we have passed the halfway mark of the three-hour ride into Paris, at around 14 o'clock.

Signor Rossini looks taken aback. I realize that now that Johanna is in her Red Sulphur mode, he cannot anticipate her actions.

"What poison did you give her?" I ask him with carefully restrained rage in Dutch, knowing that he has a rudimentary knowledge of our tongue.

To my surprise he responds. "Something totally harmless without any lasting effects," he replies breezily in French, regaining his lost composure. "I would never harm your daughter. You have no idea!" Then he reverts to his previous taciturn attitude. Johanna looks at him with the innocent eyes of a child and the power of the Source of Being, a disconcerting combination. Rossini squirms uncomfortably.

We cross the bridge near the Louvre Palace to the right side of the Seine River, riding along wide boulevards lined with trees and elegant modern mansions. I realize that old Constantijn Huygens must have received his inspiration for the grand Square in The Hague on which he built his home from places like this. Finally we stop in front of a large mansion surrounded by an impressive garden. Violin music is heard from the back of the house and there seem to be many people present. A large number of carriages line the elegant boulevard.

"You will meet *tout le monde* here," Rossini tells us. "Anyone who is anybody frequents La Voisin's masses," Rossini says softly, with an undertone of awe. Catherine Monvoisin must be powerful to be able to impress a sorcerer of Rossini's dark caliber. I look at the house with apprehension as we alight. Johanna's face is white as a sheet.

"Don't go here, Mother," she says anxiously in Dutch. "This is a very bad place."

Rossini smiles at her. "Don't worry, my child. We are with you and nothing bad will happen."

"You are the worst that could have happened to her," I bite at him. "Nothing here could be any worse than you."

"Don't go in, Mother, please," Johanna insists. But La Montespan takes the lead, and before I know it, we are surrounded by a bevy of curious nobility who treat us with the utmost respect. Princes and princesses, counts and duchesses vie for the chance to make our acquaintance, deferring reverentially to Madame de Montespan. This is going to be the last great Mass before the King's birthday celebrations at Versailles they are all required to attend. In La Montespan's honor La Voisin will conduct a second full-moon mass.

When we are introduced to Catherine Monvoisin, I instantly realize that Johanna was right. This plump, insignificant-looking, ingratiating peasant woman, with her clever eyes and incisive gaze, carries the mark of Hell. She reeks of the Devil. Father Etienne Guibourg emits the same sulfuric odor of rotten eggs. Johanna pulls my coat, wishing to leave, but the sea of nobles pulls us like a riptide to the back of the garden where the chapel is. It is crowned with inverted crosses and I realize that I shall be partaking in a satanic ritual. The mind of the diabolic cabal is turning towards the flesh and I have to get Johanna out of here as quickly as I can. A gentleman is beginning to pay disgusting attention to her and I draw her away. He looks offended. I turn back and stare at his face then down to his manhood with venomous disdain. "It is touching how much you care for children, Monsieur," I chide him. "But tonight you will not rise, I assure you," I add, putting a hex on him. He recoils under the strike of my maternal maul.

Johanna has not noticed the malodorous intentions paid her and is completely focused on leaving as soon as possible. I look around for Madame de Montespan and find her surrounded by fawning admirers plying their flattery. I can see in her eyes that it bores her to death, and she lights up when she notices Johanna.

"Will you play for us, please, my dear," she asks her – understandably, since the violin music around is utterly inane. Silence ensues, making it clear that no word of La Montespan goes unnoticed by the courtiers who live by favors like barnacles on whales.

"I would like to see the laboratory," I reply, not wishing to expose Johanna to this crowd of bottom-dwelling eel wishing to spice up their slithering desire with anything they can lay their hands on. An overwhelmingly sweet smell of perfume covers the stench of their intentions.

"In a moment, dear Madame. But it would please me *so* to hear you daughter draw down Heaven for us," La Montespan responds.

"It seems that the Master of these proceedings does not reside there," I reply coldly. The courtiers around gasp with delight, eager to watch rapiers being drawn between the most fearsome wit at court and a stranger.

Lackeys carry in a harpsichord and place it at the center of the lawn. Noticing Johanna's wistful look, I realize that this move has been carefully prepared. Music is Johanna's way of disappearing from the common world, and if we can't leave here before I have made the Lunaria elixir, this may be the only leave-taking I can offer my daughter. I nod and Johanna sits behind the keys. I see her eyes wander off to a place unseen, from where she will bring back the music from foreign spheres ordinary mortals can only hear by way of her intercession. She departs from this world of empty lust from the first moment the instrument rejoices in her ministrations. Silence falls over the garden, and minds intent on carnage lift momentarily from their fierce descent.

Having been taught by Maximo, I now can hear the stories she weaves in music. She tells us of a world where evil gets punished by breathtaking beauty that makes it wither, a land where the lust for blood is only quenched by the songs of angels. She takes us from the tears of slaughter to the eruption of Salvation in the hearts of sinners. Her music silences, if just for an instant, the cry of the loins for indiscriminate relief. A child tells us of rising above our grief to regain the innocence we once knew. Around me I see hardened eyes well up.

After Johanna finishes her transport and sits behind the keys with eyes closed in devotion, the silence remains very still until Madame de Montespan, her face in tears, begins to applaud softly like a gentle caress. For a brief respite Satan has left the garden. Then applause thunders from the crowd. Johanna smiles faintly, acknowledging the tribute, as she gets up and curtsies with the elegance purity brings. Some have to look away in order not to see the glaring indictment of their ways by the unspoiled. Soon the noise resumes, and the short hiatus is forgotten.

"I want to go to the laboratory now. I will take Johanna. My only stipulation is that Rossini will not come near," I say.

La Montespan smiles sardonically. "I've taken care of it," she responds and points to her left with a barely perceptible turn of the neck. I see Rossini talk intently with a woman I both recognize and don't. I can't place her. "She is the cousin of the Duchess of Portsmouth, Louise the Kérouaille, and is part of my retinue. They look like twins. Through her we have some modicum of control over Rossini's special powers. We know he is besotted with the mistress of King Charles, and we replace her with her double whenever he visits the Court here in Paris. He can't resist her advances. You have a free hand for as long as I bait him."

I remember Aunt Marianne catching Rossini in a glow-cloth net when he had to surrender his memory of staring longingly at Louise de Kérouaille, who in turn looked like the statue of Claudia, my husband's Virgin Mother in Dolfin chapel where the sorcerer's phantom had attacked me so viciously.

The laboratory is at the very back of the yard, bordering the adjacent lot that is wild and overgrown. When we enter, it smells like incinerated flesh. Johanna displays the abhorrence I too feel. What rites of the Devil are here performed in the name of alchemy? I see stone mortars covered from inside with a film of fatty grime, and on the floor, rats gnaw on bones that still carry flesh. What sacrifices are these?

"Mother, we need to go from here, please!" Johanna insists, her voice small like a frightened bird. I know that she is right, but I'm certain that I shall be prevented from taking her home if I don't make the elixir of youth La Montespan craves in order to bind the King to her.

"We shall work fast," I tell her, and spread the Lunaria pods on the basic wooden table at the center of the laboratory, across from the furnace that emits the stench of burning flesh as if the fires were fed with human remains. I suddenly intensely wish Mundanus were here with me! I need his calming presence in these sinister abodes of Hell. I briefly open up the small vial with the Medicine, and inhale its vapors deep into my lungs, instructing Johanna to do the same. The stench in the room vanishes instantly and is replaced by a gentle smell of springtime flowers. The Medicine instructs the nose to sense its favorite fragrances over the actual smells of the world outside. Johanna looks much relieved, and I start a search to find a relatively clean mortar and pestle without the fatty grime cover. Once I find it, I ask Johanna to grind the pods down with all of her Red Sulphur force, the way she did with Maximo when they reduced the Lunaria powder to a vapor caught by my aunt and husband in an onion-shaped vessel. I decide to repeat this experiment, because I have witnessed its efficacy in creating the lightning cloth. A short while after she has begun her work, I add some drops of the Medicine to the Lunaria powder.

Johanna has set herself to the task with the same ecstasy that fuels her music, like melting wax inspires a dancing flame. As I watch her concentrated intent with deepest love, time vanishes and the world includes just our experiment and ourselves. I find dusty glass vessels I can fashion into a funnel for the vapors arising from Johanna's labor so they can condense into the small drop of living quicksilver. I use a small, uncorked pipette to catch the vapors of Johanna's efforts. Once the condensed drop shines like a tiny silver ball in the light of the laboratory candles, I place the stopper on the vessel that now fills with milky haze. The spirit of Mercurius once more awaits my Red Sulphur daughter's command. Again I am in awe and find myself praying to Virgin Mother Claudia Dolfin for guidance and protection.

We must have been in the laboratory for several hours, for when we exit, the night of the second full moon shines brightly in silver. There is a sound of chanting coming from the chapel, and a servant awaiting us at the entrance of the laboratory leads us over to the Devil's mass. Entranced, we follow him, pulled in by haunting alien hymns.

Inside the place of worship is lit by two candles only, placed on both sides of a rectangular slab on which a young woman lies naked like a living altar-piece. Around me I hear the writhing of indiscriminate copulation – and as my eyes have gotten used to the darkness, before I can protect Johanna from this view, I see how Father Guibourg slits the throat of a silent infant and spills the blood across the body of the naked altar. I know instantly from whence the smell of incinerated flesh arises in the laboratory, and drag Johanna out of Hell. Once back under the silent silver moon, Johanna looks up and speaks softly in her Red Sulphur voice, "Mother, punish them," and she is not addressing me. With glaring certainty I know that the mortars' grime is infant flesh prepared for diabolic potions. I have never felt revulsion like this. Johanna looks at me with Red Sulphur eyes of compassion; then I turn away and vomit, while my ancient daughter holds my hand.

After some time, the satanic revelers file out into the gardens for further abomination, while uninspired violins cover the grunts and groans of this noble crowd. Their sacrifice of infant innocence completed, some still have the blood of communion and the wafer of living flesh on their lips. My hatred knows no bounds, and as I feel the sulfuric flames of my outrage, I know that Satan possesses me as well. I helplessly turn to Johanna. She pulls me down to her height and gently kisses my forehead, emptying my skull of all distress. In awe I know that I am the mother of an angel. I've always known this to be true, but as the Devil gets evicted from my heart I can feel this truth directly in my flesh.

Rossini comes up to us, obviously intoxicated, his clothes disheveled, followed by his whore of Babylon. "You made Trismosin's blanching formula," he slurs at me without expression in his voice. "It does not combine well with infant flesh, I'm afraid. They've laced King Louis' food with this concoction prepared from crushed infant bones for ten years to assure his passion for La Montespan. But it has run its course. No matter how much she rejuvenates, the lust of the King is moving on." Then unexpectedly his voice turns human and acutely sober. "Take Johanna away from here, I beg you!" There is deep concern in his voice. I am profoundly puzzled. The next instant he is taken up again with his desire for the Duchess of Portsmouth's double and his speech slurs even more audibly. When I turn to Johanna behind me, I gaze at the ghost of Mother Claudia hovering protectively over my child. Looking back at Rossini, I see his face aghast, having beheld the same vision as have I. Before my eyes, he shrivels, and letting go of the woman of his lust, he scurries off like a rodent. "Our Mother took away his power," Johanna's Red Sulphur voice speaks quietly.

"Do you have the potion?" La Montespan asks eagerly, having witnessed none of the phantom sorcerer's mysterious demise. I nod in a trance, completely devoid of any interest in this Devil worshiper before me.

"Give it to her, Mother, so we can leave this Hell," Johanna instructs me. Distractedly, I hand La Montespan the pipette.

"What am I to do with it?" she asks, irritated. "And how do I know you have not made poison?"

I turn to her and see fear in her eyes.

"You will have to take that risk," I say, intentionally breathing the bad-smelling odors in her face I was forced to inhale in the Devil's laboratory. "There is not enough of it to test it on someone else. You must inhale the entire content during the fireworks for the King you wish to keep in manacles. That is the most auspicious time for a return to your youth."

"If I die, you die. I'll make sure of that," she threatens me.

"But *I* shall be in the King's bed after the fireworks; not you," I counter with all the cruelty I can muster, wishing to punish her for all of these abominations.

ഌ

I have never beheld such opulence. The birthday spectacle of the King indeed outdoes every celebration that has gone before it, reminiscent of Nero's bacchanalia at the height of the Roman Empire, punctuated festively by the casting down the Capri cliffs of those who had incurred his wrath. This is a costume ball, with everyone dressed in Roman toga, and I have quickly fashioned my magic garments to their most flowing advantage. Now that I have decided to submit to the King's wishes, I have to overcome my revulsion, or I will remain firmly closed to his penetration and it will tear me open, ripping out my capacity for pleasure forever. I want to drive him wild so he will sign letters of free passage I have fashioned that include the mention of Giovanni Dolfin as one of those for whom these documents serve as passports.

When I had been over at Christiaan Huygens home dressed in the ways of men, I had made a concession to myself by wearing women's undergarments in which I had several pockets. In one of them I had hidden two ampules of the potion of the Devil's element fashioned by Gerda, causing lascivious effects. One vial of this aphrodisiac was to help Christiaan overcome his shyness, and the one for myself to bypass my shame. Gerda had also given me a rounded stone like the one she used to prevent pregnancy, as it was her intention to never carry offspring. Since I didn't want to become pregnant by Christiaan I had inserted the stone and had not yet removed it from my uterus. I don't think I shall ever get pregnant again. There had been ample opportunity from the frequent intercourse with Mundanus, but never did my moon cycles waver, nor did they with Aunt Marianne. Mundanus thought that over time, the Medicine prevents ordinary pregnancies, and Helvetius had agreed with him. But I'm glad I'm not at risk with King Louis, who is very prolific with his offspring, having sired over a dozen bastards. Venereal diseases are another matter altogether, the court in Paris being rife with them. But I have taken a pipette from La Voisin's diabolical laboratory and have cleaned it thoroughly so I can insert a drop of Medicine deep inside myself as protection from his putrid seed. I am very calm about it all, a matter that surprises me. Allowing myself to be ravished by a man I abhor should bring up more emotion, but it doesn't.

The King is staying close to me throughout the celebrations and I find myself to be a person of intense interest surrounded by a throng of courtiers, some of whom introduce themselves in a whisper as ones I've met in Satan's pleasure palace - hardly something to particularly recommend them to me. I hover protectively around Johanna, who has been clad in a lovely Faun costume for her performance that will lead into the fireworks. It draws interest from old Satyrs and other goats and I am ready to decimate them at their first attempt. But to his credit, I find that the King has placed Roman guards around her for both of our protection.

At the beginning of the celebration the King – dressed as Julius Caesar, leaving no doubts as to his aspirations – inaugurates a series of magnificent fountains, many of them only provisionally finished, that will become part of the most glorious aquatic art complex ever to be constructed. Bright flares of many colors give the spouting water the appearance of a burst of vertical rainbows. As forceful as the fountains is the free flow of the greatest wines from all the regions of France, having been sent to Versailles to pay homage to the King's 40th birthday celebrations.

To my relief, Rossini is nowhere to be seen. I have a faint hope that Our Mother of God, called in by my Red Sulphur daughter, has scared him off.

Madame de Montespan is glaringly absent as well, giving an open field to Marquise the Maintenon, who is already furtively being called Madame de *Maintenant*, the Lady of Now. She cavorts elegantly with the Royal bastards of Madame de Montespan, who are dressed in similar costumes as that of Johanna. I can't help but like her, and wish I could tell her the gruesome information Rossini has entrusted to me in his drunken moment. Of course she is a calculating schemer, or otherwise she would not have reached the position she is inevitably going to take up as titular mistress to the King of France as soon as La Montespan has been dealt with. But besides that, I sense a pious heart of serious intent with a genuine love of the young.

Before I can go up to her and exchange more than inane courtesies I am approached by a woman dressed as the Vestal Virgin Maxima, the High Priestess of Rome. Her costume is magnificent, made of finely woven white wool created with superlative craft. Flowing from her head, held together by four ornamental tresses of black rope with gold clasps, a pleaded scarf hangs down her shoulders, covering a jabot held together by a stunning golden broche inlaid with colorful precious stones. Her toga dress is held up by another black and gold ornamental rope just below her bosom, showing off her stern classical beauty. Wherever she walks, she spreads the crowds, like Moses parting the sea. I'm instantly intrigued and forget about my intentions to speak with Marquise de Maintenon.

The Vestal gives me a signal that she wants to meet with me away from the crowd. I walk off to a dark place behind a large fountain where there are few people. She follows me.

"Clara," she says with Aunt Marianne's voice. I am completely taken aback. This woman looks in no way like my aunt yet her voice is unmistakable. "Don't be afraid," she adds. "Since I took the caelum and our twin's blood I can change shape in the eyes of others." She briefly shows me her true form, and I'm elated. The next instance she is the unknown Vestalis Maxima again. "I place this image of myself in your mind and you see it as a vision before your eyes. That is how Rossini does it." I need to know no more and fall into her arms in the way I used to when I was young and her embrace was the only safety I had. She smells like Aunt Marianne.

"I know what you are about to do to save our daughter," she tells me kindly. "Everyone at court knows about this arrangement."

For the first time I feel the full horror of what is about to occur and begin to shake uncontrollably. I realize that I have kept the awareness of this rape at a distance by banishing it from my mind, while pretending to myself that I could handle the assault with careful preparation. But I know I have been fooling myself. I know full well that I'm about to be hurt in the most horrible way. Only my aunt's embrace and the vision of Johanna allow me not to faint right at this very moment.

"I wish to take your place," Aunt Marianne tells me. "I wish to encounter the King in your stead, in your form. My new powers give me protection. I can make him believe that he had the most wonderful night of excess he has ever experienced. Yet he will never touch me. I am so profoundly proud of you, Clara," she concludes.

Before I can express my overwhelming gratitude, I hear La Montespan behind me.

She looks rejuvenated by almost ten years, looking younger than thirty with a body that has not been ravished by seven births.

"I couldn't wait, Mme Dolfin. I arranged for fireworks this morning to celebrate the opening of the King's birthday. I took it then. And look!" She appears deeply grateful. I feel compassion for her, remembering Rossini's prescient words that her rejuvenation will have no effect upon the affections of the King.

Part Fifteen

Mundanus

Chapter Thirty-Two

There is scant air in this vaulted dungeon where I've been locked away in the Bastille for several days now, awaiting my torture. They took me here furtively by night. I crossed the drawbridge over the wide moat, looking up at the giant stone towers on either side mirroring the light of a full moon, and I felt I had crossed the Bridge of Sighs in Venice when the formidable wooden gate closed behind me. This was my last full moon as I was to be cast away to rot in this massive fortress designed to keep invaders out, and now re-assigned to hold in rejects like a constipated rectum. The stench inside reveals its purpose, and the cries from the rooms where the racks do their office offend the soul.

I have a table and they've given me pen and paper in case I wish to write my confession. The large hewn granite stones drip with constant moisture and rats are my permanent retinue. It smells dank and moldy in my cell, a step up from the corridors that give no quarter to the nose at all. Through the offices of the guard, acquired by several gold Louis coins and a convincing use of my Caelum powers, I have been able to get a letter out to Count von Waldstein in England and the Prince of Orange telling them summarily about my incarceration in the Bastille. The cast iron grilles look out at underground passageways, and the little light there is comes from one flickering torch on the weeping wall outside my cell. I have lost all track of time, not knowing whether it is day or night. Only the rhythms of the meals they bring me remind me of the cycles of the natural day outside this tomb. All I know by counting my three meals a day – of surprisingly good quality, I must say, since the Bastille is a prison for persons of interest – I know I've been here for close to a week. I'm trying to fortify myself for my inevitable encounter with the rack. I remember the stories about Cornelis de Witt, the Grand Pensionary's brother in 1672, six years ago. They broke all his bones and he continued to read Molière. He is an inspiration to me. They will try to have me betray where I keep the Red Sulphur, but I shall never tell them about the secret place behind the fire-pit in the laboratory of the Van Os ancestral home. I feel ready to die for this, passing on the Red Sulphur to my twins, the rightful heirs to the Trismosin mission. Marianne and Clara will protect them until maturity and The Twins will safeguard the Red Sulphur better and more faithfully than anyone before them –certainly better than I have – since the Stone is their lifeblood. It gives me a strange sense of peace that my mission has been accomplished. All I can do now is wait and get to know myself under torture. Yet, sometimes I feel searing headaches twist my brain and I'm submerged in a cesspool of dread. I'm remembering moments when I was in terrible pain, yet I just recall the instances but not the pain itself. It has vanished from memory. I take courage from this: that the pain of the rack may one day be gone as well. My broken bones will heal and I need to keep my pride intact. However, I have few illusions about what I shall be able to bear. The screams from the rooms with the racks, situated strategically in locations so all prisoners are present to the shredding maws of torture, portray an irresistible force. Then despair hits me and in panic I search through futures to get an inkling of what is to come, but I see nothing but darkness ahead. I'm afraid I shall tell all…

To my surprise, my warden, a stocky man of rough exterior and vicious ways covering a heart of surprising kindness, rattles my cell grill, announcing I have a visitor. I keep my mind restrained in order to have no hope in any direction. Christiaan Huygens appears from the darkness, bearing a candle. Being Clara's beloved, he is not the first person I'd wish to see right now. I stare in his face and instantly realize that the sentiments are mutual.

We sit in awkward silence.

"I know about you and Clara," I open the conversation to make our parameters transparent.

He bows his head and doesn't reply, obviously ashamed about his ungentlemanly behavior. I shall not absolve him and wait for him to speak. Yet I must admit to myself that Christiaan does not lack courage. He is putting his position at the French Royal Academy and his life in Paris at risk … unless he was sent by the minions of the King. I'm instantly suspicious, searching through the world of vision in order to find a question I might ask him to verify his intentions. I behold an apparition of Clara bearing a letter. Seeing her in the flesh, as it were, unbalances my soul.

"I've come to you with a letter of passage signed by the King. Clara brought it to me the day after the King's birthday. She and Johanna are on their way back to The Hague with a similar royal letter." He hands me a parchment signed by the King with his characteristic 'Louis' autograph drawn like the sharp teeth of high forward waves on an ocean by storm. I feel both relief over the escape of Clara and Johanna and a piercing jealousy knowing full well what transpired between Clara and Christiaan during this meeting.

"How long did she stay with you?" I can't help but ask.

"Overnight," he says softly, looking down at the floor. I loathe myself that this hurts more than the joy I feel over Johanna's safety. Christiaan maintains a respectful silence to allow me to deal with my contradictory feelings. He is kind … and he spent the night with Clara.

"Madam Schweitzer is safe as well," he tells me after some time. "She was with Johanna…"

"While Clara was sharing your bed," I complete the sentence he left unspoken. I know that I have no right to be jealous of

Clara's love for this man. God knows I have hurt her daily as my love for Marianne has grown over the years. But I realize that the heart does not reason in terms of fairness; this pain reveals my passion for Clara to me with undeniable clarity now that I have a rival who is my equal in her soul.

"So does that mean I can leave?" I ask, barely interested in his answer. The Bastille is less of a prison than is my own heart at this very moment; I expect the bone-crushing torture to be less painful than the suffering I feel as I pay back on the debt of hurt I owe Clara.

"It pains me to say it does not," he replies sadly. "I was told the letter was obtained by Madam Schweitzer from the King by trickery, and His Majesty is not aware that he signed it."

"So what is the use?" I ask him pointedly.

"If you manage to get out of here it gives you safe passage, that is all," Christiaan all but whispers, his voice crushed by the weight of his conscience

"Is Johanna in good health?" I ask him, moving my attention away from my jealousy by force.

Christiaan nods, happy as though it concerned his own daughter. I know how this childless man has adopted our twins, whom he instructs in natural philosophy and mathematics whenever he has a free moment while visiting his father's home in the Residence. Our joint concern for Johanna and Maximo softens the clutches around my heart.

"I also bring a second letter," he mentions. "It is a copy of one written to the Royal Society of France from the Royal Society in London. It is signed by Isaac Newton and Robert Boyle. It notes that the greatest alchemist of our days, Theodore Mundanus, is kept in the Bastille and requests the Royal Society of France to do everything within its power to free him. You must be Mundanus," he concludes with admiration. Even though he is unconvinced of the tenets of alchemy, Christiaan has a deep respect for Robert Boyle and even more so for Isaac Newton, who is an avid alchemist and began his interest in the Great Art under my tutelage when I transmuted lead into gold at his mother's Woolsthorpe Manor in 1665. I realize that Count von Waldstein must have thought it imperative to inform the Royal Society about my incarceration by name so my Mundanus fame might inspire their colleagues in France to obtain my release. I'm astonished about the speed of this communication across the Channel in less than a week.

"Madam Clara instructed me to tell you that she thought you should try one of Maximo's pellets. She didn't inform me what she meant."

"Her mind must have been on other matters," I remark tersely, dropping back into the claws of jealousy. Then I laugh about the complexity of the atmospheric conditions between Christiaan and me. I walk up to him and warmly shake his hand. "Fate is twisted like a bramble bush," I say. We both smile at one another.

"What are these pellets Maximo fashioned?" he asks with the curiosity of an experimentalist.

"Explosives," I tell him. "I'm afraid that if I try them here the walls would tumble upon me. They're made of the primordial power of the Cosmos."

"Light?" he asks.

"The essence of light," I say. "Before it turns into light. Pure force of creation. Alchemists named it caelum, the creative power of the blue heavens. Johanna calls it the 'invisiblizing light'. That's actually a good word for it. Maximo mixed it with the spirit of phosphorus. A very potent concoction." I realize that Christiaan discovered the wave nature of light and he might understand my explanation in his own way.

"Do you have it on you?" he asks, with the eager interest of a scientist.

I nod and distinctly feel the pea-like pellets and the amber fragments sewn into my silk undergarments. "It is ignited by the electric force. I carry amber as well."

Christiaan nods, needing no further specifics. "If I were you, I'd be willing to take the risk," he posits. "I trust Maximo. His inventions are incomprehensible and awe inspiring. The spirit of invention is already stronger in him than in anyone I have ever encountered."

"Maximo had no idea how it would work or what it would do," I counter.

"But he must have thought it useful, or he wouldn't have made it," Christiaan Huygens replies. "Maximo only makes useful things." I can't argue with him. As Maximo's teacher, he knows the extraordinary mind of my son as well as I do.

After a long silence during which we look at one another and I realize that these may be the last compassionate eyes I will see, we hear a rattle of the cast iron grill of my cell. The warden tells us that the visiting time is over. Christiaan gets up to leave.

"The Royal Society of France is doing all it can to obtain your freedom, Your Excellency," he tells me. Newton's letter must have made quite an impression for Christiaan to give me this honorific title. Needing to feel the closeness of another human being, I tentatively embrace him and we both feel awkward. "If I do not get out of here alive, please tell my wife that I love her deeply," I conclude.

"She knows," he replies. "And she loves you with equal ardor," he adds.

After restless hours during which sleep eludes me, I notice the laboratory at the Van Os family home in The Hague constituting itself around me in a dream. I'm well aware that I'm dreaming, but that does not diminish any of the experience of reality. Marianne enters and is very happy to see me. We embrace.

"You have to get out of the Bastille as soon as possible," she tells me in fast-driven speech, as if she is afraid that our dream encounter might end soon and she will not be able to get her message across quick enough. "While we were away Monsieur Delamarche has seen green light surrounding Maximo, and Venier swears it is Mantis. Maximo is unafraid, but we can't underestimate Mantis. He is at least as dangerous as the phantom sorcerer himself." She stops briefly to catch her breath. Then in an uninterrupted flying drumroll she adds, "If you don't escape shortly you'll be beheaded. I have been able to implant an interdiction on torture in the King's mind, but I have not been able to reach through to a certainty that you can't be executed." When she sees that I'm remaining in the room and the dream does not evaporate she calms down and begins to speak in her usual tone. My heart swells in her presence, and for a moment my dire circumstances do not matter to me.

"I've tried everything," she tells me by way of an apology. "But the King is a stubborn man." She pauses. "You have to come home right away," she implores again.

Instantaneously the scene shifts and I'm in a room with gold and mirrors and a romantically adorned candlelit table between two doors. King Louis, dressed in a gold brocade dressing gown is waiting restlessly, his gaze directed with single-minded focus on one of the doors. His expression is a mix between eager expectation, the frustrated annoyance of a man who won't be kept waiting, and the enjoyment of subtle torture of a slave eager to submit.

The door magnetizing the King's spellbound look opens slowly and Clara appears, her white skin dappled with candlelight. I can feel my entire body groan as I'm instantly part of the sexual craving of the King, participating in his experience, yet at the same time being fully present as myself. There is a barely perceptible sky-blue radiance coming off Clara. The King doesn't notice, his entire attention engorged to the bursting point. He doesn't notice how the glow intensifies and pulls him into a Caelum world. I know that this is Marianne in Clara's guise. It is the first time I see both my beloved spouses in a single form and I feel a dissolving feebleness. I pull upon my own Caelum powers and stay present, noting how the King faints away in an alchemical swoon and Marianne implants her demands in his mind. The King finds himself in

Caelum Heaven, a paradise consisting of many representations of Clara in her dazzling nudity. Each of these Clara-presences rides the King, who moans with an excess of pleasure until he cries out for mercy, unable to withstand the pain of rushing climaxes any longer. Then he slumps bereft in his hollow throne, a sun extinguished.

The next moment I'm back in the laboratory, Marianne still present as a naked blue-haze Clara. I know there will never again be a moment when I may love both of my women in a single body. I go over and touch her skin that sparkles like rubbed amber. In a world of the electric power where lightning strikes the heart in cataclysm, we embrace and enter a world of skin. Three souls beat in a single breast and we spiral up into the thundercloud.

Another week of meals goes by and nothing changes. There is a daily repetition of the demand that I reveal the location of the Red Sulphur, which I greet with silence. I am told in no uncertain terms that a date is being set for my beheading, which I encounter with a calm that is remarkable even to me – though sometimes at night I wake from nightmares in which I'm desperately running away from something hideous. I try to envision the future to catch a glimpse of what existence will look like after I'm dead, and feel my body give way from under me while I experience the crushing of my drowning lungs. I gasp and am bathed in sweat. I try to calm my physical fears, soothing my body as one does a dog – feeling how my spirit might soar above the terror, but refuses to leave my animal body behind. My dog is whimpering, petrified.

I'm increasingly tempted to blow my way out of this dungeon with Maximo's pea-bombs. I just have to solve the problem of the spark. If I rub the cloth and it sparks the pellet I shall surely be incinerated. Not that I mind at this point, but it does not feel like an efficient use of the explosive. I finally find a solution: I fasten a fragment of amber tied to a pellet on the grill of the high window to what I assume is a covered courtyard. I can just reach it when I stand on my table. Then I fashion two long ropes I make with strings obtained from a loosely woven woolen blanket. It keeps me busy for days. With my Caelum powers I convince my warden that I'm creating a string instrument to produce music, though my production looks like nothing of the sort. Finally I attach the strings to both sides of a long strip of silk fashioned from my undershirt. I lead the silk through two loops on either side of the amber-and-pellet combination. Then, just after one of my meals is brought to me and the warden shall not disturb me for several hours, I stand on the far side of my cell and begin to rhythmically pull the ropes back and forth so the silk rubs the amber. When I'm convinced that the construction will not come apart, I increase the speed of the remote rubbing.

When the spark strikes, I find myself utterly unprepared. Expecting a gigantic explosion ripping out the wall and producing incinerating heat, instead I find myself in a cool pale-blue spectral world of hollow transparencies. As I look down I notice vague outlines of my body consisting of the same substance as after-images when one has stared into the sun and closes one's eyes. I am in some kind of after-world, yet unrelated to the afterlife. I'm in the Caelum world before it turns to matter, when it still is just a thought-form in the outflowing mind of Creation. Everything is present as Idea; it just has not yet materialized and hardened into fact. It is a vaporous world preceding condensation and coagulation. I've seen this atmosphere inside a vessel when working towards caelum's heavenly essence, extracting it from the vegetative root moisture of the living metals. But now it seems that I myself am in the vessel and the essential world is taking place around me. I know I shall be able to walk through walls like a vapor through a porous barrier. I take a step to see if here gravity fulfills the same function as in the material world, or if it is more like a world of true imagination, as in a dream where I can fly. I instantly notice that this realm is different from imagination. Whereas dreaming consists of shapes made of solid light, it tends more to the opaque material side of reality. The transparent world in which I find myself has clear physical properties. Yet, how do I know I am not dreaming? I feel as cool as the pale blue environment and remember that the question 'how do I know that I'm not dreaming right now?' had in fact been Master Descartes' central question. He concluded that the distinction was impossible to make, and threw out all sense perception as potentially erroneous. I don't want to go his route. I decide to try out this world and move around in it to see if at any point I shall wake or if I am indeed in a realm with its own continuity, unlike dreams that eventually turn discontinuous. The coolness of my mind is driven by an excited curiosity in my heart. My emotional responses are honed by my near half a century of familiarity with Red Sulphur and laboratory experiment. The matter of whether I shall live or die is now utterly immaterial. I might die in this spectral realm, but that matters not a bit.

I take my first step and notice that I progress through the room as I would in a physical environment. My feet feel on solid ground, yet as I look down I notice only hollowness and outline. I experience the floor as being substantially different from the air above it, a different quality of density, as in the ordinary material world where a floor is denser than air. I approach the wall, and find myself entering its hollow outline. The feeling of passing through granite is like traversing thick oceanic fluids, my movements slow and cumbersome. I hope the world does not coagulate right now, or I shall find myself entombed in stone. As I reach the other side of the wall and I move again through a medium with the quality of light vapor, I indeed find myself in the expected covered inner court. While I move through this courtyard, reality begins to clot like milk curdling and the hollowness of the outlined world fills in; my body turns solid like water freezing to ice. Around me I notice guards, and they see me. I have the presence of mind to use my Caelum skills and make myself invisible by erasing instantly their memories of having noticed me, the way oblivion eradicates a dream before we have a chance to catch it. I move over to a corner of the courtyard, where the light of the half-moon is mirroring in dark silver granite. I now know that Maximo's pellets shift reality upstream, towards the source of being from where the faint outlines of reality eventually turn into our coagulated world. And I have also found that their effect does not last long - not enough to get me out of the Bastille in one fell swoop. This time I'm not afraid of a great explosion when the electric spark of amber strikes the spirit of phosphorus, triggering the caelum essence like a fuse.

I take another pellet and an amber fragment from my undergarments, and for a moment curse Clara for her expert sewing, which makes it hard to remove them without scissors. When I finally free the pellet I see a guard coming my way and have to work oblivion on his mind to such an extreme that I'm afraid it will leave him demented.

I now have to do the rubbing by hand, having no time to fashion a remote instrument. I fasten the amber to the pellet with a string of silk and start the rubbing.

When the spark strikes once more, I notice how my hand and arm reduce to outline and my body turns hollow in a solid world. I have become invisible, but the world around stays unaltered. I don't know for how long this invisibility will last, so I move as quickly as I can to where I assume the drawbridge to be along which I entered. Within a short period, I must admit that I'm lost in a virtual labyrinth. By the time I get to the seventh corridor, my body returns to its ordinary visibility. I walk up to a guard and silence him with my mind. He shall not be able to use his voice for several hours. I demand he point me in the direction of the main gate. When he refuses, I put my hand on his forehead and strike him with an excruciating headache. He looks at me cross-eyed. "Point it out to me and I'll let go of you," I whisper, with an ominous threat in my voice. I know that I can crush his brain and kill him in an instant. My faith in my powers has returned.

I take out the final pellet and rub it. Again my invisible self replaces my solid body, and I decide to follow the hand gesture of the unfortunate guard, who is writhing on the floor in implacable migraine. I walk through the wall, feeling the thick substance resist me. It takes a great deal of effort to reach the other side. I know I will not have the energy to cross thick stone walls too often. At the end of this corridor, there is an ironclad door. Diving through that barrier costs even more effort, even though the door is thinner than the wall. I'm quickly getting exhausted.

But in the far distance I see the gates I recognize as the ones leading to freedom by way of the Bastille Bridge of Sighs. I have the energy to cross one more wall, one more obstacle, and I gather all my strength as I approach the final gate.

I lunge my invisible body forward and get stuck in the middle of the wood, unable to go forward or backward, my legs in the Bastille, my head and torso outside. As my body takes on its density again I realize that I'm about to be cut in half. A red haze collects like a funnel in front of my eyes. I can feel the wood cleave my body like an ax, and I'm ready to die. My last awareness before the searing pain robs me of my consciousness is the face of Ricaldo Rossini, concentrated in great effort as he tries to free me from the maw-betwixt before I'm sliced.

When I regain consciousness, Ricaldo Rossini stands in front of my bed.

"How did I get here?" I ask, confused. In my back, I still feel the memory of being cut in half. My recollections stop with the certainty that my life is about to end.

"I knew you were about to escape. I didn't know how but you were going to leave by the front gate. That's all I could foresee," Rossini replies, almost pensive. "When I saw your torso seep through the gate I realized that you had been able to move closer to the world of Ideas from which physicality congeals. And I saw that you were in the process of turning back into matter."

I remain silent, realizing that he is right.

"So I used my Caelum powers to momentarily de-materialize the gate, pushing it back up the chain of reality to its original ideation before its descent into matter. I was able to push your body back inside in the fraction of a second it took before the gate re-materialized. Then I showed a letter signed by the King to the guards at the gate, who of course didn't notice any of my fierce struggles with the hierarchies of reality. The letter autographed by King Louis allowed me to visit you on the night before your execution. I followed the guards as they took your senseless body back to your cell."

"Why did you save me?" I exclaim in accusation. "It would have been better if I had died right there."

"One might think so indeed," he replies calmly. "You shall be beheaded tomorrow. The King has decided that if he can't have the Red Sulphur, no one should. I told him that there are others who know where it might be. But he is outraged and feels completely betrayed by Clara. He pleaded with her to stay and become his next Montespan. I can only describe him as heartbroken. He is seeking his revenge on you, now that Clara is back home and under the direct protection of Prince William. The King is beside himself and can't be reasoned with. He's even more enraged now that the Royal Society of England is trying to secure your release. He will execute you publicly just to spite them and destroy Clara. The Red Sulphur no longer plays any role in his mind. Many have come to intercede to save Theodore Mundanus. A great wave is washing throughout Christendom. The natural philosophers see you as one of their own, a great experimentalist. They call your execution a willful blow against natural philosophy and science. You even seem to have friends in the Church. The King had not counted on this gale of resistance and is even more infuriated, calling on his divine right to decide over the life and death of his subjects. He considers you French, for some unfathomable reason. Even his private physicians have tried to change his mind. But to no avail… He has defiantly stated that he will attend the public execution, calling on all of Paris to attend. He's making it into a lurid spectacle."

"That must give you great pleasure," I bite at him. "You freed me because you want to enjoy my beheading so you can go and find the Red Sulphur for yourself. That's all you've ever wanted. But you won't get far, Rossini. Marianne is now stronger than you!" I welcome the fact that I shall die in public and will have a chance to shame the King with my final words. A fury rises to my eyes, blotching the grey cell with red spots.

Rossini remains silent.

"You really have no idea who I am, do you, Zanni?" he says gently after some time in a voice I recognize, carrying waves of past.

"Don't you dare use my father's voice," I yell at him. "What do you want from me? Isn't my death enough for you? Get out! Warden!" I yell loudly. "Get this man out of here immediately!"

"Wait," Rossini responds with disconcerting calm, blocking the sound of my voice before it reaches the corridor. "Wait, I need to show you something." Realizing the futility of my screams, I stop yelling for the warden. The corridor remains still and my jailor does not appear.

In front of my eyes, Ricaldo Rossini begins to transmute. I don't know if his shifting shape happens only in my mind or if he is actually changing. His back is bending and he is aging by 30 years within a moment; his features melt like wax, and when they reset, I look into the face of my father, Maximo Theodore.

"Stop it!" I yell, and I lunge at him with blind force. His daring to use my father's guise is the most vicious act Rossini has committed on me yet. I want to rip his guts out and stuff them down his throat. He holds me off with the calm ease of a skilled master able to deflect one blinded by fury. With a light twist of my wrist, he unbalances me, and the force of my thrust propels me against the stone wall. I scramble back to my feet and attack again, my outrage without bounds. Predictably, the same event occurs;

this time Rossini looks like a man who watches the unfolding of a tragedy.

"Zanni," he says with gentle melancholy, "How could I know what your father looks like forty years after he was last seen by anyone? And yet you recognize my older incarnation without effort as your father."

"You've changed shape before. You've abducted Johanna in my guise; you've come to Gerda as her brother Peter. I hate you."

He lowers his head, shame written on his face. "I knew Peter since I had killed him. So I knew what he had looked like recently."

"Why did you kill him?" I scream, feeling again the full extent of Gerda's pain.

"I needed his liver because there was a residue in it of the Red Sulphur Medicine you used to heal his broken arm. I would have died without it. I replaced my dying liver with his. My liver had been ruined by my constant ingestion of Red Sulphur." He pauses, tortured expressions filming over his face. "When I left Venice to go in search of your mother Claudia I took a small slice of the Stone along with me, not expecting that I would need ever greater amounts to accomplish the same thing: descend into the Underworld where she resides to be with her. I didn't know I could become possessed by Red Sulphur like a slave. I used ever more and began to run out. Then I started looking for women who were enough like your mother in appearance so I could reach her Underworld abode by way of their bodies. It took less Red Sulphur. While I was enslaved by Red Sulphur, I was constantly pursued by the green insect you call Mantis, who hid in the cellar of Dolfin Palace and had been there ever since anyone can remember. He was even more deeply under the spell of the dark powers of the Stone than I, and desired whatever Red Sulphur I had left. I had been told by my father that the green insect had lived in those cellars for generations and was after the Stone. My father revealed a prophecy to me that had been passed along for generations: *In the future, Twins shall be born whose blood is made of Red Sulphur; their power for good will be legendary*. I found out that just as I needed Claudia's physical effigy in order to stay close to her, Mantis took possession of humans to continue his presence and survive forever. Venier was only the last in a long line of carriers. I do not know who or what Mantis is, but he is the most dangerous being of all. Mantis has been waiting for the birth of the prophesied twins so he can take possession of them and his power shall be limitless. He has kept himself alive in order to ultimately capture The Twins. He has waited centuries for them to be born. His ability to see futures is much better honed than mine. He can see far. Compared to Mantis, I am but a blind child. You have to protect Maximo and Johanna, Giovanni."

I can't help but admire his cunning. His story has an eerie plausibility, even though the facts he is relating are more outrageous than the stories about vampires told in Bohemia.

"I must admit, Rossini, you have a capacity to warp the mind I have never seen before. You know, of course, that I shall never believe a word you say." I'm still looking for a way to catch him off guard and strangle him. My rage has reached the temperature of feverous delirium.

Suddenly emerging from the wall, my mother Claudia emerges in all the beauty I remember, just like her Virgin Mary statue in Dolfin Chapel.

"Stop all your conjuring, Rossini!" I hiss. "Implanting the image of my mother in my mind will not help to convince me."

"Just listen," he says quietly. I plug my ears with both hands, but my mother's voice echoes quietly through the inner chambers of my skull.

"Zanni, please listen to your father," she says gently, in the melodious alto voice I remember so well. The timbre reminds me of Marianne. Is this shadow play of illusions never going to end? I cannot help but hear her no matter how much I try to choke all sounds that attempt to enter my ears. I wish I were beheaded already. But maybe that is itself a trick conjured up by the all-powerful Phantom Sorcerer, who plays my emotions like a musical instrument. Maybe there is no beheading either.

"He speaks the truth," she continues. "I have told him that the only way he can expiate his heinous sins and regain access to my presence is if he sacrifices himself for you. He has taken on your guise before. I told him to do so again and offer his head in your stead under the henchman's sword. The Red Sulphur has complete dark mastery over his soul and he can only regain freedom through an ultimate act of love. He has agreed. When you see your father's head roll off his shoulders, you must believe his words. For us it is the only way to find ourselves together as consorts in the Underworld. Only in this way can he set things right. I have told him this and he agrees. You must go home immediately to protect our grandchildren against the powers of Green Mantis. He is biding his time to choose the best moment when he can capture The Twins and rule both Darkness and Light. He possessed soul after soul for centuries and has coagulated all the thirst for power of which we humans are capable. He wants to be the Lord God Himself and he needs to be stopped!"

The face of my old father, to whomever it belongs, is stricken with remorse. "I have always blamed it on being addicted to Red Sulphur. I've seen what it did to the Green one you call Mantis. I've seen how depraved he became over the centuries. How he just became a mere maw of craving. I said: that is what is happening to you, Maximo, and it is an irresistible force. So when I took the liver of the boy to survive, I did it without reservation like a man in a drunken stupor who cares about nothing." His head hangs low. I feel overwhelmingly tempted to believe him, though I know at the same time he's involved in the highest form of trickery: the lies you speak while convinced you're speaking the truth. "But then," he continues in barely a whisper, "I realized that there *was* choice. Actually it was the spirit of your mother Claudia that convinced me." He grows silent.

"He came to me in the home of shades where I was waiting his return with the usual lassitude of the dead," my mother's ghost – or whatever this conjured presence might be – continues in a plaintive voice that echoes a remoteness I do not know. Before my eyes a landscape begins to form that is white as snow, a cloudy world of transparencies who sit around in unfathomable waiting. Among them I discern my mother's ghost with eyes devoid of recognition, a gaze that does not register. In the distance I see Maximo Theodore appear in outline. He remains distant while coming closer. He's an inhabitant of another realm though not a total stranger to this world of white haze. I notice an awakening in the cataracts that hide my mother's retina; they dissolve as warm recognition shines forth paradoxically in this cold world of vaporous death. I see my parents merge like fluids in a glass alembic. I am moved that their love persists in the Beyond, and in the backwoods of my mind the possibility emerges that truth is being revealed. Emotions clamber for priority and disturb my vision of this afterlife. I have to cool them in order to watch my parents' scene unfold. I breathe in deep and placidity returns. Like watching mirror images in a silver lake I notice my mother looking lovingly at my father's bent figure, much like the one revealed by the phantom sorcerer just moments ago.

"It has to stop, Maximo," I hear my mother Claudia say to my father. "We all can feel the powers of the Green One rise. Even in this remoteness his presence is now felt. We are disturbed. Just Zanni can protect The Twins. Without him there is only cataclysm in all realms of existence." My father bends his head. I see a pale pink glow, incongruous in this barren world, arise from her chest and envelope him with a love that has broken the bonds of death. Deep within my soul I feel a glacier melt as my love for the parents I knew so well as a child comes out of hiding. I remember my father bringing home the two ivory boxes from the Holy Land. They now radiate with undeniable affection.

"My soul dissolved in the vitriol of shame. It corroded everything." Maximo Theodore continues. "But even though it hurt like the tortures of Hell I realized that I could feel again. Red Sulphur had made me numb so green raw sulphur could satisfy its hellish craving for bliss. I had followed Marianne to The Hague to be with The Twins; and when I looked at Johanna and at Maximo with Claudia's overwhelming love for them I knew for a fact that Green Mantis was going to cannibalize them if they were not protected. I abducted Johanna in your form and I could feel the love of a father for his daughter that came with inhabiting your simulacrum. I drugged her and saw the blankness in her eyes. That's when the shame became stronger than the craving, when all this love – your mother's, yours and now also mine – overwhelmed the craven addiction and I might have followed your mother's command. But I relapsed. Finally at a Devil's mass I attended delirious with depravity, Johanna called in the heavenly Mother with all her Red Sulphur power and I was crushed by Claudia with one withering look. You must believe me Zanni." He looks at me with eyes both pleading and in full surrender. He will take my verdict as truth.

I remember my days with him on the Lagoon. How we talked about Red Sulphur and he told me about its majesty; and its pitfalls! He must have known already then that he was in danger. I suddenly realize that this is why he left. He was trying to protect me from the infection that was taking over his soul. His search for my mother was a search for salvation. He knew he was doomed. The tragedy of his condition rises before me with undeniable clarity. This is true. Even if this is all a grand performance by raw sulphur craving for its Red Sulphur opium, the words the raw craving uses derive from truth itself. I see the eyes of my mother, full of love. She nods and keeps nodding as her image turns misty and retreats from this world, vanishing. Her final presence says: "Forgive!" My heart grieves. I don't want her to go. I want to keep her with me forever. For just a moment I can feel the hot imperative that made Maximo Theodore set out on his journey to find her. He could not breathe without her. Now I myself am suffocated by her leaving and I gasp. In the ultimate distance I see my mother Claudia Dolfin give me a nod that briefly makes the cosmos shudder. Then she is gone.

I know that it is not only my father who will sacrifice himself for me, but that I too have to sacrifice the hatred I feel for all he has caused, my hatred for the phantom sorcerer that had kept me going during my trials here in prison. Yet, can I reach through to that forgiveness? I realize that I shall never forgive the deeds, but I must forgive the man. There is no other way. I stare at the prison wall, enveloped in dilemma. Then in the distance into which my mother had vanished I hear music. It is a song played by Johanna, not on a harpsichord but directly on my heart. I hear all the music that inspires her, hear what she hears. I love my daughter with such passion that it turns my head towards my father. All I can do is repeat the nod with which my mother left me. Then I quickly look away to avoid seeing the gratitude in my father's eyes. His gratitude makes me complicit. I need to block it out but I cannot.

It becomes very still around us, wrapped as we are in primordial silence prior to sound. I notice that the whole Bastille is shrouded in stillness, all torture silenced, as the world before time envelops us all. I close my eyes and darkness cools my senses. All vision ceases. My world has come to closure.

When I open my eyes I behold myself.

"Give me your clothes, Zanni," Father-in-my-guise demands. "And take mine. I'm wearing a very large wig so you will remain unrecognizable." I'm utterly stunned as he gently undoes my outer garments and puts them on his person, while covering me in his giant wig and dressing me up in his flamboyant garments. I feel the last shreds of my resistance wrestle with the certainty that this is indeed my father and that my mother's presence has been real. Yet I cannot fully embrace these facts as truth.

"Warden," he calls out in my voice. My jailor comes this time. "My guest is leaving. Give him a golden Louis, Rossini," he tells me, pointing at the left pocket of his jerkin I now wear. "This man has been good to me." I do as I am told. The warden bows and guides me away from my cell; as I look back my simulacrum calls out to me: "Take care of The Twins. Beware of Mantis!" His words echo in my soul, as I walk out of the Bastille a free man.

Here I stand hidden behind the curls of a grand wig, close to the front of the spectacle that will culminate in the beheading of

Theodore Mundanus. The King has taken his seat and has distributed coins to the masses, who cheer him with great applause, looking forward to a good beheading. Since hangings are the usual manner of capital punishment while decapitation by the sword is reserved for nobility, this execution is more of a delicacy. It also is a sign of reluctant respect paid to Theodore Mundanus by the King.

When Mundanus is led to the scaffold, erected in a large square so thousands can partake in the festivities, the crowd starts chanting wildly, demanding an instant gruesome death. The blood thirst of crowds knows no limits. I see his face that is mine searching the crowd. In a trance I briefly raise my hand, long enough for him to notice me. His whole body relaxes instantly; with a smile on his face and religious transport in his eyes he goes down on his knees, hands bound in front of him, his back proud and straight. His only request is that he not be blindfolded. As our gaze locks I am aware that I will know the ultimate truth after the sword has come down. He knows that the last vestiges of my doubt lie in these scales of destiny. We both hold our breath. The crowd grows silent like a congregation before an altar. The face of Mundanus looks straight at me and I back at myself. The verdict will be swift.

Then the sword comes down and onto the wooden scaffold rolls the old head of Maximo Theodore.

Made in the USA
Middletown, DE
18 September 2022

73469758R00161